D1505613

Chhibber, Preeti, author.
Spider-Man's bad connection!

2023
33305256684873
ca   09/01/23

SPIDER-MAN'S BAD CONNECTION

WRITTEN BY

PREETI CHHIBBER

MARVEL

Los Angeles   New York

To Samir for saying, "Heck yeah"

© 2023 MARVEL

All rights reserved. Published by Marvel Press,
an imprint of Buena Vista Books, Inc. No part of this book may be
reproduced or transmitted in any form or by any means, electronic or
mechanical, including photocopying, recording, or by any information
storage and retrieval system, without written permission
from the publisher. For information address Marvel Press,
77 West 66th Street, New York, New York 10023.

First Edition, September 2023
10 9 8 7 6 5 4 3 2 1
FAC-004510-23194
Printed in the United States of America

This book is set in Caslon 540 LT Std/Adobe
Designed by Catalina Castro and Madison Ackerman

Library of Congress Control Number: 2022952007
ISBN 978-1-368-05770-7
Reinforced binding

Visit www.DisneyBooks.com
and Marvel.com

SUSTAINABLE FORESTRY INITIATIVE
Certified Sourcing
www.forests.org
SFI-01681

Logo Applies to Text Stock Only

CHAPTER ONE

Spider-Man is swinging through the streets of New York City, grinning under his mask. It's a new year, and he has to admit, he's feeling *fine*. The teeth-chattering cold weather isn't even bothering him because over his suit he's got on a matching woolen scarf and winter hat courtesy of his girlfriend, Mary Jane Watson. She presented them to him over the holidays.

"You know, for your *night* job," she said, and grinned prettily when she handed over the box.

He flies forward, up past the Empire State Building, fist tight around a web-line. The skyscraper is still lit up red and green despite the fact that it's been the new year for a few days already. He should know, considering he rang it in right on top of that building with MJ by his side. As he thinks back to it, Spidey can almost feel the reverberations of the fireworks.

It was viciously cold while they were sitting there, just the two of them. But they'd brought extra blankets and very thick winter coats; MJ had even managed to bring up two thermoses of hot chocolate. Peter had his mask off, and the green-blue-and-yellow hat was doing a great job of keeping his ears warm. MJ was flush against his side, and her head was tilted down and leaning on his shoulder while they both looked out at the fireworks going off over Times Square. They were only minutes into the new year, and Peter was glad that he was spending it here. He hoped it was a good sign for the year to come, if you believed in that sort of thing. Which he would, if it meant his year would have way more MJ time. He turned to look at her; she was still facing the fireworks, and her face glowed in the bright, tiered lighting around them. Her eyes were *actually* sparkling. Peter had to stop himself from pinching his own hand to make sure he wasn't dreaming.

"We have to do this every year, you realize." MJ's voice had a laugh in it. "Nothing else is going to compare to this view, sorry to say, Spider-Man."

Peter grinned and put his arm around her.

"Mary Jane Watson, I promise you that we will come

back here to watch the fireworks for as long as we both shall live."

Suddenly, a tingling at the base of his skull breaks through the memories, and Spidey swings to a stop, settling into a crouch atop a deli sign. His spider-sense vibrates at a dull frequency and then goes silent. He looks down at the sidewalk below him. There's nothing that he can see; it's a quiet side street. Someone's walking toward the intersection at the end of the block, and all the windows are dark. A movement across the way catches his eye, though. It was too quick to see, but it *looked* like someone was there and then they weren't. He drops to the ground to cross the street. There's an ATM with its screen bright blue outside of a darkened storefront. There's an error message on the screen that says NO CASH HERE in big block letters. He sees a few bills dropping from the cash dispenser, floating softly down to the concrete below. His lenses narrow as he takes it in. There's a thick metal chain circling the machine, presumably so no one can run out with it while the owners are away. But he can't see anything else. Spidey steps closer and sees it— *There!*

A small, filled-in black circle sits on the side of the machine. He groans, a warm puff of air coming out through his mask as a tiny cloud in the cold. The circle is exactly the same as the others, about four or five inches in diameter and solid black. But with some kind of paint he's never seen before. It looks like it's part of the plastic encasing the ATM, not like someone drew it there. He takes out his phone and texts MJ.

> **FOUND ANOTHER ONE.**

Three dots pop up. Spidey thinks that she must have been waiting for him to check in and can't help the smile breaking out across his face. It was nice to have a partner in crime. *Well, not crime. Vigilantism? That does* not *roll off the tongue. . . .*

Then her reply pops up.

> **SHOW ME!**

He takes a picture and sends it her way. She replies quickly again, telling him she'll add it to their folder. She sends one more follow-up.

> **I DON'T KNOW HOW THIS PERSON IS DOING IT, BUT THEY'RE GOING TO HAVE TO GET CAUGHT AT SOME POINT. AT LEAST ON SOMEONE'S CAMERA OR SOMETHING? MAYBE THE CIRCLE'S THE RESULT OF SOME KIND OF TOOL . . . BUT NOTHING I CAN FIND. I EVEN WENT TO THE HARDWARE STORE TO DO SOME DIGGING! THERE IS NOTHING THAT LEAVES THAT KIND OF RESIDUE.**

Spider-Man stops to look at the ATM again. It's so strange. His gut is telling him there's *something* going on, but none of the clues add up to anything. There have been some minor stories in the paper about a slew of ATM robberies, but so far no one has been able to figure out who might be responsible. There's a loud honking down the street, and Spidey starts. He looks around one more time and finally interlocks his hands behind his neck and sighs in frustration. *That's that. My spider-sense is quiet; there are no discernible clues around. I must have* just *missed the guy.* His phone lights up with another text, and it's MJ asking him when he's going to be heading back home. He types out *Now!* and hits send.

He kneels down to pick up the leftover cash and shoves it under the locked door of the store before turning around to shoot a web at a fire escape a few stories up and launch himself into the air in the direction of Forest Hills.

MJ is sitting in her room with her desk lamp on. It's *very* late. She's in her coziest robe and pajamas and might be struggling to keep her eyes open. *How does Peter stay up so late all the time and not collapse in the middle of the day?* she thinks. He should be back soon based on when he replied to her. She brings up the photo he sent on her phone and takes two fingers to the screen, pinching out to zoom into it, hunting for any clues she might have missed the first five times she did it. But there's nothing—just a regular old ATM with that same strange circle graffiti.

Maybe it's a calling card. . . .

An alert pops up on her phone reminding her about her required reading, but MJ just makes an irritated sound and swipes it away. She stares intently at the image again before finally shaking her head, frustrated. There has to be another connection. No one is *this* good. Her visit to the hardware store was a complete bust—the clerk just called her "little lady" and laughed at her questions. MJ is still furious about it. There's a tap at her window, interrupting her thoughts. She jumps up to open it, and there's Peter grinning at her, sticking to the side of her house. *Am I ever going to get used to this?* she wonders. He's taken the time to change out of his suit and into a warm sweater and thick sweatpants, but he's kept on her gifts to him, the scarf wound tight around his neck and the hat pulled low over his ears. She steps back, and a rush of cold air follows him into her room. She shivers and shuts the window before any more can get in. Then she turns and flings her arms around him, and he's hugging her back.

"Hi," she says.

"Hi," he replies.

MJ takes a step back and sits down on her bed while Peter takes his place on a beanbag near the bedroom door.

They've been doing this for weeks now, all through winter break, and it's become a habit at this point.

"So, this ATM guy is really annoying," MJ says.

Peter laughs, and MJ bristles. He puts his hands up placatingly. "I'm just glad I am not doing this alone. I would have been driving myself up the wall trying to figure it out," he says. "I know we'll get there, though. You're really good at the investigative part. I'm just the muscle," he jokes, flexing an arm.

MJ throws a pillow at him, and even though she knows he could have dodged easily, he lets it hit him before taking it and resting it behind his head. "Peter, you better not be coasting just because I'm here to help!"

"I'm not, I'm not! I just know we'll get there. I have faith in us." And he says it with such certainty that it makes MJ feel warm all over. She decides to change the subject before he notices her blushing.

"Anyway," she says, looking at the wall to compose herself, "can you believe school starts the day after tomorrow? I haven't even touched the reading we were supposed to do over break." Her head twists back at Peter as he lets out a monster of a groan.

"Don't remind me. I am not ready to start getting up so early again. And I haven't even *thought* about the reading." He rubs a hand over his face, like he can already feel how tired he's going to be on the first day back in classes.

"I'm glad we have that group study with Dr. Shah to work on our project first thing, though. The rest of my schedule is rough." He slides the hand down his face. "I can't believe we only have the one class together."

"Sorry," MJ says apologetically. "I had to work my schedule around my internship with Councilman Torres. But," she adds with a sly smile, "at least classes will be a lot easier without a weird alien thing taking over our entire lives?"

"Speaking of which, any luck on finding that last cell phone? I did some digging on my end, but you're . . . definitely better at this part," Peter says, voice hopeful.

MJ bites back a sigh, thinking of their experience with the arc lamp, the alien meteor, and Sandman a few months ago. Part of figuring out *how* the alien matter had worked had been on her—she'd realized it was somehow living in the phones of anyone who connected to the Wi-Fi at the Museum of the Moving Image the day she'd been there. That had been why she'd been so furious and couldn't get a handle on her anger. There were still three phones unaccounted for by the time Peter had fought Sandman and the strange alien at the New York Hall of Science and successfully destroyed the arc lamp. Together, they've managed to find two of the phones . . . but the third is still missing. She shakes her head, and Peter's shoulders fall just the smallest bit.

"It's been months, though!" MJ is quick to add. "We would have heard something by now. Right?"

"You're probably right," Peter agrees.

"We can keep looking, but I think we've done everything we can do," MJ continues. "Honestly, at this point, if anyone even says the words 'arc' or 'lamp,' I'm immediately convincing my parents to go on a no-technology-allowed-vacation." She's trying to lighten the mood and feels good when Peter lets out a bark of laughter. She's glad they *can* laugh about it now. Turns out taking down a secret alien, using an actual criminal, is pretty emotionally—and physically—exhausting. Especially when it involves a lot of research and Peter having to fight both Sandman *and* the mysterious alien thing at the New York Hall of Science without *anyone* finding out. Not to mention the fact that it has taken her weeks to get comfortable around her phone again without being worried about the thing controlling her emotions! She side-eyes the device sitting on her desk and edges away from it. *Mostly comfortable*, she thinks.

Peter's laugh is loud, and he slaps a hand over his mouth, eyes shifting toward MJ's bedroom door. She shakes her head at him but stands up to walk to the door just in case. She opens it and peeks outside, and the hallway is still dark and quiet. The other bedroom doors don't show any light underneath, and she knows they're safe.

She turns back to Peter and agrees. "Just what I

thought. My mom and aunt are *dead* asleep. Nothing ever wakes them up. One time the fire alarm malfunctioned and went off, and I *still* had to go wake them up."

Peter nods and grins, reaching up to grab her hand. "Sounds good to me," he says, pulling her down to join him.

She falls, laughing softly, and they spend a few seconds as a tangle of limbs before situating themselves next to each other, with Peter's arm tight around her shoulders. MJ pulls her phone out again and brings up the photo so they can look at it together.

"I can't believe we can't figure this out after five different times spotting this thing." She frowns, pinching and zooming again.

Peter narrows his eyes at her screen. "Wait, zoom in a little more." She does, and he points at a small line next to the black dot. "Is that anything?"

She brings the phone close enough that her nose is nearly touching the screen. "No. I think that's just someone leaving a scratch on the machine with a key or something. Sorry, Pete." She feels him shrug, and she settles back into the seat.

"It was a long shot; I think I'm just trying to reach for stuff at this point."

"We'll figure it out," she says, echoing his earlier sentiments. "It's what we do."

There is something . . .
   Home is near us; we can feel it.
Home is near us.
     But we're too weak. Too weak to find
it. Too weak to battle . . .
 SPIDER-MAN.
THIS IS SPIDER-MAN'S FAULT. BUT WE ARE TOO
WEAK.
   Remove him, remove him. We will remove him.
Find another problem. He will not see us.

CHAPTER TWO

"Hey, Pete, how was break?" Randy Robertson's voice hits Peter's ears just as he steps into Dr. Shah's mostly empty classroom. It's the first Monday back in school after winter break, and the morning has already been a rough one for Peter. It wasn't that he was surprised that he missed the bus, but he was a little put off that the universe had decided to add insult to injury by having a bird poop on his shoulder. He went home to change and then had to swing through the icy air to make it to school on time. He usually doesn't mind a quick web through Queens and into the city. . . . *It is just so cold outside!*

"Hey, Randy, I can't complain," Peter jokes, walking

toward his desk. Randy tucks a loc behind one ear and gives him a bright, welcoming grin. Peter's glad to see his friend again. "You?" he asks, dropping into the seat next to Randy's.

Their other groupmates—MJ and Maia Levy—have their heads bowed next to each other in the seats ahead of them, but MJ cuts a quick glance at Peter and smiles, reaching a hand back to grasp his. Maia waves at him but continues whatever she's saying to MJ. Peter returns the wave, shooting MJ a soft grin back. MJ and Maia became fast friends after Peter and MJ ran into Maia at a protest a few months earlier, and they realized that even though it didn't seem like it on the surface, they both had a ton of stuff in common. His cheeks warm remembering the day. It was his and MJ's first date and had been *almost* perfect . . . *if it wasn't for some C-list panda-themed villain showing up and ruining everything.* . . . Peter clears his thoughts before tuning back in to what Randy is saying.

"Mine was great. We went to California to visit family—"

"Oh, yeah, your dad mentioned that was happening." Peter works with, well, really *for* Randy's dad, Robbie Robertson, at the *Bugle* as a student intern. Randy nods, unsurprised at Peter's interjection.

"He was as into it as I was. Because the Robertson men were thrilled at how awesome it was not having to wear forty-seven layers on Christmas Day." Randy pulls at his sweater to emphasize how irritated he is, accidentally snagging a loose thread, which ends up looped around his finger.

"Tell me about it." Peter laughs, thinking of how insulating his suit is under the long-sleeved T-shirt *and* sweatshirt he's got on. He'd left his parka on while he swung to school, even though he knows it makes his legs look like toothpicks and that *someone* is going to make fun of him on the internet. *Worth it.* He looks back at the empty teacher's desk behind them. "Where's Dr. Shah?" he asks, wondering if he's already missed his chance to at least pretend to be on time.

"No idea," Randy says, looking down at the small hole he's created in his sweater and frowning. "I was the first one here, and he hasn't been in, as far as I know. I mean, I guess it doesn't really matter since we're his only students, right?"

"I guess," Peter says. The four of them are supposed to use Dr. Shah's class this semester to get their OSMAKER project ready for the competition in October. They are going to be representing Midtown High in the Oscorp-backed competition, and Peter still can't quite believe Dr. Shah actually chose their team to represent the school. But he said he loved their idea of combining activism and tech in a social platform designed to connect activists involved with similar causes. Peter just really hopes they can deliver. If they can win, it could mean a full ride to college—his internship at the *Bugle* might pay him money, but it doesn't pay him college-tuition money.

"If he wants to sleep in, I get it." Randy's teeth show when he smiles, bright white against his dark skin. Then his expression shifts into one of excitement. "Oh, actually, while I was in Cali, my dad got me a meeting with a Dr. Camacho—he's a professor of social justice at CU. I got to ask him those questions we wrote out before break, and once I type my notes, I'll send them around to everyone."

"Awesome," Maia said as she and MJ look back to join their conversation. "Peter, you were going to talk to some-one, too?" she asks, pushing her dark hair back from her face. Maia was new to the school last semester, but MJ had shared over break that it felt like Maia was a permanent part of their budding friend group.

Peter nods. "Yeah, there were some climate activists getting interviewed by the *Bugle*, so I got to tag along and they answered some questions. And," he adds, feel-ing accomplished, "one of them gave me their email and said we could ask them things whenever we wanted. They loved our idea for the activism-connection app!"

"That's great, Peter!" Maia says. "I was watching an interview with Norman Osborn the other day, and he said Oscorp was really focusing on growing their mobile userbase this year . . . so I think the fact that this is an app could really give us an edge. You know, this might actually be fun," she says, but there's laughter in it and Peter knows she's kidding.

"Whatever," MJ says, "you're the most excited out of all of us because you are a nerd for this stuff."

"Takes one to know one," Maia shoots back, and now the laughter is out loud. MJ and Maia fist-bump.

"You guys *both* went to, like, ten different meetings over break—and you loved it," Peter says. He's glad Maia and MJ get along so well, but he is definitely out of his depth with some of the minutiae of how the local government works. "Did you hear of anything good that we could ground the program in? Like, what our sample cause could be?" he asks, mostly for Randy's benefit, since he and MJ have already discussed it.

"Yeah!" MJ says. "I showed you the site the other day, for some local greenery groups?"

Maia pulls her tablet out and types in the address. The screen loads a surprisingly professional-looking homepage, the words *Go! Go! Gardens!* spread across the top.

"So they . . . build gardens?" Randy asks. "Just . . . anywhere?"

"Specifically, in empty lots," MJ says. "So, lots the city just hasn't dealt with, or some evil landlord is hoarding to try and artificially hike rent in the area somehow—I didn't totally get it, just enough to know it's wrong." Maia drags her finger along the screen and pulls the bottom of the page up. There's a link that says *Get involved!* at the tail end.

"That is what my manager, Kayla, at the *Bugle* would call 'below the fold.'" Peter lifts his hands and makes air-quotes. "Like, it's less important than the stuff at the top, but it feels like it should be more important?" he asks, waiting for his friends to agree.

"You're not wrong. I'm terrible at this stuff, and even I know no one's getting through all those paragraphs to click the volunteer button at the bottom," Randy says, frowning.

"We thought the same thing," MJ says. "So we pitched them on our program, and they're down for us to include them in it and use it as a sample!" She and Maia slap a high five. "We're gonna *kill* this OSMAKER thing. The other teams better watch out."

"That's good to hear." Dr. Shah has finally arrived, walking in and setting his backpack on the ground next to his desk. He sounds strange to Peter's ears. His voice is flat, and the energy he usually brings to the classroom just isn't present—his shirt is rumpled, and Peter can see dark stubble on Dr. Shah's chin, dotting its way up to his bushy mustache. It's strange: his teacher is usually fastidious in his appearance. But now he just looks tired. "Let me know if you need any help, but otherwise I'll leave you on your own." With that, he turns to the ancient computer on his desk and starts typing at the keyboard.

Maia's face is twisted up, and even Randy looks discomfited by their teacher's mood. Peter frowns. *He didn't even ask about our break.* Peter catches MJ's eye, and she nods, like she can tell what he's thinking. Even with the weirdness Dr. Shah has brought into the classroom, Peter can't help but feel a quick burst of joy at that.

"I guess . . . we'll just keep going?" Randy asks. Maia and MJ both nod in agreement.

"Yeah," MJ says, shooting Dr. Shah a quick side-eye. "It looks like we have a ton of notes to go through—here are the packets Maia and I pulled together."

Spider-Man fidgets a little to get comfortable. He's sitting on the parapet of an old building on the Lower East Side, looking down at the sidewalk below and eating a quick snack. His mask is pulled halfway up his face, leaving his mouth free to inhale a couple of churros the churro lady gave him. Apparently, he'd stopped a mugging for her a few months ago. He grins. The *Bugle* may not like him, but *New Yorkers* did.

"Hey, spider-jerk! Get off my roof!!!" *Okay, maybe not all New Yorkers . . .* The shout comes from two or three floors below him, and a head pokes out from a window. Spidey leans forward to try and see who it is, but they're hard to make out through the grates of the fire escape. "I said leave!"

"Okay, okay!" Spidey calls down, though he's shoved the remaining churro in his mouth, so it might be too full for the guy to understand him. He swallows and immediately regrets not grabbing a water bottle when the food gets stuck somewhere between his throat and his stomach. He makes a fist and bangs it against his chest. "Any chance I could get a glass of water?" he calls down. *Can't hurt to ask.*

"If I had a hose, I'd give you a glass of water all right! I read J. Jonah Jameson. I know what you're like!" the man yells back, and Spidey groans. Someone must be a fan of Jameson's latest editorial in the *Bugle*: "SPIDER-MAN: WEB-HEAD DESECRATES LADY LIBERTY!" *It was a single string of webbing on the torch, and it dissolved within an hour!* Unfortunately, J. Jonah Jameson runs the *Bugle* and can write whatever he wants. Or at least, that's how it feels to Spidey. It sometimes makes things awkward when he is pretending to be normal intern Peter Parker at the newspaper headquarters. Suddenly, a sound on the grate just below him gets his attention.

"Jeez, sorry, I'm leaving!" he says, pulling his mask down over his face. He throws out his hands and presses both sets of his middle two fingers against his palms. Webs shoot out, and he grips them tight, swinging . . . right across the street to sit on the building opposite. He settles himself down and finally sees the older white man who had been screaming at him. He gives him a quick nod and a salute. The man actually sputters. Spidey's not sure he's seen literal sputtering before. He lets out a quiet laugh and then pulls out his phone to send off a quick, snarky tweet.

SpiderManEnWhySee

Ever seen someone get so mad they can't even get words out bc I just saw this guy . . . put four wheels on him and he'd be SPUTTERING along *#Jokes #IGotEm*

He laughs to himself again and hits send, even though he doesn't have high hopes for this one going viral or anything. No one seems to like his jokes as much as he does. Maybe he should find Pun-Twitter. He makes a mental note to ask MJ if there *is* a Pun-Twitter. He's about to close the app and shove the phone back in his suit when he sees a notification pop up for a direct message. *Maybe someone really dug that joke, after all!*

Spidey opens up the messages and sees a note from a user just named USERRRR021985342. There's no profile picture, either. He and MJ had a long talk about anonymous accounts and how to do some digging to see how real it is. Before reading the message, he clicks through to see what this account's page looks like. It leads to more red flags. There's no bio to speak of, and the account was created *today*! Under his mask, Spidey bites his lip. He drags his thumb along the screen and swipes back to the message. As he reads it, his lenses go wide.

> Hello Spider-Man. You don't know me. But I want to help you. Don't ask me where I got the info, but there's going to be a bank robbery tonight at Manhattan Financial in SoHo, on the corner of Thompson and Prince Street. Please catch them before they can do any harm.

USERRRR021985342

What in the . . .

Spidey takes a screenshot and texts the image to MJ. The speech bubble pops up immediately.

> LET ME LOOK THIS PERSON UP ON MY END,
> BUT IN THE MEANTIME, YOU BETTER CHECK IT
> OUT! JUST BE CAREFUL. IT COULD BE A TRAP!

"Who'd want to trap *me*?" Spidey says to himself. Then he shakes his head. "Wait, it's like Aunt May always says, don't ask questions you don't want the answers to." Spidey *thwips* out a web and starts swinging his way west, past the tourists shopping and over Broadway. The bank is still open when he flips onto an adjacent rooftop, so he settles down to keep watch.

Hours later, Spidey has to admit it. *It's possible that I've been had*, he thinks. MJ called him earlier to say she couldn't find anything on the anonymous user who'd sent the bogus tip. It looked like they'd set up the account using a public computer, or maybe something that would bounce their IP around; she wasn't sure.

"I'm going to start watching YouTube videos on how to crack hackers," she said, joking, but Spidey could hear a note of truth in it.

"MJ, you don't have to become a digital detective or anything," he replied. "I appreciate the thought, but we'll figure this out in a way that doesn't eat into the other eight million things we have to do." He grimaced, thinking of how he still hadn't written up his interview notes to share with the rest of their OSMAKER group.

"All right, all right," she said. "I guess then it's probably my bedtime—I'll have my phone next to my head, though! Call me if *anything* happens." Spidey agreed, said good night, and then went back to watching. And watching. And *watching*.

Once the bank gets locked up for the night, he has a brief moment where he thinks that *maybe* something will finally happen. But all he gets for his hope is a rat running across the expanse of roof behind him, and the fact that no one is around to hear the painfully embarrassing yelp he lets out when he sees it. Eventually, Spidey calls it. There's been no sign of anything in the hours since the last security guard made his rounds inside the building, so Spider-Man texts MJ to let her know that the stakeout was a bust. Then he starts the long trek home, furious at the anonymous user who wasted his night. *Never gonna trust anyone on the internet ever again.*

The next morning, Peter wakes up with a crick in his neck. His phone is chiming. It's not his alarm, though. Mary Jane's sent a series of texts.

> **PETER! CHECK THE BUGLE!**

> **PETER PARKER! WAKE UP!**

> **OMG PETERRRRRR**

She's sent one final text, and it's a screenshot of the *Bugle* homepage. Peter clicks on the image and zooms to the bottom right corner. In large letters he reads *SoHo Bank Robbed at Dawn*. Peter drops his phone onto the bed and puts his head in his hands. *Crap.* In the midst of rubbing at his face, he realizes something. Peter grabs his phone again and opens up Twitter, immediately navigating to his messages. He goes to click on USERRRR021985342 and—*oh no!* This user's account has been deleted.

What had been a blank profile the night before is now a defunct profile.

Peter twists his fingers into his sheets in frustration. He needs to find out who this user was and *how* they knew about the robbery!

CHAPTER THREE

Dr. Jonathan Ohn is conducting an experiment—
something he's used to doing, even if he doesn't get to
experiment so often these days. Right now, he's at home,
standing in his underwear, staring at his reflection in a
full-length mirror. There's a hiss behind him as one of the
ancient silver radiators kicks on, and he lets out a sigh of
appreciation. It is *cold* in his home right now. He goes back
to looking at his mirror image. From head to toe, his skin
is a stark chalk white, except for where it's dotted with
various sizes of black spots that move across his body. He
can shift the black spots so he can see a pair of white eyes,
and the thinnest line that can imply a mouth, but his nose

and lips are camouflaged into his body. He concentrates, and the spots on his face merge and become one large black circle, removing any semblance of a face. From the desk next to him, he picks up a pencil and pushes it into his face. There's no pain—the pencil simply vanishes into the darkness. With a mere whim, he can decide if the spots are solid or work as waypoints from one to another via a portal dimension. Focusing, he pulls a spot from his skin and throws it at the wall, pulling at it until it's large enough for a person to go through. Then he takes a deep breath and wills all the spots to move down to the center of his chest.

He feels their energy pushing and pulling, until he finally he opens his eyes and sees his old self in the mirror again. He looks like he used to look when he was a scientist, forced to tiptoe his way through the mundane day-to-day life of a nobody. A nobody who couldn't amount to anything, whose peers never gave him the respect he knew he deserved. The image staring back at him is tall, white-skinned, and blue-eyed, with a wide pink mouth— albeit with a large dark circle marring his torso. He sneers at the face. That's not him anymore.

"Let's see how long I can keep this disguise up," he says before getting dressed and wrapping himself up in a warm coat. He walks to the spot on the wall and steps through. Then John—*No, I'm the Spot*, he self-corrects—is in the portal dimension. It's a mix of dark and white all around him, and there are millions of spots, each going to a new place, each going somewhere *he* decides. He's found he has to know where the other end leads in order to not end up in a sticky situation, but that's been easy enough. As long as he concentrates, a spot'll open wherever he needs it to. The Spot knows he *can* use the black discs that normally litter his skin, these petrifying polka dots that cover him entirely. He's tested them on a few ATMs in the city, pulling out cash in the dead of night. But those are stagnant and easy enough—though the last time he did notice the bug swinging around and had to make a quick exit after briefly considering starting a fight. He wants to go bigger, see what they can do. He finds the void he's looking for and steps through it directly into a dark closet in the Union Square subway station.

The Spot pushes the door open slightly and sees two MTA workers walking his way. He hastily closes it, counts to five, and then reopens it. *The coast is clear!* He slips out the door and heads up the stairs. At the top, he cranes his neck over the crowds to find the weekday chess players and starts walking in their direction. Picking a table at random, he stands in front of it, watching two old-timers play the game. But he's splitting his attention. That's the next part of the experiment. How many things can he focus on while still maintaining the large black hole covering the center of his chest, allowing him to look like an average human being again? A man at the table near him just moved his bishop to C5 and hit the timer button with a mittened hand. The other player will need to move something to protect his queen.

"Okay, Mr. Chiang, I see what you did there," the man mutters into his scarf. He leans forward and stares, thinking through all his options.

John looks at the board and tries to consider what he'd play if he were sitting in that seat. He can feel it as the hole in the center of his chest ripples. He pulls the spot back and holds it still. There's a bead of sweat that drops down the side of his face. Taking a step back, he moves to take a seat on the low steps facing 14th Street. A block south, he can see the bright lights of the movie theater on the corner. He hugs his middle, more to keep the spot in place than from the weather. The cold isn't really bothering him as much as it used to before he'd changed. Before his most successful experiment.

Slowly, and focusing really hard, John pulls a small part of the black disk away and moves it up from his chest to his shoulder and back down his arm until he can see it poking out from under the edge of his coat sleeve. He itches to dip his finger inside, see what's on the other end, even if he knows the answer.

"Ow!" he yelps as someone's steel-toed boot catches him in the hip. "Watch it!"

In front of him, an angry-looking white kid turns around and glares at him. "You watch it, old man," the teen spits out. "Shouldn't be sitting on those steps anyway," he adds before spinning away and stalking toward the theater.

John considers the kid from behind and grins suddenly. This is the perfect opportunity to test out these new powers of his and see how good these hole things are against a moving target. He looks at that same small disk on the edge of his wrist again, then pulls it forward onto his palm. Resting the other hand against the concrete, he pushes himself to his feet, walking at a swift clip to catch up to the rude kid. They're already by the glass theater doors, and John has to run so he can bump hard against the kid's shoulder as he goes by him, seamlessly dropping the spot on his hand into the kid's pocket.

"Hey!" The kid flips around and shoves John. "Quit it!"

But John's already moving away, and his cheeks apple out in a wide smile. He ducks into the comic book shop across the street and stops in a quiet corner. He pulls another dot down his body and onto his wrist before flinging it onto the wall, just behind the rack. It's perfectly round, matte black, and about the size of his fist. Exactly five centimeters wider than his fist, actually. He looks around quickly; there's no one near him. And John pushes his hand into the spot—now a hole—and he can feel his hand go through the strange dimension he'd seen when he'd finally had the courage to pop his head inside one of the black spaces, and then he feels the rough texture of jeans against his fingers. He grabs at whatever he can and pulls hard. His hand is back in his eyesight now. In it, he's grasping a phone and a wallet. "Jackpot," he says to himself.

Now the Spot knows that even if the target is *moving* he can still get into the spot no matter where he is. *Take that, kid-who-shouldn't-kick-adults-and-then-call-them-old-when-they're-not-even-old!* He grips the phone tighter in his hand. *Maybe I should show that kid up even more. I could probably do some real damage.* Staring at the phone, he sees a trickle of white popping out from under his sleeve, and he banishes the thought, pulling the white and black back into the hole sitting in the center of his chest. *No!* He shakes his head and takes a quick wipe at his forehead with the edge of his sleeve to clear away the damp. Then he opens the wallet, pulls out the cash, and drops the wallet on the ground. He shoves everything into his pockets—the cash, the phone, and his hands—and walks out the door, heading up the street back to the subway in Union Square to make the trek home to his apartment down on Canal Street.

He leaves the dot on the wall behind him, knowing from his limited experience that it only works if he wants it to work. All that's there now is what looks like a black dot painted on the wall. This was a good night, the Spot knows. He whistles as he takes the steps down into the station two at a time. Deep in his thick winter coat, the phone buzzes, but the Spot doesn't feel it.

CHAPTER FOUR

"I'm so sorry!" Spidey says as he swings feetfirst into a mugger. There were three of them, masked and harassing an old Black lady and trying to grab her purse. The *Bugle* gave every employee a pair of Bluetooth headphones for the holidays, and Spider-Man has made quick use of them under his mask. "I didn't know when you said 'partner,' you meant for Spanish. I thought you meant for patrolling." His sentence is punctuated by swift punches to the thief's midsection. Spidey pauses and looks up because just one punch should have sent this guy reeling. But the *giant* robber is staring down at him with an ugly grin.

"Wanna try again, spider-kid?" he sneers.

Spider-Man crouches low, and under his mask, he makes a pained expression. *Why is there always one annoyingly strong robber in a group of thieves?* He makes a fist and punches up hard, catching the guy's chin in an uppercut.

"It's Spider-*Man*!" he yells at the point of contact. "Get it right!"

In his ear, MJ is speaking.

"Argh, I really needed—"

"What was that, MJ?" Spidey asks, throwing another punch.

"Nothing—never mind! We need better code words, maybe? I hate that we're only a week in—"

"And we've barely seen each other. Yeah, it *sucks*," Spidey says, landing in front of the heap of bad guys who are now finally out for the count. He shoots some quick webbing at their hands and feet. "Excuse me." He walks up to the old lady, who is glaring at the pile of thieves behind him. "Are you okay?" he asks her.

"Yeah, I'm all right, honey. Thanks for the assist. Have a candy." And she pulls out a hard caramel wrapped in clear plastic and places it in his palm, curling his fingers back over it.

"Oh, uh, thanks," he says, and holds it tight in his fist.

"Now you have to eat it or she'll feel bad," MJ jokes into his ear.

Spidey takes a step back and waves. "Stay safe, now!"

"I think I should be saying that to you!" the lady says back to him with a laugh. "You go on. I'll get these children dealt with." And Spidey is extra glad to not be one of the bad guys because it's clear that woman means *business*. He shoots out a web and springs forward, swinging his way downtown. Something occurs to him.

"Hey, MJ, what do you call a group of thieves? Like a group of crows is a murder, right?"

"Where are you going with this, Peter?" she asks, and Spidey can hear the tired acceptance in her tone. He holds in a laugh.

"A cutpurse of thieves? A pickpocket of swindlers?"

"Oh my god," she groans. "I think the jokes are getting worse."

"I try." And this time he lets the laugh loose, following it with a whoop as he swings by a coffee shop littered with people bundled up in their parkas and peacoats. The crowd cheers hello, and Spidey feels warm in his chest. "I'm sorry for the mix-up," he says right as MJ says, "Sorry about the confusion."

There's a beat and it's quiet on MJ's end, and Spidey's stomach twists, but then she's laughing and he's laughing and it feels okay. He knows they'll need to work on how to be extra clear so they can keep everything straight. *Maybe MJ's right about those code words. . . .*

"Hey," MJ says, interrupting his thoughts. "Do you think I could come with you on patrol next time?"

Spidey swings into a flip and lands on a sign above an Italian restaurant.

"Oh, uh—uh," he stammers. *What if she gets hurt?* "It's pretty boring and it would be *awesome* to have you here . . . but it can get dangerous, though?" he asks at the end, even though he knows the answer, but hoping to soften the blow.

"I mean, obviously if there's something *dangerous* and super villainy happening, I'd tap out. But I don't know if you've noticed, Peter, I'm pretty good at handling myself. Besides, I want to see what it's like for you!"

Spidey stands and crawls up the side of the building to the roof, where he takes a seat, letting his legs hang over the edge. He surveys the city below him and nods. *MJ's right. She should get to see this part of my life, too.*

"Okay, you know what?" he says, and is surprised to hear a very baritone, decidedly non-MJ voice answer him.

"What?" He hops up and turns around to find a man and a woman sitting at a rickety porch table on the roof behind him.

"Ahhhhh— I . . ." he says, and then draws it out in a long syllable to cover up the fact that they'd surprised him. "Uh, nothing. Nothing. Just talking to myself."

"Nice save, Pete." MJ giggles into his ear. His cheeks go warm.

"That's great, Spidey," the woman says. "But you're kind of killing our moment here."

And then Spider-Man takes in the wrapped rose on the table, and the glasses full of some dark liquid. He puts his hands up and walks backward to the edge of the roof. "Sorry about that!" Spider-Man says as he steps onto the edge. "Hope the rest of the date goes well, though!" he calls as he launches himself forward and *thwips* out a web, catching it when it sticks to a ledge high above him, and swinging forward. In his ear, MJ is cracking up, and Spidey can't help but grin. "Okay," he cuts in, "next time we go out on a date, it's gonna be a *spider-date*."

"Yes!" MJ squeals, and Spidey can picture her sitting in her room fisting her hands and grinning ear to ear in her polka-dot pajamas. "Okay, okay, I have to go, Maia and I are video-chatting about next steps for the project—but call me if there are any black-dot updates . . . or if you get another weird DM from that anonymous account."

Spidey had almost completely forgotten about that account. He hadn't gotten any more messages on Twitter that weren't just people telling him he was bad at pretending to be Spider-Man.

"I will," he says to MJ. "But I feel like it was a fluke."

"Why does that feel like a famous-last-words moment?" she says, and then her voice goes up: "Oh! Gotta go, I'm officially late calling Maia. Bye, Peter!"

"Hey, Maia!" MJ waves as Maia walks up to join her on Jewel Avenue. They'd chatted the night before about their part of the OSMAKER project, but the more they talked about the community garden idea, the more they'd wanted to make their own!

As they were saying their good-byes, Maia stopped and said, "We should try to do one of these, right?" And MJ had responded with an enthusiastic yes. So now here they were after an epic Google Mapping session to check out some of the empty lots they'd seen in Forest Hills.

"Hey, lady!" Maia replies as she gets closer. She's got a camera case slung across her black puffer coat and a knapsack on her back. "This weather is *no joke*. Should we be doing this in the spring?"

MJ's thankful for the warm scarf wrapped around the lower part of her face as an icy wind blows her hair back. She shakes her head at Maia's question. "Nah, if I've learned anything from shadowing Councilman Torres, it's that local government is *slow*. If we get an application in now, *hopefully* it'll be ready for this summer." She threads her arm through Maia's and pulls the other girl forward. "Let's go look at some dirt!"

Maia laughs in response.

They make their way up and down a few streets and take pictures of potential lots and note addresses, but nothing feels quite right. But finally, Mary Jane turns a corner and they find it. "Maia! Come look at this!"

Her friend jogs a little to catch up to MJ and stops by her side. There's no scarf around Maia's face to hide the smile that's blooming across her features. "MJ! This is awesome!"

The lot they've found is just west of the familiar facade of the Forest Hills library, and it's about the size of three brownstones in a row. There's a chain-link fence in front of it, so MJ presses her nose through a gap to see as much as she can.

"It's so big!" she says finally, picturing all the plants and paths they would be able to fit in the space. "And it's so close to the library!"

"Hold on, I'm writing down the address," Maia says, pulling off her gloves and typing into her phone. "Okay, got it." She joins MJ at the fence, peering in alongside her. "I think this could work, if we can get it. Should we . . . just go print the application right now?" she asks, her eyes sparkling. "It feels like kismet that we're right next door to a place that has a printer," she jokes.

MJ laughs, but she doesn't *not* believe it. This lot feels right.

"Let's do it," she says, and they head into the warmth

of the library. The librarian waves at them when they come through the door, and they send her a chorus of hellos before heading to the computers.

"Okay . . ." Maia sits at the machine closest to the printer. "I think we have to go to the NYC GreenThumb site, and that has all the forms."

"I love that that's what they decided to call it," MJ says, sitting in the chair next to Maia's but leaving the computer in front of her untouched.

"Same," Maia replies, already at the site and navigating through the links. MJ pulls her phone out of her pocket and scrolls through her messages while Maia reads through the webpages. There's one from Peter, and MJ can't help the smile pulling at her cheeks.

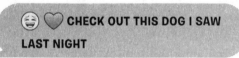

CHECK OUT THIS DOG I SAW LAST NIGHT

His text is accompanied by a picture of a French bull-dog in a Spider-Man onesie, and MJ covers her mouth to stifle the laugh that's threatening to come out of her. She sends back a quick note asking Peter if he should be getting licensing money. She sees three dots pop up, but before the reply comes through, Maia speaks up next to her.

"Found it! And printing the applications now. It's a ton of pages, so maybe we can go through the application together at school? I'm visiting my girlfriend, Dani, next weekend, so I won't be around to do stuff."

There's an apology in her tone, but MJ doesn't think she needs it. She thinks back to asking Peter about joining him on patrol.

"That will be fun!" she says, trying to let Maia know that it's not a big deal without focusing too much on it in a way that would be embarrassing.

"Yeah, I'm really looking forward to it. We don't get to see each other as often as we'd like—you and Peter are so lucky going to the same school!"

MJ tucks a strand of hair behind her ear and nods in agreement. "We definitely are, but between my internship and his, and schoolwork, and barely any classes in common, we haven't had a chance to actually hang out in, like, a week." *Not to mention the night job*, she adds silently.

The computer dings to signify their sheets have printed, and Maia walks the short trek to the printer to grab their application. Together, they bow their heads over the thick stack of paperwork.

"Maybe he can help us with this garden thing, too?" Maia asks, gathering the paperwork.

MJ makes a noncommittal noise before adding, "He's got a lot going on already."

"True, I'm not sure he has the organizational skills to add anything else to his plate." Maia laughs before looking down at the papers in her hands to scan through the questions. "This all seems easy enough. . . ."

"Wait, does that one ask who owns the lot?" MJ wonders, pointing to a question near the bottom of the sheet.

"Shoot, yes. Let's see. . . ."

MJ's now seated in front of the computer they've been using, and her fingers fly across the keyboard as she searches for the lot's address. They comb through a few pages of results before finally finding an extremely generic-looking site that claims to hold the ownership rights.

"KRT Technologies? What would a technology group want with an empty lot?" MJ asks.

Maia's face is screwed up in confusion, and she shrugs. "I have no idea. What does their site say they even do?" She leans forward to look at the About page MJ has landed on. "'A company committed to a bright, new future by way of synergy, organization, and unique solutions,'" she reads off.

"What the heck does *that* mean? That's a lot of words to say basically nothing."

"Yeah, I think my dad calls this corporatespeak," Maia says. "I don't really know what that means, but this feels like it. Right?"

"Right," MJ agrees. "A whole lotta nothing." She hits back and googles the company name plus the words "year" and "established." "Huh," she says after the results load. "KRT Tech has only been around for, like, three months. And it doesn't look like they have any real physical address. This is weird."

"Find out where the URL is registered," Maia says.

MJ taps the keyboard again and reads through the URL registry. "It's some address in Vancouver." She frowns. Something about this is rubbing her the wrong way. "I don't like this. It's giving me a bad feeling."

"Hmm, I think my mom might know someone who might be able to help us figure this out," Maia says, tapping a finger against her chin. "Let me do some digging with her, and I'll tell you what I find out."

"Okay, cool," MJ says. *But I'm going to do some digging on my end.*

We feel it,

   we feel it,

      we feel it,

we feel it.

   It's here.

      There is something here for us to use. Home.
It has us. It's with us. It's near the island.

      So weak. Need help.
Find help. Found help.

      The plan. We have the plan.

CHAPTER FIVE

Peter yawns loudly, not bothering to cover his mouth. He's alone in the records room at the *Daily Bugle*, filing away some photographs his manager, Kayla Ramirez, had passed to him. He really prefers getting to write social copy for his Spider-Man pictures, but unfortunately, the internship can't just be that. He also helps with all sorts of things around the office. He looks through the stack of pictures in his hands. Most of them are just of random things—sporting events, a plane landing, the Oscorp building Christmas tree, the Museum of Modern Art's latest exhibit—but as he's flipping through, he's surprised to find a picture he'd taken of himself from a few months earlier, just after the Sandman stuff. *Are these technically selfies?* Peter thinks, holding on to the printed photo. It's one of his better action shots. He's got one leg high, flying toward a bad guy off-screen. . . . *Who was it again? Oh, yeah.* Peter rolls his eyes remembering. *That old dude, the Vulture or whatever. More like the Buzzard, considering what a buzz-kill he was.* Peter snickers to himself and then moves to find the filing cabinet for *S.* Locating it, he pulls the drawer open and riffles through the folders, finally spying one for *Spider-Man, falling.* Peter's face takes on an affronted look, and he opens the folder to see a litany of photos, all of him falling in increasingly embarrassing ways.

"What the heck?" he mutters to himself. Pulling the folder out of the drawer, he turns, like he's considering taking it, but then he lets out a deep sigh and turns around to put it back. *No, Pete, you can't steal from your place of work. Even if you really want to.* He drops the folder back in and then resumes looking at the rest, trying to find the right places to put all these pictures. *Spider-Man, action; Spider-Man, eating—ignoring that one; Spider-Man, first appearance?* Peter's eyes widen, and he pulls the folder out. Opening it, he spies an article on top.

MAN SPIDER SPOTTED IN LOWER MANHATTAN

BY J. JONAH JAMESON

A man dressed in a red-and-blue onesie with a spider-web pattern swung through the streets of the Lower

East Side late last night. The costumed hero stopped no fewer than four crimes across the avenues of our beloved city. It makes this reporter ask what other good can this Man Spider do? The potential this has for making our communities feel safer, just because someone special is watching out for them, is paramount.

It's a short piece, and dated some time early last year. It must have been *right* after everything that happened with Uncle Ben. Peter runs his fingers along the paper and feels the raised ink of the printed words absent-mindedly, thinking back to those early days. He furrows his brows and rereads the author's name. *Jameson wrote this?! What happened to him?!*

This time, Peter does take the folder—*I'll put it back, but I have questions that need answers!* He leaves the rest of the photos on the desk in the records room and takes the elevator back up to his space next to Kayla. He crosses his fingers while he's in the elevator, hoping that she'll be there. When he sees that she's seated at her computer, he lets out a sigh of relief.

"Hey, Kayla?" he asks, taking his seat at the desk behind hers.

The click-clacking of the keyboard pauses when she swivels her chair around to face him. "What's up, Peter?" she asks, and he passes her the folder.

"I found this downstairs and I wanted to ask . . . Well . . ." He hesitates and rubs a hand against the back of his neck. His eyes dart this way and that, looking for the right words. Finally, he settles on "What happened?"

Kayla's opened the folder and is skimming the short article. As she gets further along, her jaw drops open.

"*Jameson* wrote this?" she asks. Frowning, but more in thought than anger.

Peter nods. "My thoughts exactly. Did you know he used to like Spider-Man?" He can't help it, and he starts bouncing his knee.

"I had no idea—it must have been before I started working on that beat. I honestly barely remember pre-Spidey days. I know he's only been doing it for a little while, but it feels like he's part of the city now."

There's a quick flash of joy across Peter's features before he settles them back into a careful neutrality. Kayla hands the folder back to him.

"I just wonder what—"

"Spider-Man did to make Jonah so mad?" Kayla interjects. "Me too . . ."

If Peter is being honest, he hasn't considered that as an option. But when he thinks back to those early days . . . *I did mess up a lot back then. Maybe I* did *do something to lose Jameson's trust in me. I must have disappointed him somehow.* The thought makes something in his stomach curdle, and he tries not to let his anxiety show on his face. *Well, if he liked me once, maybe he can like me again. I just have to be better.* Peter nods to himself, resolved.

Kayla's turned back to her computer. "I am dying to know more about this, but I'm on deadline with this piece," she says over her shoulder in apology.

"It's okay," he says, getting up to head back down to the records room and finish filing the photos. He feels strangely buoyed by the find. *I can get Jameson back to liking Spidey!*

A few hours later, Peter hits the down button in the elevator bank and steps back to wait. He has to get home so he and MJ can *finally* have some time to hang out together one-on-one. A loud *ding* sounds out signifying which elevator is coming, and Peter moves to stand in front of it. The doors open, and Peter's stomach twists again. Standing in the small space is none other than J. Jonah Jameson. For once, Jameson doesn't have his standard look of absolute fury on his face. He looks kind of calm. Peter steps in and takes a deep breath.

"Hello, sir."

"Hm? Oh, it's you. Good to see you working hard, kid," Jameson says, and Peter is elated. Jameson's *never* complimented him before. Peter squares his shoulders and musters his courage. *I've gone toe-to-toe with Otto Octavius,* he thinks. *I can do this!*

"Sir . . . I was in the records room earlier, and I found an article you wrote. . . ."

At this, Jameson turns to face Peter fully. He's nodding and looking at him appraisingly. "Yeah? What piece was it? Had a killer write-up about Phantom back in the day. Almost got me a Pulitzer if that other hack hadn't won. Whole thing's rigged," Jameson adds, nearly as an aside.

"No, it was about Spider-Man—back when he first started." Jameson's face shutters. He turns away, and Peter can see his eyebrows come low over his eyes. But he's made it this far, so he keeps going. "I just wanted to ask if something happened? It seemed like you were kind of . . . okay with him back then?"

"It's nothing. Leave it alone."

"I was just wondering about the . . . change in direction?" Peter tries hopefully.

Jameson hands are in fists balled at his side, and Peter realizes he's made a mistake.

"Don't talk to me about that spider-freak, kid," Jameson says in a quiet voice, and it's way scarier than when he's yelling. Peter's about to apologize when the doors open. Jameson takes one step out and then turns back to face him. Peter swears he can see Jameson's mustache quivering in anger. "In fact," he spits out, "you're fired! Don't bother coming back!" And then, without another look in Peter's direction, he turns away and speeds off.

Peter's so shocked he doesn't make it out of the elevator in time, and the doors close on him. In the reflection of the elevator's brass door, Peter sees his own face fall, and he closes his eyes to the sight.

Oh no . . .

"And stay out!"

The Spot watches as a gigantic man carries someone out of the Café With No Name and throws the wayward patron onto the street. Pulling at his collar, the Spot thinks about his tactics. He's got to get inside that building. He deserves to be inside that building. He's been here since early evening, waiting for the sun to go down and for the street to get quiet.

"Jeez, you don't have to be such a jerk about it." The man in the street is standing and rubbing his backside in pain, glaring at the bouncer, who doesn't deign to turn around, much less respond. Even in the dark, the Spot can see the injured man's pained expression. "Jerks," he repeats to himself before walking away, limping slightly. Spot does not want to end up in that situation. He has to go big. He's been here, sitting on a bench across the street from the café in Lower Manhattan, for about an hour. To his disgust, most have gotten in *fine*.

I had to walk by the place four times before I even felt safe sitting across the street, and now someone like freakin' Stiltman just walks in! Stiltman?! That guy hasn't done anything in the last year but get beat on by a tiny bug man in a red-and-blue onesie.

Spot's blood is boiling, and he has to take some deep breaths to calm down. He can feel the void deep in his chest wavering under his shirt, and he has to keep it together. *Stiltman!* he thinks again, frowning deeply. But that settles it, and the Spot stands, crossing the avenue with a purpose and halting in front of the worn, unremarkable door. There's no sign and no indication that this is anything significant. Even the dirty awning above the door is completely free of any words, but Spot knows a power hub when he sees one. He's been itching to up his game, and word on the street is the Café With No Name is where that can happen.

The handle is dull and black and the paint on the door is peeling around it, but Spot holds on to it tight and turns, pushing the door open with a bang. The streetlights from outside stream in, and Spot has the briefest chance to see dark forms flinching and turning away at their tables before the huge form of the bouncer steps between him and the inside of the café. Spot looks up . . . and up . . . and up at the man before him. A white man with dark brown hair, who could be anywhere from twenty-five to fifty-five and is probably three hundred pounds of solid muscle, glares down at him with disgust.

"What the heck do you think you're tryin' to do here, buddy? This ain't a coffee shop; that's two blocks away." He crosses his arms and continues to look down his nose at the Spot. Something in the Spot's chest roils . . . and it's not his Spot World calling. It's a dark fury, radiating out from inside of him.

"What do you mean what am I doing here? I'm a super villain," Spot says, not without a little pride. "I stole, like, four thousand bucks, easy, in the last three days."

The monster man's eyebrows go up in mock surprise. "Oh, you hear that, guys?" he calls back into the dark of the shop. "Four thousand bones this guy says he stole. Four whole thousand," he repeats, sneering at the Spot. Behind him, Spot can hear the mocking laughter of the hidden patrons. Then the bouncer leans forward and in a menacing tone says, "You're not ready for this, *guy*, so get outta here."

"I have a right to be at the CWNN!" Spot shouts out. "I'm as much a big bad as any of you creeps!"

"No one calls it that. Get out," the bouncer says, and Spot hates that he can hear disgust dripping in his voice. It makes his insides curdle, and he feels like screaming. Instead, he takes a step backward out of the doorway.

"Fine," he spits out. "I'll leave. But you'll be sorry."

With that, Spot spins around and is proud that he doesn't flinch at the sound of the door slamming behind him. He stalks away and digs his nails into his palms, trying to keep it together. *How dare they? They don't know who they're messing with.* He makes his way up the block, when a strange calm comes over his face and he turns suddenly to the right into an empty alley. Picking his way among the debris and trash, he finds a space that's a ways off from the busy street. Focusing, he lets the black hole at his chest break off into tiny spots, and he's in his new form again. He pulls a spot up on the wall in front of him and smiles a smile laced through with contempt. *I'll show them*, he thinks, and hops into the hole. He's calculated exactly where he needs to land for maximum impact, so when he gets to his Spot World, he takes a moment to look at all the black holes littering the white all around him. Then he finds the right spot and steps through it.

And falls straight down on top of the bouncer who had stepped into the room away from the front door.

"WHAT THE HECK?!" the bouncer screams, yanking at the Spot and pulling him off his back.

"AH!!!" the Spot cries.

But he doesn't even have a chance to see anything other than a huge white fist heading directly toward him. And then he's out.

John is staring at his laptop in shock.

"I've solved it. I've *solved* it!" He whips his head

around to find the room empty of his colleagues. Only Val remains, a young Nepali woman who's a part of the same research team. "Val, I *solved* it," he says again.

She nods absent-mindedly. "That's great, John." But she doesn't ask him anything. She doesn't seem interested in seeing his brilliance.

John frowns at her. "Don't you want you to know what I solved?" he asks her.

Val finally looks at him. She closes her notebook and stands, moving closer to look over John's shoulder at his screen. "What did you solve?"

"Interdimensional travel," he answers, with more than just a hint of smugness. "I think, using this equation"— he points to his screen—"I can give people the ability to use their own energy—the electrical impulses in their own bodies—to move through space nearly instantaneously."

But Val doesn't look nearly as impressed as he is expecting. "John, you can't use this for the grant. They need something from us that they can use in six months . . . not . . . decades. This would take decades of trials."

John scoffs. "You don't think I can do it."

"I don't think you can *ethically* do it," Val corrects him.

"What does *that* mean?" John asks, his voice dangerous.

Val takes a step back from him. "Nothing, John. Never mind," she says. She heads back to her station.

The quiet in the lab is awkward, disrupted only by the soft sounds of Val packing up her things. John is seething.

He knows what the others say about him, how they mock him—that he cuts corners, that he doesn't follow the rules—but they don't think about how, throughout the history of science, people have broken rules as a path toward greatness. That's the path John should be on. Instead he's stifled at every turn by "rules" and "regulations." It infuriates him. He stares at his laptop screen again. He has it all written out in black-and-white, a path toward self-teleportation. He resolves to make this work . . . even if he has to test it on himself. He'll prove them wrong, prove to them all that he has a mind worthy of respect. Worthy of adulation.

John will remember this moment. He'll think of it when he's standing in the Spot dimension for the first time and staring at the potential around him, and he'll laugh. The anger comes later—after he's been kicked out of the university, after he loses his funding. That's when he promises to do whatever it takes to get what he's owed.

When the Spot comes to, he's lying outside in a heap on the sidewalk. He shakes his head, clearing out the memories of his old life. His body is aching, and he groans. He cracks open one eye and blearily watches the bouncer's shoes as he walks away. Spot can hear the soft *shwww* of the bouncer dusting his hands off.

"I don't know what that bizarro costume is, and I don't care. If you wanted to sneak in, you shoulda changed your coat at least. Come back when you're a real criminal, weirdo," the man says without turning around, and then he walks inside the CWNN and closes the door hard behind him.

"You'll be sorry," Spot croaks out, but he knows no one hears him. He rolls onto his back and takes in a lungful of air. The sky is dark above him, but the lights of the city blot out any stars other than few a faint dots. For a second, Spot wonders if he'd be able to go all the way to space if he wanted. He chuckles, but there's no humor in the broken sound. Slowly, he drops a spot next to him on the ground and rolls into it, moving through Spot World and back into his apartment with a soft *thud*. He lets out a puff of air and moves to sit up, but immediately hisses in pain when he tries. His head is *aching*.

There's movement to his right, and he realizes he's landed in front of his mirror. There's no proof of the altercation on his white and black-spotted skin, but curious, he pulls the spots inward and is pained to see a deep black bruise forming around the right eye of his old face. He lets out a loud cry of frustration and slams a fist against the floor. Then he lets the tightness at his chest go, and he's back to being the Spot.

"They'll all be sorry," he says, biting. "They'll wish they showed me some respect today." It's like the lab all

54

over again, underestimation and too-easy dismissal. The Spot has had enough of that to last a lifetime—this is his chance for a do-over, to be somebody, and he isn't planning on wasting it.

For a few minutes, the only sound in his apartment is his own heavy breathing. But then something catches his ear. He turns his head, following the sound. It's a slight buzzing. The Spot pulls his own phone out, but it's silent. The buzzing continues.

Standing, he looks around the room. On his desk, there's a muted glow. He walks toward it and finds the cell phone he'd taken off the kid a few days earlier. There's a moment of surprise that the power is still on, and strangely, there's no phone number, just one word flashing at the top of the screen: ANSWER ANSWER ANSWER ANSWER.

Unable to hold in the same curiosity that led his body to where it is now, the Spot picks up the phone and slides his finger across the screen.

"Hello?" he says.

A reedy chorus of voices comes through the weak speaker and into his ear.

"We know how to get their respect."

CHAPTER SIX

Peter stands outside of a brownstone on the Upper East Side. Their OSMAKER group agreed to meet at Randy's this week since the Robertsons have a dinner tonight and Randy is worried about being late for it.

Peter rings the doorbell once and starts praying that Mr. Robertson won't open the door. "Please be Randy, please be Randy, please be Randy, please be Randy," he repeats to himself over and over. He hears the latch give inside, and in his pockets he crosses his fingers. He's not ready to see Mr. Robertson yet, not just after having been uncere- moniously fired by J. Jonah Jameson in the elevator just the day before. The door in front of him swings open showing a grinning Randy, and Peter lets out a sigh of relief.

"Hey, man! You're the first one here," Randy says, stepping aside to let Peter inside. The entry hall is cozy and clean. Peter sees a raised board off to the side with shoes on it, so he kicks his own off while Randy gestures to a line of hooks on the wall. "You can put your coat and stuff up there. My room's on the second floor."

"Cool," Peter replies, pulling off his layers and hanging them up. He shoves his gloves and hat into the pocket of his parka and finally runs a hand through his hair when he's finished to get it to some semblance of a normal hairstyle. When he finally turns to face the interior of the house, Randy's at the end of the foyer, waiting for him at the bottom of the stairs, grinning. Peter walks past the living room and kitchen to join him.

"Are your parents home?" he asks as they walk up the flight of stairs, hoping his nerves don't show.

"Yeah," Randy replies, a few steps ahead of him. "But my dad's busy in his office working on some last-minute story someone just turned in for the Big Man. And I think my mom's helping my sister with her homework." He shrugs as they make it to the top floor. They bypass a closed door on their right, and another on the left before making it to Randy's open bedroom door. "Come on in," Randy says. "Take a load off." Peter takes his backpack and drops it onto Randy's floor, then moves to take a seat at the desk. Randy falls backward onto his bed.

In his back pocket, Peter's phone buzzes. He pulls it out and sees a text from MJ.

> **SRY! MAIA AND I ARE ON OUR WAY AND'LL BE THERE SOON!**

"MJ and Maia are running late, I guess," Peter says after reading it, and from his bed, Randy laughs.

"That's fine with me. We can wait to get started then." He picks up the remote off his nightstand and turns on the television mounted to the wall at the end of his bed. "Have you played the new *Executioner's Promise*? It's set in ancient Greece, and it is *suuuuper* bloody." Randy's pulled both controllers out and is holding one out to Peter. Grinning, he takes it.

"No! But I've been wanting to. Can we do co-op?"

"Def," Randy says, hitting a button on the controller to turn on the gaming console. Peter loses himself in the game for a few minutes, following Randy's character through a series of battles and puzzles. They're about to enter the Minotaur's cave when Pete hears Randy's mother's voice from the hall.

"Right through there, girls."

"So yeah, my mom's still trying to figure out who in Canada owns that freakin' URL," Maia is saying as they walk through Randy's door. *Canadian URL?* Peter thinks. *What are MJ and Maia up to?* MJ follows Maia into the room, and Peter puts the controller down and gets up but then immediately sits back down. *I can't hug MJ in front of everyone.* His face reddens, and he grins and waves awkwardly instead.

Peter's looking at her like he doesn't know how to act, and MJ tries not to giggle at his discomfort. They really are still figuring out this whole couple thing, but sometimes it's funny. Like now, she was guessing he got up to give her a hug and then realized he didn't want to do it while Randy and Maia were around and potentially get teased about it. *I wouldn't have minded, though*, she thinks.

"Hi, Peter," she says, shooting him a soft smile so he knows.

"Hey, Pete," Maia says in a louder voice, dropping her bag on the floor and jumping onto Randy's bed next to him.

"What's this about a Canadian URL?" Peter asks as he stands up from his seat. "Here, MJ, you can take this. I'll sit on the floor." She starts to protest, and he waves her away. "It's fine. I need to switch it up anyway." He grins, crouching into a familiar pose before sitting down on the carpet.

Then she processes his first question. *Oh no, I can't believe I forgot to tell Peter about that weird company we found.* She and Maia lock eyes, and she knows it's too much to get into right now if they want to wrap up their OSMAKER work before Randy has to leave for dinner.

"I'll tell you about it later. It totally slipped my mind," she says, and Peter's face falls just the tiniest bit. But he brightens up so quickly, she isn't even sure she saw it.

"I'll hold you to that," he says, and looks like he's about to say something else, when Maia claps her hands.

"Should we get started?" she asks when everyone turns to her.

"Dang, Maia, big teacher energy coming out over here," Randy says, rubbing at his ears. "That clap was *loud.*"

"I have, like, a hundred cousins, man. You have to be loud in my family." Maia laughs.

Peter's pulled his backpack next to him and is rummaging through it. He pulls out a notebook and opens it up to find a series of papers shoved into the back. "Sorry," he says, handing them each a few pieces from the packet. "It's a little crumpled, but I was in a hurry—"

"Pete, you're *always* in a hurry," Randy jokes. "It's fine. We can still read it."

MJ looks down at the papers in her hand and sees that they're printouts of app mock-ups and submission forms that Peter has created for their activist portal.

"Peter, these are *great*," she says truthfully. His cheeks go wide with a smile, and he rubs at the back of his head in a now-familiar gesture.

"They are. I love this one that's the form to connect to other activists. We may want to double-check the language, but it all looks really good from just a skim of it," Maia adds, bouncing her heels against the edge of Randy's bed. Her bright wool socks leave little threads of blue on the white bedspread. She grimaces and leans forward to brush them away. Randy gives her a look like, *What are you doing? Don't worry about it*, and MJ laughs a bit.

"Thanks," Peter says, looking down at the notebook in his hands. He's missed the entire exchange. "I looked at a few of the sites you guys mentioned last time, those groups you went to see? Just kind of culled the ideas from there and put them together, to be honest."

"Considering that's the whole point of this app, to pull it all into one place and help people from multiple areas, that makes sense, bro." Randy nods, reading through the sheets. Then he leans over and finds his own binder on the floor next to his bed, pulling it up with him as he settles back into a sitting position with his legs stretched out long in front of him. "Okay, so what I did . . ."

They work for another hour or so before Randy's mother calls from somewhere else in the house.

"Randy! I hope you all are wrapping up soon. We'll need to leave in about twenty minutes!"

"OKAY, MOM!" Randy yells back, and everyone else covers their ears.

"Dude, you called *me* loud?" Maia says, grimacing and moving to scooch off the bed.

Randy follows her, and Peter's already moving to put his things back in his bag.

"I have no idea what you're talking about." Randy laughs. "Oh, Pete, before you leave, do you wanna go to the *Bugle* together next week? We can get the train after school." MJ's packing up her own things and doesn't hear Peter's response, but it's strange because he's only a few feet away. She turns to look at him and realizes he's deliberately mumbling it into his bag. Apparently, Randy didn't hear, either. "What'd you say?"

Peter looks up, and before answering, he lets out a deep sigh. "I said I got fired."

What?! MJ has no idea what he's talking about and is stunned. Randy and Maia both look as shocked as she does—Maia's stopped pulling her things together and Randy is clearly at a loss for words. MJ opens her mouth to ask Peter what happened, when a deep voice breaks into Randy's room.

"Fired?" Randy's dad, Mr. Robertson, must have been walking by when Peter answered, and he's stepped into the room and has his hands on his hips. "What do you mean, 'fired'?"

Mr. Robertson opens the door to his study and waves Peter in.

"Go on, take a seat, Peter," he says, pointing at one of the bright yellow armchairs in the corner. There's an identical pair to its right, with a small wooden table between them. Peter holds in a heavy sigh and walks in, taking the proffered seat. *This is so awkward!* Mr. Robertson settles down into the other chair and leans forward, bracing his elbows on his knees. His glasses have slid down low on his nose again, and Peter is reminded of the first time they chatted all those months ago, when he'd interviewed for the internship position. Peter's knee is bouncing in a sharp, fast rhythm, and he spreads one hand over it willing it to stop, but his nerves aren't listening to him today. Mr. Robertson gives him a long look before leaning back into his chair.

"Do you want to tell me what happened?" he asks finally.

So Peter looks down at the floor and twists his fingers and tells Mr. Robertson the whole story without looking up once. When he's finished, he hears a strange sound come from Mr. Robertson's direction, and he looks up and his eyes go wide. Randy's dad is . . . trying not to laugh? He's got a fist tight against his mouth, and his eyes are glistening. *What the heck?* Peter's eyebrows furrow, and his pride protests Mr. Robertson's reaction. Mr. Robertson must see it on his face because he immediately sobers and pulls his hand away from his mouth.

"I'm sorry, son. I don't mean to laugh, but . . ." He pauses, like he's trying to weigh his options on what to say to Peter.

"But?" Peter prompts.

"Peter, you've just been through a rite of passage," Mr. Robertson says, finally settling on an answer. "This is, unfortunately, a J. Jonah Jameson standard thing."

Peter is shocked. "Sir, with all due respect, that is . . ." He hesitates, unwilling to be outright insubordinate.

"Really messed up?" Mr. Robertson asks, with a knowing look on his face. "I wish I could give you a better explanation, but sometimes there isn't one. Jonah is . . . Well, Jonah is Jonah, and I promise you that you are categorically un-fired. Just so you know," he says, laughter back in his voice, "if you hadn't shown up for your next shift, Jonah would have fired you again . . . and then gotten mad when you didn't show up. Kid, Jonah's fired everyone in that building more times than I can count, and I'm not sure he's *actually* ever fired anyone. Doesn't have the heart, if we're being honest."

Peter scrunches his nose and frowns. "I hate that a

lot, Mr. Robertson," he says. "That feels like someone's allowed to behave badly just because they're in charge."

"You're a very thoughtful kid, aren't you, Peter?" Mr. Robertson asks in response, *and* without really responding to Peter's comment, he can't help but notice.

Peter shrugs. "I don't know, sir."

"You can call me, Robbie, Peter," Mr. Robertson says.

"I'll . . . try, sir." Peter grins, but it's shaky. He's had a stressful twenty-four hours. "I do appreciate you telling me I'm not fired. But . . . can I ask you why Mr. Jameson gets *so* mad about Spider-Man? Like, don't get me wrong!" he says, raising his hands up, palms out. "I'm really glad that my captions aren't getting edited anymore, but . . . he *fired* me just for asking about it."

Mr. Robertson sighs, and the heavy breath breaks the room's quiet. "I can't tell you the whole story, Peter, because it's not mine to tell. But once upon a time, Jonah lost someone very close to him, and I think he's just upset, or maybe even hurt, that he didn't have the Spider-Man to save that person."

Peter's heart drops into his stomach, and he has to stop himself from recoiling. That's something he understands deeply. He knows that no one should have to live through a loss just because there wasn't some super hero around where he needed to be. He thinks of his own family. He thinks of Dr. Shah losing his wife and daughter.

"Oh," he says quietly.

Mr. Robertson nods. "It's not fair—I'm not saying that at all—but grief does funny things to people."

"I get that," Peter says, without really thinking, staring off at nothing in Mr. Robertson's study. He doesn't want to see Mr. Robertson's face shift to pity and is thankful by the time he looks up again to find the other man's expression is carefully neutral.

"Randy told me about what happened with your family, Peter, and I'll just say I'm sorry for your loss, and we can leave it at that."

"Thank you, sir," Peter says, moving to stand up. "But I think your wife is going to kill me if I make you late for dinner," he jokes weakly. Mr. Robertson does him the favor of laughing, though, and Peter's spirits are lifted slightly.

"You're not wrong, son, you're not wrong." Mr. Robertson puts his hands on his knees and pushes himself out of the chair, gesturing for Peter to follow him as they exit the room. "Come on—let's see if I can get some of Martha's brownies into your backpack before you go."

CHAPTER SEVEN

It's been a few days since their last OSMAKER meeting, and MJ is sitting in the school media center on her free period working on her part of the project. She scribbles in her notebook and glares at the page. Working on this project isn't nearly as exciting by herself. She isn't *really* upset about it, and the rest of her team all have solid excuses. Randy is at an away basketball game, Maia is at her grandmother's for a few days, and Peter is helping the yearbook out with some club photography. And . . . Dr. Shah is absent again. They've only been back at school for a few short weeks, and it's already the third time their teacher hasn't made it into school.

I hope everything is okay. . . .

She stares at the blank piece of paper again. She's supposed to be organizing their thoughts into a coherent welcome page, but she can't help but be distracted. She and Peter still haven't had time to talk about what happened at his job. When she asked him about it, he grinned and said, "It turns out I'm not fired! It was all a mistake." And then he went out on patrol, and she had to study for a calculus test, so they couldn't even talk on the *phone. He still hasn't taken me on patrol with him, either! He's probably putting it off because he thinks it's too dangerous*, she grouses. There is also the strange DM about the bank robbery from earlier that is bothering her. And Peter hasn't asked her about her project with Maia . . . though she knows she can't really be upset about that. Patrolling or talking about her garden thing? There is no competition. Besides, MJ and Maia have made no headway on figuring out who the mysterious company is behind KRT Technologies, and it is driving her bananas. Finally, she slams her notebook closed with a huff and stands up to move to one of the computers. Logging in and bringing up her email, she clicks on the compose button.

SUBJECT: Empty lot follow-up?
Hello Councilman Grant,

I'm emailing you to follow up on the query
I sent last week per Councilman Torres's

recommendation. I'm the intern in his office. I was wondering if there's any way my friend and I can start a community garden in an empty lot if we can't figure out how to contact the company who owns it?

Thank you so much for your help.
Mary Jane Watson

Just as she hits send, the library's loudspeaker rattles to life, and MJ is surprised to hear *her* name come out of it.

"Attention, students. Would Mary Jane Watson please report to the principal's office?" The school secretary's voice is crackling and loud in the empty space, and MJ flinches. The few heads that are in the library swivel in her direction, and she slouches as she stands, pulling her bag up and over her shoulder in one motion before heading to the door. She tries to remember if there's anything she could have done to warrant a trip to the principal, but nothing is immediately coming to mind. At least not for this new semester. She makes the fairly long walk to the main office, passing by lockers and closed classroom doors. It's still early in the school's first period, so the halls are quiet and she's thankful for it. MJ finally makes it to the office and walks in, and the secretary ushers her into Principal Pettit's office.

"He's waiting for you," he says, gesturing to the door.

The man himself is seated behind an old wooden desk and staring at something on his phone. His bald head is white and shiny under the fluorescent lights, and MJ has a momentary hysterical urge to laugh, but she keeps her face smooth and pleasant.

"You asked me to see me, Mr. Pettit?"

He looks up from his desk and startles, like he hadn't heard her come in. "Oh, Ms. Watson, yes. Sorry to pull you away from class, but I have something to discuss with you." He opens a desk drawer and drops his phone into it. "Please," he says after shutting the drawer, "have a seat."

MJ sits in one of the two chairs in front of his desk and slides her backpack onto her lap, hugging it to her chest. *What is going on?* she wonders. *What could I have even done?*

"Do you know why you're here?" Principal Pettit asks, employing the oldest trick in the book. MJ knows that that's the fastest way to incriminate yourself, so she just shakes her head no. *Plus, I really don't!* Principal Pettit folds his hands and rests them on the desk, leaning forward to look at her. She thinks he might be trying to look sympathetic. "We've had some complaints from Councilman Grant's office."

"*What?*" MJ can't help it; the question bursts out of her, and she leans backward at the force of it.

He nods, frowning, but thoughtful all the same.

"They said you've been harassing the councilman."

"I . . ." MJ is gobsmacked. "Mr. Pettit, I sent two

emails asking if Maia and I could start a community garden. I'm . . . sorry?" she says, but unsure of why she's apologizing.

"It's all right," the principal says, and MJ can feel her face start to heat up. But not in embarrassment. MJ is *mad.* "But you'll need to stop doing it. I know you've been talking to Ms. Nguyễn about starting a new club—what was it, Work Together? We won't be able to approve it if we keep getting complaints about harassment. It won't do to get the school in trouble with local politicians. They can make a *lot* of trouble for us. Is it worth it for a little garden?"

MJ is too stunned to speak. *I can't believe he's talking to me like this. Like what we're trying to do doesn't matter!*

"Actually"—he turns his chair and looks out the window at the quad behind the school—"what if we give you both a plot here, at the school, instead?"

"Sir," MJ says, trying to keep her voice steady, "we're nowhere near Queens . . . how would a community garden at this high school help *my* community residents?"

Principal Pettit gives her an assessing glance before turning away. "Sorry, Ms. Watson, I wish there was more we could do. But I'll really have to ask you to refrain from contacting the councilman's office about this again."

MJ sighs. She knows this won't go anywhere if she tries to fight right now. She needs to make a plan. "Yes, sir," she says dejectedly.

The principal spends a few more minutes with her, but MJ barely hears what he says until he tells her she's free to go. The minute she's in the hallway, she pulls her phone out and shoots off a text to Peter and then to Maia telling them what happened. She leans against the wall just outside the main office and puts her head back, looking up at the ceiling above without really seeing it. She's not quite ready to go back to the library.

I can't believe they threatened me just for sending a few emails!!! There has to be something else going on. . . .

We are getting stronger.
  We are.
And we can feel our home.
    It's close.
      Closer than space.
Closer than it was.
    He can help us. The man with the spots.
    He can find it.
We can feel it and he can find it.
      He can take us there.
The other—the other—the other will stop the spider.

Spidey swings up 3rd Avenue. He's pretty far downtown and, if he can, he wants to get closer to a subway that will get him home faster than trying to swing across a bridge in this icy weather. It's been a pretty quiet night as far as crimes in the city go—he stopped two guys from harassing people in the streets, walked an old man home with his groceries, and stopped a holdup at a corner bodega. All pretty light work, truth be told. He'd be in a great mood if he wasn't so preoccupied with what happened to MJ. He flings an arm forward to shoot out a new web and grabs hold of it with two hands, sticking his feet out straight ahead and letting the momentum carry him up and forward into a flip before he *thwips* again. He spies a pizza place he likes on the corner and grins under his mask: He's already up to 52nd Street! He turns pensive again, considering what MJ has told him.

How could some actual grown-up politician go after a kid like that?

When she texted, he was in the middle of taking the French club's photo. One of the members thought it would be hilarious to buy five *pounds* of Brie and have it sitting in the middle of the group. It smelled awful, like it had been sitting in the girl's locker all week. *Actually, it probably* had *been sitting Marissa's locker all week*, Spidey thinks. *Gross.*

The second he read MJ's text, he faked a bathroom

incident and got out of there. He's still a little embarrassed over having to mime "Stomach problems, gotta go" to the yearbook editor, but there are few things he isn't willing to do for Mary Jane.

He found her sitting on the floor outside the media center, furiously texting Maia. When he walked up to get closer, he could see that Maia was sending her messages back in all caps, and was gratified to know that at least MJ had more than just him on her side. She looked up when she saw him; her cheeks were flushed, and there was a deep wrinkle right between her brows, they were drawn so tight together.

"Can you *believe* what he said to me?" she whispered in a heated voice when he leaned against the wall and slid down so he was seated next to her.

"I am so sorry, MJ. This is the *pits*. What can I do to help?" he asked, taking her free hand in his.

MJ shook her head. "No, this is *my* problem . . . and Maia's," she added as she looked down at her phone, which had lit up again, before meeting Peter's eyes again. "But I appreciate it. Maia and I are going to go to a town hall Grant has scheduled," she said, and squeezed his hand.

"Well . . ." He took a quick look around to make sure they were alone, and then leaned close and whispered, "If you need you-know-who to do some strong-arming." He flexed one arm and smiled goofily. It had the desired effect, and MJ started laughing in quiet, stifled huffs.

They sat together on the floor the rest of the period, and luck was on his side, or maybe he got some of MJ's usual luck, because they didn't even get caught.

Now, as Spidey flies through the air, he's still thinking about what he'll do if he *does* need to get involved. *I can't actually use the suit to intimidate a politician, but I can be there for MJ when she needs me as* me. *She did mention that town hall.* . . . He's up near 70th Street now, and swings to a stop, soaring up and landing softly on the ledge of a skyscraper, in between two floors. He sits, crouching on his toes, and pulls his phone out to type a quick message to MJ.

> HEY, LET ME KNOW WHEN YOU NEED ME AND I'M THERE. WHAT TIME DOES THE TOWN HALL THING START? I GOT YOUR BACK, EVEN IF YOU DON'T NEED IT BC UR AMAZING <3

Smiling under his mask, he hits send and then presses the button on the side to darken its screen. As he goes to slip it inside his suit, he sees the screen light up again and pauses to see what she's written. But it's not MJ; it's a notification for a direct message from some account called TheSpideyCode0285. Spidey's lenses narrow as he stares down at the screen. *What the heck is a Spidey Code?* He swipes the phone back open and opens up the application to read the message.

Hey Spidey. I can't tell you who I am, but I made this code to help you. It tells me where crimes are happening in the city in a more . . . cohesive way.

TheSpideyCode0285

Spider-Man continues reading the message, shaking his head. This sounds ridiculous.

I know you probably don't believe me, even though it was me that sent you the tip about the bank. I should have known the time. But I made the code better. There's a burglary that's going to happen at the ESU Science Center in the next 20 minutes. Trust me on this and get up there so you can stop it.

TheSpideyCode0285

That's the end of the message. Spider-Man clicks through, and like the last time, there's no picture and no other information on the profile. He stands and paces back and forth on the thin ledge a few times. *Should I go?* Then he remembers what Mr. Robertson told him about Jameson: He had lost someone because there was no one there to help him. *Can I take the chance that something like that might happen again?* Decision made, he launches himself off the ledge and back into the streets, webs flying and on his way to Empire State University.

It takes him twenty harried minutes to make it there, and by the time he's on the scene, his fingers are numb with cold, but the minute he lands in front of the science building, he knows he's made the right decision. Even if the alarms weren't already blaring, there's a steady buzzing at the base of his skull. He takes in the broken window two floors up and the sounds of something crashing. Then, all of a sudden, Spidey clutches at his head and leans forward—his spider-sense is overwhelming! There's something coming.

CHAPTER EIGHT

Spider-Man crouches and flips high into the air just as a huge figure barrels toward him, missing him by mere inches. Spidey lands on the sidewalk, low to the ground and hand stretched out, ready to web whoever it is that just came for him. His lenses go wide as his brain tries to compute what he's looking at. It's a man in some kind of apparatus with huge legs and a tail, and what looks like a dark ski cap with large, high-standing animal ears on his head. The metal of the legs and tail and chest piece are shining blue-gold in the campus lights. There are golden wires popping out from a pack on his back that seem to be powering the suit.

"Um, hi?" Spidey says, using one hand to wave. The guy hops high and spins, landing so he's facing Spidey. He's got a large square jaw and no mask to speak of, so Spidey can see his white skin, thick dark eyebrows, and beady eyes. He's got a nose that's clearly been broken more than once, and Spider-Man gets the feeling that even if he looks ridiculous, this is not a guy he wants to hit him. Not only because of the massive legs and tail the metal suit of armor gives him. Suddenly, it hits him what animal this thief is supposed to be. "A kangaroo?" he asks, disbelief etched across his tone.

"Yeah, whaddya care?" the kangaroo man spits out. Spidey narrows his lenses as he sees that the man has a black case strapped to his back.

"I mean, it kinda seems like you're robbing this school, and a lot of us frown on taking from higher education. My girlfriend told me they just cut a ton of funding to this department, so I don't think they can really take the hit right now." Kangaroo man's eyes go thin, and he growls something indiscernible. "I . . . did not understand that, Kanga," Spidey says, and then slings out a web directly at the man's face. As Spider-Man expected, the Kangaroo jumps high to avoid it, and Spidey shoots a second line of webbing at the tail, pulling down hard so that the metal-suited man crashes into the concrete on his back. "Or do you prefer *Roo*?" Spidey yells as he jumps toward the thief, fist-first. Unfortunately, the Kangaroo is ready for him.

Spider-Man's fist connects with a powerful set of feet that push out and send him flying thirty feet backward. It would have been farther, but a lone tree stops him and Spidey crashes to a halt against the bark. Woozily, Spidey gets to his feet and shakes his head, trying to clear his vision.

Vaguely, he can hear the Kangaroo yelling from where he left him on the sidewalk. "No, no, no, if you broke this case, we're both in trouble, you stupid bug!!!"

Spidey bends his knees and springs forward, covering the distance between them in two quick leaps. He sees Kangaroo fiddling with the case that had been on his back, trying to open it to check on its contents. Spidey doesn't like what he's just heard the man say.

"What does that mean, Mr. Kangaroo Man?" he asks, landing a few short feet away. He's careful to stay out of range of the armor's powerful kicks. He's remembering how terrifying kangaroos actually are with their brute strength.

"Nothing!" the Kangaroo yells, but there's panic in it. "Why don't you get the heck outta here?!"

Spidey frowns. He has to figure out how to take this guy down *and* figure out what he's doing here.

"Can't we just talk this out?" he says, buying time. "We can sit down, have a one-on-one. Wouldn't you like that?"

The kangaroo man's brows furrow in confusion. "I— What?" Then his face shifts back into anger. "You're just trying to confuse me! I heard about you. I know *all* about you! We crooks know how to look out for each other." And then he launches forward and spins in the air, aiming to swipe at Spidey with his tail.

"Aw, do you guys have a club?" Spidey asks, jumping and spinning out of the way, landing crouched on the guy's shoulders. He pulls at the headpiece. "I gotta ask . . . do the ears do anything, Mr. Roo?"

"ARGH!!!" The Kangaroo reaches out and grabs the center of Spidey's suit and yanks him forward, flinging him away. "MY NAME IS KANGAROO!" Spidey stands up on the lawn where he'd landed, triumphant. In his hand, he holds the case that had been on Kangaroo's back.

"I honestly don't really care, man," Spidey says, dropping the case behind him. "But I can't have you going around robbing schools. It's really not cool. And I don't think kangaroos want you giving them a bad name!"

Kangaroo's face is red, and his whole body is shaking with fury. He crouches low to the ground and jumps high up in the air. Looking up and watching Kangaroo's form fall back down to land, Spidey can see that he's standing on the bull's-eye.

"Okay," he says to himself, watching Kangaroo fall from above, "in five . . . four . . . three . . . two . . . ONE!"

And a split second before the Kangaroo makes impact, Spidey jumps to the right and throws out a hand, punching into the metal leg of Kangaroo's suit—hard. The thing crumples under his super-strength, and the joint where it was connected to the torso cracks in half. Kangaroo is left hopping on one leg and falling slightly over to his right.

"Gah! Can't—keep—my—balance!" Kangaroo yells, and Spidey takes the opportunity of the thief's distraction and shoots quick bursts of web at the man's chest. He grips the strands and pulls hard as he jumps up and over his marsupial-lite assailant. He lands and immediately turns around to watch Kangaroo fly up and land flat on his back, groaning. Then Spidey sprints forward and pulls at the gold wiring coming out of the pack on Kangaroo's back.

"And I'm guessing these are the hydraulics that keep that suit working . . ." Spidey says as he yanks them out one by one. There's a soft hiss of air, and the Kangaroo stops struggling.

"Why you gotta be so mean about it?" Kangaroo says weakly from his spot on the ground.

Spidey frowns at him, even though the thief can't see it. "You . . . What? You were robbing the school, and then you called me a stupid bug. *And,*" he adds, pointing at him accusingly, "you said that all your criminal friends are gossiping about me! Plus, between you and Panda-Mania, you New York City criminals are really starting to ruin cute animals for me." He shoots a few webs at Kangaroo, securing him tightly. Then his attention shifts to the black case Kangaroo had been holding.

He walks to the bag and leans down over it. He unzips it carefully and pulls open the two sides to reveal a black cylinder with a giant red biohazard sticker on it. *That's not good!* Spidey zips the bag back up and looks to his right and then to his left. He's surprised that he still hasn't heard any police sirens heading his way, but shrugs. Maybe they were busy. He gives Kangaroo one last look before heading in the direction of what he hopes is ESU campus security.

"You stay here—someone will come get you. It was not nice to meet you," he says to Kangaroo, and then walks off to figure out who needs to take this scary biohazardous canister of *something* and put it somewhere safe.

Swinging back home after making sure Kangaroo was dealt with and putting the canister back in the hands of the professionals, Spidey ruminates over the night.

I don't like the sound of criminals having conversations about me, even though I guess it makes sense . . . and I can't believe this Spidey Code thing was real!

He realizes something and swings to a stop somewhere near 72nd Street. He glances at the street sign. He's got a stash of clothes nearby, he knows, but it's late enough that it will probably still be faster to web his way home than wait for a subway. Even if it is freezing. First things first, though. He pulls out his phone and types out a quick message to TheSpideyCode.

Thanks for the tip, TSC 👍. But I gotta ask how you did it? How did you know Kangaroo would be there?

Great. Full disclosure: I didn't know who would be there, just that there was probably trouble. And there's more where this came from, SpiderMan. I'll be in touch.

TheSpideyCode0285

Great. Oh and uh, there's a hyphen.

?

TheSpideyCode0285

In Spider-Man. There's a hyphen.

Oh. My apologies. Talk soon.

TheSpideyCode0285

The messages leave him feeling unsettled, and not just because that hyphen thing was awkward. *I've got to start letting that go,* he thinks. But there's something familiar about the way the Spidey Code was writing to him. And yet, something totally strange. He takes a screenshot of the exchange and texts it to MJ. She'll definitely be able to help him figure out what's making him feel so weird about it. The reply is nearly instantaneous.

👀 WANNA COME BY MINE ON UR WAY HOME? LETS THINK THROUGH IT TOGETHER

Peter sends back a thumbs-up and puts his phone away before launching back into the air. At least he'll get some hang time with MJ out of this!

Peter climbs into MJ's window, pulling his hat and mask off in one fell swoop as he steps onto the carpet. MJ's moving to greet him already, and he envelops her in a tight hug.

"Hi," he says, grinning.

"Hi," she says, with a matching expression. She pulls back slightly to kiss him once and then retreats to her seat. "Are you feeling okay?" she asks.

Peter tests his joints again and moves his head this way

and that, pulling off his glove and running a quick hand over the back of his head. "A little bruised, but nothing too bad. That healing kicked in, and the guy really only got me with, like, one good hit." He's lying to her a little bit. He can feel a small abrasion at the back of his head, and there's a dull ache to it, but he knows it will be gone by morning.

MJ nods. "Good," she says, looking at him warmly. Next to her, she's got the family laptop on her bed and already has TheSpideyCode0285's profile pulled up. "So, this whole thing is making me nervous," she says, frankly, tapping one glittery blue nail against the keyboard. Peter sits on the floor in front of the bed so he can see the screen when MJ turns the computer his way. "Should you really trust someone you don't know? I think that's how horror movies start."

Peter's mouth quirks up in a half smile. "You're not wrong. But the intel was good," he says, shrugging. MJ twists her fingers in between her hands, which Peter recognizes as a sign of MJ's anxiety. He reaches up and puts his hand on hers, stilling her movements. "Are you okay?" he asks. "Is it . . . about Pettit?" After that time in the hallway immediately after MJ's meeting with the principal, they didn't have a chance to talk about it any more.

MJ looks away and bites her lip before turning back to him and shaking her head. "No, no, it's fine."

"MJ, you don't have to—"

"Peter, this Spidey stuff is definitely more important

right now. We have to figure out who this person is, and why they're helping you—*how* they're helping you. How did they know that the school was going to be robbed?"

"You're *sure?*" Peter asks, hoping he can get across how much he means it. "Your stuff is important, too! I don't think some creep council person should be able to go after a high-school kid like that."

"Peter," MJ says, and there's a finality in it. "The Spidey Code could be a bad guy."

"The Kangaroo dude *did* say that other criminals were talking about me . . ." Peter acquiesces. *Maybe she really doesn't want to talk about the principal.* . . . Peter isn't sure, but he doesn't want to push MJ somewhere she isn't comfortable going.

Peter is nodding his head, and MJ ignores the twist in her stomach. She thinks he *probably* doesn't think his stuff is more important than her stuff. *But it's true! How do I compete against men in robot kangaroo suits trying to steal majorly scary stuff from the science department at Empire State University? Where does a community garden stand next to that? It sounds ridiculous.* She can't help but feel uncomfortable at the idea that their problems are unequal. She knows it isn't fair, but sometimes life isn't fair.

"Anyway," Peter is saying, pulling her out of her

reflections, "I guess we have to keep an eye on this person, but if they keep telling me bad guys to go after, they can't be all bad, right?" he ends, hopeful.

"I don't know," she says, hesitant to rain on his parade but wanting to be honest. "What if it's, like, a mob boss or something trying to get you to take out his competition?"

Peter's face pales. "Do you think so? I didn't even think of that."

"You don't watch enough gangster movies, clearly," MJ says with a small laugh.

"And you do?" Peter asks, grinning and standing up to join her on the edge of the bed.

MJ closes the laptop and pushes it behind her. She takes Peter's hand in hers and plays with his fingers, pulling them forward and curling them into his palm. She can feel him smiling beside her.

"MJ, now you're twisting *my* hands. What's going on?"

"We should just go have a fun date night one night," she says, surprising herself with the idea but warming to it. "Forget all this annoying real-life stuff for just a *night*."

Peter shifts his hand so he's holding hers now. He squeezes it once. "This time you're *really* not wrong," he repeats, and MJ rests her head on his shoulder.

"Just fun stuff, one night only," she says.

"Just fun stuff," Peter agrees.

CHAPTER NINE

A paper ball flies out from one of the dark holes situated on the Spot's living room wall. Seated on his couch, he grabs it out of the air and flings it right back into another hole, only for it to fly back in from the first one again. It's gotten more instantaneous. He can do it without thinking now, getting things directly from one place to another without a long stop in Spot World. He repeats this action two more times and then finally looks at the phone sitting on his coffee table. It's been a few days since the last call. The voices said the thing about getting respect, and then the phone had died. He's been waiting for them to reach out again, and today they finally have.

"So," he says, "who are you?"

There's a tinny whistle coming out of the speaker, and then that same chorus of voices speaks. "We are The Faithless. We are powerful. We are The Faithless."

The paper ball flies through the air again, and the Spot grabs it before dropping it onto the table next to the phone. He leans forward and looks down at it.

"That doesn't tell me anything. Any two-bit jerk can call himself whatever he wants. Who *are* you?" he asks again.

"We are The Faithless," the voices repeat on the phone. "We are not of this planet."

"*Aliens?!*" The Spot picks the phone up and nearly shouts in excitement. "Aliens! Honest-to-God *aliens*!" He almost wishes he was still an employed scientist, if just to see the looks on his colleagues' faces. He's made first contact!

"We are . . . We are more than just this word. We are kings and queens and conquerors," The Faithless say.

The Spot replaces the phone where it was, and then he stands to pace. It's an action that reminds him of the old days. "And you 'kings and queens and conquerors' need . . . my help?" he says, a greedy grin cutting through the bottom half of his face.

"Yes, yes, yes," the voices say. "You have the ability. You have the portals. You have it, and we need it to get home."

"You want me to find a hole to space?" The Spot has never tried to get to space.

"NO!" the voices yell. "Under. Underneath. We can feel it and direct. Under."

The Spot pauses, confused. "Under what?" he asks. "Underground?"

"No. Under the island. Under this city."

"Ooooh, under*water*," he says, returning to the couch and leaning against the back and putting his arms behind his head. He picks his feet up and crosses them on the table. "I could probably get you there," he semi-bluffs. He's never tried going underwater, either. "But what's in it for me? What's in it for my *name*?" he says, and his new ever-present anger is quick to bubble up in his gut. "What'll help me show all those jerks at the CWNN that I'm worth the entry, that I could rob circles around those lazy, good-for-nothing . . ." He trails off, revisiting his earlier embarrassment and fury.

"We can get you power. Power. You need power to build. Reputation."

"I'm listening. . . ."

"Four nights from now. Four nights. A big-money move . . ." The Spot listens as these untethered voices tell him about a bank move happening tomorrow night. His eyes grow wide and the spots on his body quiver, and he realizes what this means.

"I'm gonna be *rich*. And *everyone's* gonna know that

I'm a player," he croons once they've relayed the details. Then he leans forward, resting his elbows on his knees. "How are you gonna keep me from getting caught? The police? Or, ugh, Spider-Man." He spits the name out with unconcealed disgust.

"Police? Easy. Distractible."

"Spider-Man?" the Spot asks again. It's who he's really worried about. He's heard about how the costumed freak had taken out heavy hitters.

"Also distractible. Handling. Have plan for Spider ongoing." There's something strange in their voices, but they keep talking before the Spot can hit on what it is. "You help us. You help us, and we help you," the voices say.

"Listen, if this works out, I'll get you home, I'll get you to the White House, I'll get you wherever you need to go, my new and knowledgeable friends." The Spot stands and stretches his arms above his head before hanging up. "And if it means that I knock a few wise guys down a few pegs, then more respect for ol' Spot."

"Okay," Maia says, passing out their packets. "I pulled everyone's notes together and read through them, and used Peter's mock-ups to create a pathway of what our actual app could look like—I got my little cousin to design it for me."

"By which she means, she blackmailed him by threatening to tell his parents about how he's been getting detention for skipping class," MJ says, the corner of her mouth hitching up in a smirk.

They're sitting in their study hour with Dr. Shah and going over the OSMAKER materials. Peter notices that even though Dr. Shah is there in class, he doesn't seem particularly present. Their teacher looks kind of . . . *haggard*, Peter thinks. *Dr. Shah looks rough.* He's been quiet the entire time, too. When he arrived, after Peter, he mumbled a greeting and immediately took a seat at his desk, gesturing for them to work on their project. That was a half hour ago. Peter sighs and looks over the sheaf of papers in his hands. He thinks about what Mr. Robertson said about grief. *It* does *do funny things to people.*

"Do we . . . need to come up with an actual name for this thing?" Randy asks after glancing through the packet. "Like, could your cousin be coerced into making us a real logo?"

Maia gives him an appreciative glance.

"That's a good idea, Randy," she says. "I like it!"

"Me too," MJ says. "We could really make this thing if we win, and we'll need a name for it, won't we?"

Peter nods in agreement. "How about . . . A Helping Hand?" he says.

Maia frowns and shakes her head no, Randy mirrors her, and MJ grimaces and then shoots Peter an apologetic smile.

"Feels a little old-lady, dude. Not to be mean," Randy says.

Peter laughs. "It's fine! I'm probably not the best person for this."

"No! There are no bad ideas, but we'll find the right one," Maia says. "Let's all brainstorm this week, and when we have our first class next week, we'll each bring a list of ideas and vote on the best one."

Peter makes a mental note to remember to come up with any kind of list so he doesn't seem like he's slacking. MJ is already writing it in her school planner, and Maia has a reminder list up on her tablet and is typing into it.

Peter looks at Randy, who taps the side of his head. "All up here, my man." He grins.

"Ditto," Peter says. Then he adds, "Mostly," after MJ shoots him a dry look.

Before anyone else can say anything, the PA system above Dr. Shah's desk lets out a loud stream of static.

"*Yikes,*" Randy says, covering his ears. Everyone in the room follows suit, and they all collectively glare at the small brown box.

"Hello, students!" a loud voice booms through the

speaker. "This is Dr. Osei, your favorite practical-science teacher *and* the head of the Midtown High Microbots team. I am excited to share that we have been gifted an incredible, er . . . gift of a brand-new city grant. Every single student at Midtown High will be receiving a school-owned tablet to use. This is all possible thanks to an anonymous wealthy donor, but they wish to remain *anonymous*, so don't try looking for them!" he jokes awkwardly. "But new tablets!" Then the PA goes quiet.

It's silent in the room for a beat, and then Peter, MJ, Maia, and Randy all start cheering and clapping.

"We each get a *free* tablet to use all year?!" Peter says. "That's amazing!"

"Seriously. I can finally do research without having to ask my mom to use the computer," MJ says, her teeth showing in a bright, wide smile.

"Will you all please *shut up*?!" Dr. Shah's loud voice cuts through their glee. Peter is stunned. He whips his head around to stare at his teacher. Dr. Shah has his eyes closed and two fingers at his temples, steadily rubbing in small circles. The deep bruising under his eyes seems even more pronounced. The room is deathly quiet. Peter looks at his friends, and they all look equally stunned and uncomfortable. Finally, Dr. Shah opens his eyes and sighs. "Sorry . . . I'm sorry, kids. That wasn't kind of me. I think I didn't get enough sleep last night, that's all. Up late grading, that exciting teacher life," he jokes. But no one laughs.

"You're right to be happy—it's so great that you're all getting tools to make your education easier."

Peter locks eyes with MJ, and she nods slightly. *This is weird*, she seems to be agreeing.

"Wish I was rich enough to donate two thousand tablets to some high school," Maia finally says, and Randy lets out a loud laugh.

"Yeah, yeah," he says. "Okay, let's get back to it, we only have, like, ten more minutes left in class. I gotta know what I'm supposed to do next."

Peter's listening, but he can't help but glance over at Dr. Shah's desk again. His teacher is turned away from them, looking at his computer screen. But Peter isn't sure he's seeing anything at all.

Spidey runs over the rooftops, trying to catch up to the mugger he can see on street level, holding on to someone's laptop. TheSpideyCode0285 has him all the way down in Sheepshead Bay after telling him they think someone's about to work over an electronics shop in the area. Turns out it was just one guy lurking around a coffee shop waiting for an innocent writer to go to the bathroom so they could lift their computer.

Still a crime! Spidey thinks, leaping from one building to the next. The downside to working in Brooklyn is there are too many areas where the buildings are too low to swing. He and MJ haven't really settled on whether TheSpideyCode0285 is good or bad, but Spidey doesn't want to risk not listening and ending up missing something big again.

"Please stop!" he yells down in the direction of the thief. "Is this guy like a marathon runner or something?" he huffs to himself. "Yeesh."

It does not have the desired effect, however, and the man below keeps running. He sees him take a hard right down the next street, and Spidey is gratified to see a *very* tall tree around the corner. Pointing his arm straight out, he presses against his palm and the web flies free, sticking to a high branch. Spidey fists his hands around the line and jumps, the momentum sending him moving fast enough that he can let go and fly forward, catching the thief right around the midsection.

"*Oomph!*" he says, going down hard onto the ground. Spidey hears the crunch as the laptop hits the sidewalk and winces at the sound. *That's not good.* He pushes himself off the thief and stands up. The man rolls over onto his stomach, and Spider-Man finally gets a good look at him—his white skin is dirty and reddened by the exertion, and his pale blue eyes are glaring at Spider-Man. Underneath his beard, his lips are pressed into a thin line. The laptop lying next to him seems like a lost cause—the metal casing is bent and there's a large crack along the top.

But the thief's backpack is bulging, and Spidey's lenses narrow. He webs the man's legs to the ground and pulls on the backpack. "Hey! Don't!" the thief cries out, but Spidey ignores him, unzipping the bag. His lenses go wide when he sees what's inside.

"There are *ten laptops* in here. How were you running so fast carrying *ten laptops* . . . ?" He pauses, dropping into a crouch and pulling the man's wallet out of the backpack, reading out his name from his driver's license. "Brett?" The man, Brett, lets out a loud groan, and Spider-Man hears a quiet *thunk* as his head falls back resting against the concrete. "Pro tip, Brett? Don't carry your own wallet around in a bag full of stolen goods. Now, why don't you tell me what you're doing with ten laptops . . . ?"

It turned out that Brett, the lone laptop thief, *is* kind of a crime ring in and of himself. He's been lifting computers all over the five boroughs for *months* and then carefully portioning them out to used-technology stores around the city. Which means Spider-Man has the conundrum of either leaving the man webbed to the sidewalk with what looks like a bag full of free laptops *or* sticking around to keep the laptops safe and risk running into cops, who, for some J. Jonah Jameson–shaped reason, hate his guts.

Somewhere behind him, a loud bell rings as a door opens, and Spidey looks behind him to find a short white man, thick around the waist with a head full of white hair, looking at him. He has the name of the shop behind him across his T-shirt—DMITRI'S.

"Um . . . hello?" Spider-Man waves awkwardly.

The man says something rapidly in what sounds like Russian and then points at Spider-Man and says, "Spider-Man!" with a grin.

"Thank you?" Spider-Man says, unsure of what his gratitude is for, but it seems like the right track when the man smiles wider, then points up at the shop and back at himself. "Dmitri?" Spider-Man asks.

"Yes!" Dmitri says. And then adds, "We are fans of Spider-Man!" in thickly accented English. He points behind him again, and Spider-Man looks closer to see a hand-drawn version of his mask taped inside the front window. Oh, he must have helped this man at some point!

It occurs to Spidey that this could be the solution he's looking for. He pulls his phone out, brings up an app, and speaks into it clearly. "Can you wait here and make sure no one takes these computers? And call someone to help deal with this thief?" He presses a button and lets the phone translate his sentence into a robotic-sounding Russian. Dmitri nods, while frowning at Brett, who is watching the exchange with an increasingly frustrated look on his face.

"Don't look at us like that, Brett. You wouldn't be here if you just left that lady's laptop alone."

"You suck, man."

Spider-Man decides not to dignify that with a response. Instead, he thanks Dmitri for the help, and then slings himself up onto a rooftop to keep an eye out and make sure Dmitri does actually call for help. After he hears the sounds of sirens coming closer, he finally feels comfortable pulling his phone out to send TheSpideyCode0285 a message.

> Thx, wasn't exactly right, but was a smalltimer stealing a bunch of laptops. Seemed kinda convoluted imo but I got em. Thanks for the tip.

> Every time you give me more info, this will get better. New gig for you: there's going to be an altercation on a Manhattan-bound Q train when it's going through Flatbush.

TheSpideyCode0285

> How will I know which car to be in?

> Either the third or fourth car, but it's the Q that will hit Flatbush at 8:48 PM.

TheSpideyCode0285

Spidey looks down at his phone and sighs. This is going to be impossible. *How am I supposed to know which car to choose between three or four?* He swings to the nearest Q station at Neck Road and flings himself up to the open-air station. There are five stops in Flatbush—he just has to figure out what train to get on. In the distance, he can see a train coming up from the Sheepshead Bay stop. He needs to get on a train that's going to roll into the Avenue H station at 8:48 p.m. *I need to get a train that's here at 8:40* . . . he thinks, doing the math in his head. Spidey checks the time on one of the digital schedule boards; it's currently 8:37 p.m. *That's lucky.*

He's the only person on the platform, so there's not much to go on when the train rolls to a stop. TheSpideyCode0285 told him it was the third or fourth car from the front, so he jogs to those doors and jumps in just before they close again. He hopes he chose the right one. In front of him, a little kid's mouth drops open and she points.

"Spider!" she says.

"Yes, yes, spider," the mom repeats, not really listening and continuing to scan her phone screen.

Spidey looks around. There doesn't seem to be anyone who wants to make trouble. Everyone on the car is sitting quietly reading or listening to something on their headphones; there are a few teens on the far end having a lively conversation about anime, Spidey thinks. In true

New Yorker fashion, no one is paying attention to him.

He leans a hip against the divider to the right of the doors and crosses his arms, settling back to wait, and hoping he's not wasting his time. He's close enough to the end of the car that he'll know if something goes wrong on the next one over. They bypass a few stations and finally enter Flatbush eight minutes later. The train rolls to a stop at Avenue H, and Spidey steps out to let people off the train before getting back in. No one new steps into either car at that stop. The woman's voice comes on asking people to stand clear of the closing doors, and then they're off to the next station. Again, Spidey goes through the motions. He steps off, steps back on, and this time, there's a few new people in his car and none in the fourth. Still quiet, still in their own worlds, ignoring their fellow subway passengers. This happens two more times, until, finally, they roll into the Church Avenue station. The doors open, and before Spidey can step off the car, someone barrels into him, screaming, "MOVE!"

A white man in an oversized trench coat shoves Spidey without looking at him. On the platform, a woman is yelling, "STOP HIM! HE STOLE MY PURSE!"

The doors close, and the man's looking at the woman still standing on the platform through the window. He's laughing. Then he turns back to face Spider-Man, and he gasps.

Spidey grins under his mask. "Hey, man, heard you got a new purse," he says, on the cusp of laughter.

"Oh, come *on*," the guy groans. "What are *you* doing on the *Q train*?!"

CHAPTER TEN

Peter is at the *Bugle* standing near the copy machine waiting for the PowerPoint deck he's put in to finish duplicating and collating. Kayla asked him if he'd feel comfortable presenting a social media update to some of the team since he'd been driving so much of the content in the last few weeks. Peter was surprised and pleased to be asked. His nerves went into overdrive when she told him who would be attending the meeting.

"I can't believe I have to present this to Mr. *Jameson*," he says to himself, rubbing at his eyes. He hasn't seen Jameson since that horrible elevator ride, and despite what Mr. Robertson had said, he isn't sure Jameson won't refire him the minute he sets eyes on Peter. The whirring of the machine is loud, so for a moment, Peter doesn't realize he's not alone on this side of the floor. Then Ned Leeds's voice breaks through.

"Yeah, I just don't know what Spider-Man's doing, Bets."

Peter perks up. *Why are they talking about Spider-Man?* Peter edges closer to the corner and takes a quick peek. The printer alcove is just off one of the break rooms, and he spies Ned and Betty Brant standing close together near the coffee machine. There's dark liquid pouring out of the machine and into the pot, but neither of them seems to notice. Ned is leaning against the counter, and Betty's just in front of him, so Peter has a clear view of both their faces. He glances down and is surprised to see them loosely holding hands. *That's new. . . .*

"I did see that he was all the way down in Sheepshead Bay this week," Betty says, shaking her head. "It's so weird."

Peter furrows his brow and frowns, finding himself standing at the center of offended and confused.

"This isn't like him—almost makes me feel like it isn't the actual web-slinger," Ned jokes. "Usually there's some kind of pattern to it, like he's in that part of the city and those are the crimes—but he's never gone so far off course and completely missed the major crimes."

"Yeah, one-offs, I get. But he scooped up a subway

purse snatcher and a petty thief?" Betty's mouth twists. "While in the city there were two separate bank heists and a whole organized-crime shoot-out in the middle of Wall Street."

"So, so weird," Ned says, repeating Betty's earlier sentiment. "Are you going to dig into it?" he asks.

"Maybe . . ." Betty says. "It feels like *something*, doesn't it?"

Ned nods in agreement.

"And I'm sure Jameson will be all about anything Spider-Man's doing wrong." He laughs mirthlessly. "So you'll definitely get the pitch approved."

Betty shrugs. "I'm not for or against him, really. But he *is* newsworthy," she says, her eyes sparkling and her lips quirking up at the corner.

What's so funny about that? Peter wonders. *Adults are weird.*

Ned laughs. "Right, *newsworthy*. Anyway, are we still on for dinner tonight?" he says, changing the subject.

Peter takes a step backward, returning to his spot in front of the machine. There's something making him queasy, and Peter can uncomfortably admit to himself that it's probably guilt. *There's clearly something wrong with TheSpideyCode0285's system if it has me missing all that stuff! How many other big things did I miss because I was listening to a computer? But whoever is feeding me this info said it will get better. . . .*

Peter groans, rubbing his palms against his eyes.

If we can get it to be perfect, it will help with the focus and make me more efficient! No more sitting around on rooftops or swinging randomly hoping I'll run into someone who happens to need help. Maybe I can even start planning things again. Maybe I should ask TheSpideyCode0285 if there's an update to the system. . . .

He pulls his phone out of his pocket and opens the app to send the mysterious stranger a message. His fingers are poised over the keys, but he wavers, unsure. In front of him, the printer makes a loud whining sound, and Peter startles out of his thoughts. There's an error message on the screen, and Peter lets out a frustrated noise, shoving his phone back into his pocket before kneeling down to pull at the doors on the side of the printer. There's a sound of light footsteps coming around the corner, and Ned and Betty wave to Peter as they walk by.

"Hey, kid," Betty says.

Peter returns the wave but doesn't reply, letting the printer play distraction so he won't have to pretend to not be irritated by what he's overheard.

"Man, Jameson really needs to spring for some new supplies," Peter hears Ned say as they walk away. "That thing is, like, eight million years old."

Even annoyed as he is with them, Peter has to agree. It takes him ten more minutes to get the printer restarted and another twenty to gather and double-check all the collated decks. By the time he makes it back to his space, it's nearly time for him to go home. He drops the stack of pages onto his desk and falls into his chair with a huff.

"Having that good a day, huh?" Kayla says without turning around, but Peter can hear the joke. He smiles wanly. Then he straightens and leans forward, an idea occurring to him.

"Hey, Kayla," Peter says.

She must hear the seriousness in his voice because her fingers still and she turns her chair around to face him. She has her braids pulled back into a bun high on her head today, and she's got on a tailored red pantsuit and a made-up face. Peter remembers she had her own meeting with the bosses that morning.

"What's up?" she asks.

"Do you know if there's any way to figure out who is behind an anonymous Twitter account?"

Kayla's face shifts into a pensive expression, and she taps a manicured nail against her chin. It looks like she's running through a knowledge-base in her brain. Finally, she refocuses on Peter and asks, "Can I ask why?" Then she leans forward. "Are you being bullied, Peter?"

Peter nearly laughs at the question, thinking of Flash Thompson and his meanspirited name-calling. *I wish Flash was my biggest problem.* Instead of saying any of that out loud, he just waves his hands and says, "No, no, of course not. I'm just curious."

Kayla gives him a knowing look. "You're lucky I know you, Peter. Anyone else asking that question—who wasn't such a clearly good kid—I'd think *they* wanted to start an anonymous account to bully someone." She laughs. "But that's because I work in the news and know how terrible so many people are."

Peter is aghast. "I wouldn't!"

"I know, I know! Sorry," she says. "It's kind of like gallows humor. We laugh so we don't think too hard about the horrible things." She shrugs. "*Anyway*, to answer your question . . . you might want to ask one of our tech reporters. I don't really know enough about the actual workings of that stuff to tell you. But let me . . ." She turns back around to her desk and flicks through a few screens before finally finding the information she's looking for. She pulls a bright pink sticky note off the top of a stack and jots something down and then passes it back to Peter. "Here, get in touch with Swapna Subhaiya. She's one of our top tech reporters, just let her know I told you to contact her."

Peter take the note and glances at it—there's a name, phone number, and email address. He pockets it, smiling at Kayla. "Thanks, this is a huge help," he says, even though Kayla can't know how much. *I'll look her up in the system before I leave, and Ms. Subhaiya's going to get a visit from her friendly neighborhood Spider-Man.*

It's pretty early in the afternoon when Spidey swings by a fancy-looking apartment building in midtown. He's come directly from finding Ms. Subhaiya's address at the *Bugle*. *I swear I'll only use the system when I* really *need it*, he promised to the universe as he wrote down the information. He lands across the street and starts counting the windows, finding the one he's looking for, five down from the top of the building and three to the right. If the map is right in his head, that should be apartment 1503. He slings out a web and flies forward, crouching against the wall just to the window's left. The sound of the city below him is loud, and he doesn't think anyone is paying attention on the ground to something going on this high up.

"Hey, Spidey!" Across the way, there's a window washer waving at him. "Big fan!" the man yells, pointing at himself.

Spidey laughs and waves back. *Right, can't forget about window washers.* "Thanks, man!" he yells back, grin wide under his mask. "Appreciate the support!"

Next to him, there's a sound as the window slides open and a loud, angry voice cuts into the air. "Excuse me, could you please stop *screaming* outside of my window?"

Spidey's head twists to look at who's talking. There's an angry old white woman in a bathrobe glaring at him.

"Swapna Subhaiya?" he asks uncertainly. The woman's entire demeanor changes so quickly it gives Spidey whiplash.

"*Oh*, you're looking for that wonderful South Indian

couple a few doors down?" she asks. "Sorry sweetie, you've got the wrong place. You want three windows *that* way," she says, pointing in the opposite direction. Then she grabs something from inside her apartment and holds her hand outside the window. She waits a second and adds, "Well, open your hand!" Spidey removes one of his hands from where it has been anchoring him on the side of the building and holds it out to her questioningly.

She drops two hard candies into it, and Spidey almost drops them in surprise. *How come all these old ladies are giving me hard candy??*

"One of those is for Swapna, so don't eat them both, Spider-Man."

"I . . . won't," he says haltingly, mildly affronted. "I'll give it to her."

"See that you do. Now go away, I'm in the middle of a Keanu Reeves marathon."

Spidey laughs to himself and crawls along the wall in the direction the woman had pointed, counting until he arrives at what he hopes is the right window. He raps loudly on the glass and then sits back to wait.

A few minutes later, the window opens and a handsome Indian man with a starched white collar and thick dark hair pokes his head outside.

"Oh!" he says, surprised. "I thought . . . I thought it was going to be a bird." He looks confused.

"Nope, just me," Spidey says, raising his hand in

greeting. "Oh, uh . . ." He holds out his fist, and the man hesitantly reaches out an open hand. Spidey drops one of the candies into it. "I knocked on the wrong window, and a lady asked me to give that to you."

The man laughs and pockets the candy. "Ah, yes, Ms. Burnside." Then he shakes his head. "Wait, this is weird, right? Do you usually knock on strangers' windows?"

Spidey shrugs. "If I have to," he says, and then his tone goes serious. "And I really do have to."

The man nods once but still looks unsure. "Is . . . there some kind of crime happening in the area that I can help you with?" he says, doubt lacing through his voice.

Spidey shakes his head no. "I actually am looking for a reporter named Swapna Subhaiya?" he asks hopefully.

"Oh! You want my wife," the man says. "I'm Kabir Subhaiya. I'm sorry, Spider-Man. She's actually in San Francisco right now reporting on one of those giant, monster tech companies."

The apology lands heavy on Spider-Man's ears. *Argh, I really needed to talk to her.* "That's okay" is what he says to Kabir, though.

"She'll be back in a few days." Kabir pauses. "Is there . . . ? Uh, do you have a phone number or something I can pass along? Sorry, I don't know how this whole superhero thing works." He apologizes again.

Spidey can't help but let out a slight chuckle. *I don't know, either. Let's be real.* "Hm, a phone number . . ." He tries to remember if there are any minutes left on the free VPN phone he's set up, but he doesn't think so. "I don't have one that I can share, but I can just come back." He shrugs and moves to spring off the building before turning to Kabir suddenly. "Oh, wait! She can DM me on Twitter—I'm SpiderMan-E-N-W-H-Y-S-E-E."

Kabir mouth opens and a loud, short laugh comes out. He slams his jaw shut immediately and looks horrified. "I'm so sorry! Sorry!" he says. "I just . . . I thought that account was super fake."

Spidey's lenses narrow, and under his mask, a frown mars his face. "What? Why?" he asks, trying not to let the annoyance show in his voice.

Kabir lifts his shoulders and his hands come up in a placating gesture. "Well, there are just a lot of typos and reposts of cool *Bugle* shots. It seemed like someone could easily fake it. Sorry, really," he says, and it sounds like he does feel bad for thinking it, so Spidey cuts him some slack.

But that doesn't stop him from adding, "You try to type while you're swinging high speed down the street *and* you're wearing gloves."

"That's fair." Kabir grins. "Sorry," he says again, through the smile.

"It's fine," Spidey says, resigned. *This would be what people are thinking about my actual account. They probably think one of the fake ones is real.* "So, anyway . . ."

"I'll tell Swapna you're looking for her," Kabir says.

"Thanks," Spidey replies. "It was, uh, nice meeting you," he adds awkwardly. *I never know how to end these.*

"You too, Spider-Man. Thanks for the candy," Kabir says, laughing again. He steps back and closes the window.

Spidey pushes off the building and shoots a web out, letting the momentum of the swing carry him forward. *If I don't hear from Ms. Subhaiya by this weekend, I'll come back and try again. Now I gotta get to MJ's!*

MJ holds Peter's hand as they step off the G train and into the Metropolitan Avenue station.

"I can't believe we both missed the Nassau Ave. announcement." Peter is laughing.

"I know we said our next date would be patrolling," MJ says. "But I am glad it's actually not." Peter's eyes go wide, and she's quick to add, "I do want to go! Just . . . I want a break from it all first. Just get to have fun and no *weird* life stuff at all."

"I think we can handle that?" Peter says, only kind of sounding like he's asking a question.

Tonight is their fun date night, and MJ is excited. There's a crowd of people around them, and toward the end of the platform she can hear music playing. It sounds like a fiddle and a drum, and MJ squeezes Peter's gloved hand in hers.

"Let's stop and watch!" She grins. "Usually it's that guy who plays those terrible Rolling Stones covers down here. This actually sounds like a real band."

"Oh man, I hate that guy," Peter groans. "He's so loud and *so* out of tune. And he yelled at me once."

Then he steps forward through the crowd resolutely so he and MJ can weave their way closer to the group busking. When they come into vision, MJ can see it's a woman playing the fiddle and a man using his hands to drum against a large plastic box. The combination is surprisingly jaunty, and they both spend a few minutes enjoying the music alongside the crowd.

"Maybe we were *supposed* to miss our stop at Nassau so we could hear this music?" MJ says.

"Kismet." Peter grins.

When the song ends, MJ lets go of Peter's hand and steps forward to drop a few dollars into the open case at the fiddler's feet in appreciation.

"Ready to head up?" Peter asks when she makes it back to him.

"Yup," she says, taking his hand again. "Let's go. I think the Museum of Food is still only, like, a ten-minute walk."

"Good," Peter says, using his free hand to pull his hat down over his ears and his scarf up over his nose.

MJ bites her cheek to keep from laughing. In his black parka and winter clothes, Peter kind of looks like a burnt marshmallow. "Peter." MJ grins. "It's not *that* cold.

Plus"—she leans closer to whisper—"you're usually in *way* less layers. This will be a piece of cake."

"I appreciate your belief in my ability to not complain about the cold, but I regret to inform you, you are mistaken." Peter laughs as they step up the stairs and out into the cold Brooklyn weather. MJ starts pulling Peter east on Metropolitan so they can turn onto Lorimer Street toward the Museum of Food and Drink. There's an exhibit on the American diner that she's read about online. *How could we go wrong learning about food?*

Out of the corner of her eye, MJ sees Peter's hand come up and rub his nose. She turns to face him and sees that it's already bright red. *And cute.*

"Can you believe that a few months ago we were fighting a secret, invisible alien?" Peter says, apropos of nothing.

"Can you believe a few months ago you didn't know I had a crush on you?" MJ responds, smiling and biting at her lip. Peter stumbles and then blushes, and MJ releases his hand so she can tuck her arm around his and walk closer together. "I got you." She grins.

"I can't," he says a few minutes later.

"Hm?" she asks.

"I can't believe you had a crush on me," he says, looking away.

"Peter Parker, you're a catch," MJ says, laughing before she adds, "And so am I."

"No disagreement here," he says, stepping closer so he can knock her shoulder with his.

"Good," MJ says. Then her eye catches something and she points. "Oh, look!" There's a small street market down a little side avenue to their left. She and Peter detour to look at the booths. While they're walking, Peter asks her if there's anything new going on with the garden. "Oh, I don't know. It's all so weird," MJ answers, holding up a leather wallet with her initials on it. She puts it down after a few seconds. "Maia and I have had no luck figuring out *why* we'd get in trouble for asking about that lot, and we can't figure out who KRT Technologies is, or why they want that lot in the first place. Everything about it is giving me bad vibes."

"Oh, you know what?" Peter says, pulling her away from the booth they'd been in to a more secluded area. "You know how I told you about that reporter I'm talking to, or trying to talk to," he amends. "She's a tech reporter, I bet I could ask her about that URL, too!"

MJ gives him a half smile. "That would be really helpful! We're at a complete roadblock with this stuff. There is that town hall coming up, but it would nice to be able to look at this from multiple angles. . . ." *He's not doing extra work if he's asking someone he's already talking to*, MJ reasons. "Oh, and I hope you're still taking this Spidey Code person with a grain of salt, by the way," she adds. "I still don't trust them. I think it's weird they sent you to Sheepshead Bay last week."

Peter nods. "It could be weird, or it could be them working out whatever system they're using. I just wish I knew who it was!"

There's a loud buzzing coming from Peter's pocket just then, and he pulls out his phone. MJ can't see the screen, but Peter's face falls as he reads it.

"Night job?" she asks.

"Night job," he says, and she can see the apology on the tip of his tongue.

"This is the life. I get it, Pete. Really," she says, untwining their arms and batting at his coat softly. She tries not to let the disappointment show on her face.

Peter's eyes dart in that way she's come to recognize and appreciate, when he's trying to find the exact right thing to say, or trying to understand something. "Thanks, MJ. I am *very* lucky that you're my girlfriend. Definite rain check on the food museum and *fun*," he says, and leans forward to kiss her quickly before turning to find a place to suit up. *Or peel off some layers*, MJ thinks.

"You are, Peter!" she says after him. "But come see me after!"

CHAPTER ELEVEN

The Spot is crouching on a rooftop overlooking a quiet city street. It's just after four in the morning, and dawn is on the cusp of the horizon. He's frowning, looking down into the empty, quiet street.

"This better be for real and not some new way those jerks at the CWNN cooked up to torture me." He rolls his eyes. "Not that that makes any sense because how would they know that I would pickpocket that kid and end up with that phone? No, this *has* to be real." He falls back on his haunches and picks at the rooftop. *Although*, he thinks, *there are a lot of really bad, powerful people in that café, and who knows what they're capable of.* "I mean," he continues talking to himself out loud, "my whole body is covered in interdimensional portals now!" There's a thread of desperation in his voice, but he shakes it off. He needs to be confident and ready for this. He spent a few hours getting as prepared as he could on his own—using his scientific mind for researching heists. He has a pretty good idea of how this could go, as long as he hasn't been lied to about the opportunity.

Just then, there's a sound below, and he stretches to peek back over the ledge on the rooftop. A massive black armored truck turns onto Varick Street, heading farther downtown. He waits to see if there's more. Two minutes go by and the truck is followed by a single black town car, as if the security firm that planned this decided they'd rather not call attention to the job at all and instead rely on anonymity and lack of people on the streets in lieu of an extra security detail. The Spot smirks because it doesn't matter either way for someone with his special skills. He waits a moment for the truck to roll to a stop at the signal and then makes his move. There's a large black hole next to him on the roof. He gets on his knees and pushes his head and shoulders in so that he can pop up from the asphalt directly below the truck. There's a pair of wire cutters in his hand already, and he pulls at a thin black wire and cuts it, then takes the opportunity to slash the two front tires. There's a loud sound of air hissing, and a *thunk*.

The Spot pulls back and is on the rooftop again. The light turns green, and the Spot's gratified to hear the growl of an engine paired with no movement. Two men in tactical gear get out of the front of the truck. They're wearing thick helmets with the visors pulled down and bulletproof vests, and they're dressed completely in black, head to toe. One yells something to the other, and the Spot knows it's his chance. The driver kneels to look at the rapidly flattening tire while his partner moves around to guard the back door. *The joke's on them; they'll never see* me *coming.*

This time, the Spot hops fully into the hole, landing in the Spot World. He takes a moment to look around at all the floating black disks around him, jumping directly toward the one he needs. It's down a little ways and to his right. In this space, all he has to do is to crawl through it, and then he's inside the back of the security truck. It's a tight fit because the Spot finds himself completely surrounded by dozens and dozens of large lockboxes. There's a low light in the back of the truck allowing him to see. He drops a hole on one lockbox and dips his hand in, pulling out a fistful of beautiful, shining emeralds. His eyes go wide, and he grins, his face glowing green with the gems' reflection. Dropping the emeralds back into the safe, he tries another box. This time it's *diamonds*. He picks one more at random, and he's elated to see it's more jewels. That means he won't have to worry about silly things like logged security codes on cash, or fencing iconic art, or anything like that. Jewels are more difficult to trace. At least according to the research he's done.

The Spot places a large hole on the back door of the truck. He's got more than enough time; there's no reason for the men to open the back any time soon, but still he hurries all the same. *No reason to tempt fate*, he thinks, shoving a stack of the lockboxes into the hole, where they slide directly from the Spot World into his apartment. It takes him no more than eight minutes to get through nearly all the boxes in the truck. He's reaching for the last two when he hears a sound, and in front of him, he can see the mechanics of the door start to move. *They're coming in!* He starts vibrating with excitement, knowing that he's going to get away with it. Throwing the last two boxes before him, the Spot flings himself forward and into the dark hole. Then he's safe and in his Spot World, the last two boxes already sliding forward into the portal leading to his apartment. The Spot follows them through and sees the boxes of jewels littering his space. He sits down, surrounded by his loot, and starts laughing in joy. He's done it.

The stolen phone rings from its spot on his coffee table, and he swipes at it, answering the call.

"Hello, partners!" he says before they can say anything, unable to hide his joy. "I think this is the beginning of a long and mutually beneficial relationship. If this is what you can get me, I don't think I have anything to lose."

"If this is amenable. Amenable. We can do more than

this, more than paltry rocks. If you help us. Help us find home. We can help you get more."

The Spot's wide smile takes on an eerie, maniacal glint. "And then everyone'll know my name," he says with heat. "Everyone will be worried about *me* messing with *them*."

"Infamous. We can make you infamous. Respected. Feared," the voices say, and they seem louder somehow.

"I like the sound of this," he says, leaning back against the lockboxes full of pay dirt and running his hands along the sides of the stack next to him. "This is exactly the kind of break I deserve."

It's working. We are closer.
But still so far.
This one is stronger than the last. Smarter.
We will need to be careful.
He cannot leave us.

"MJ, I got two guys who were hilariously trying to steal an actual subway car, stopped three separate bodegas from being robbed, *and* waylaid a dognapper after he tried to swipe some lady's prized poodle in Central Park."

Peter and MJ are walking to the bus stop. He's surprisingly energetic for someone who didn't get to bed until five in the morning, but it was a busy night. Next to him, MJ is holding his hand and nodding along, but she's been quiet and it's beginning to rub at Peter the wrong way.

"Isn't that awesome?" he says, trying to pull her into the conversation. She finally looks at him and nods, smiling, but it's not convincing. "What is it?" he asks, deflating.

"No, Peter, it is really amazing. Seriously," she says, and her voice is soft.

"But . . . ?" Peter prompts. They turn at the signal, still a few short blocks away from their bus stop. A fierce and fast wind picks up; Peter uses his free hand to pull his scarf up.

"But," she says after the wind has died down, "that was all on the list the Spidey Code person or whatever sent you?" She tucks a piece of hair behind her ear and then pulls her own hat back down. Her hair is all over the place, and her cheeks are a bright pink against the white of her face. She's beautiful on this very frigid February morning, and *I look like freakin' Rudolph the Red-Nosed Reindeer.* He sighs.

"Yeah . . ." he says out loud. "That's why it was so productive! I usually only get to help, like . . . one or two people tops. Although I definitely can't have that many late nights consistently." He's interrupted by a huge, well-timed yawn. When he's finished, he grins lopsidedly. "You see what I mean."

MJ laughs, a small sound that carries in the cold air. "Five is *very* late," she agrees. "You're lucky today's a pretty easy day. But . . ." she says again, and Peter tries not to let his frustration show on his face. He wants her to be happy that he's doing so well, and is confused by her resistance. "Well, you missed a pretty big thing last night, Peter."

"Huh?" he asks. He'd been later than usual waking up that morning—which was saying something, considering his usual routine wasn't exactly the picture of timeliness—and he hadn't had a chance to look at any news online, so he has no idea what she's talking about.

"There was an *actual* jewel heist," she finally says in one burst of excitement and a tiny bit of disbelief.

Peter is thrown. "A *jewel heist?*" he repeats, dumbfounded. "A jewel heist?!" He lets go of MJ's hand so he can rest his palms against his eyes and block out the world for a second. "I missed a jewel heist," he whispers to himself. "Mary Jane, did anyone . . . get hurt?" he asks after dropping his hands to his side. His whole body is tense.

"No! No, no one was hurt. Sorry, I should have led with that," MJ says in a hurry. "They're not releasing a ton of details, but I *know* no one got hurt. I just . . ." She takes his hand again, and they resume their walking. "I just think this Spidey Code person has an agenda, and that it's something to think about."

Peter shrugs. "You might be right. I probably shouldn't rely so much on something I can't see. I'm gonna send them a message, though, and see what they say if I ask about the jewel thing."

"That's not a bad idea," MJ agrees. All of a sudden, her eyes go wide and she points. "Peter, the bus!" Their school bus is passing by them, and they've got at least another block and a half to make the stop.

"Shoot!" Together, they sprint down the street, huffing and puffing by the time they make it, just in time for the doors to open. Their bus driver, Ms. Betty, grins at them both, eyes lively, and her dark skin looking vibrant in the morning light.

"Good morning, kids!" she says, laughing. "I hope that run was a good wake-me-up for you both."

"Ms. Betty," Peter says, breathing heavy as he passes her by to walk down the aisle, "someday, please tell us your secret as to how you are so awake so early in the morning."

In response, her laughter follows him down to the empty seat MJ's commandeered for them in the back of the bus.

"Definitely no more super-late nights," MJ says. "I can't take this kind of stress before school even starts." But she's grinning, so Peter knows she's not upset.

"Deal," Peter says. He drops down into the seat next to her and digs to pull his phone out of his pocket. "Okay, let's message our supposedly benevolent Spidey Code helper." MJ hums in agreement. He pulls up a link to the story about the missing jewels and pastes the URL into a new direct message.

> How'd we miss this???

"Okay," he says. "Done and done." He presses a button to turn the phone screen off and slides it into his backpack instead of attempting to finagle it back into his coat pocket while he's bundled up and sitting down.

"Good," MJ says. "Now, in other news, please don't forget that town hall with Councilman Grant is tonight. Maia and I are going to go and see if we can get any answers."

Peter grins and puts his arm around MJ. "I am *there*. The minute I leave the *Bugle*, I'll text you to meet up."

CHAPTER TWELVE

This time, when he gets to the Café With No Name, the Spot doesn't wait around to work up the nerve to go in. *I'm not some no-name nothing. I'm somebody.* He walks right up to that same dirty old door and opens it, letting it bang against the wall with a loud *thud*. He takes a step inside. He's forgone any sort of semblance of his old look, and is now covered head to toe in black spots.

The same bouncer from earlier comes into view and narrows his eyes. "Ain't you the same road trash as before?" he sneers. "I told you, you're not welcome here."

The Spot puts up a finger in the bouncer's face and steps around him. He just needs one extra second, and the bouncer's confusion buys him the time. In full view of the quiet clientele, he shoves an empty fist into a hole in his chest and pulls out a full one. Then he lets a bunch of tiny, shiny diamonds fly into the room.

"Are these . . . ?" he hears someone say—and another: "This is from—"

"*That* guy?!"

The bouncer's just behind him now, but the Spot can feel the man wavering. The mood has turned, and it's in the Spot's favor.

"I believe you're about to tell me I'm good?" the Spot asks, without turning around.

"Yeah," comes a gruff voice. "Yer good." And then the heavy footsteps walk back toward the entrance.

"That's what I thought." The Spot takes the CWNN in—there aren't a *lot* of people, and the space is dark, but he thinks there are some recognizable silhouettes. The one at the far end of the café, at a table that's being given wide berth by everyone who walks in that area, is particularly familiar with its sharp angles and rectangular shape. The Spot doesn't head that way, though, opting for an empty table along the wall. An old man with dark-brown skin comes over to him, holding a notepad. He must be a waiter. The top half of his face is scarred to pieces, and he's got a full white beard covering the bottom half. He puts a pen to his notepad and starts speaking. "That's some entrance, new guy—"

"It's *the Spot*," the Spot corrects him in a professional voice.

"The Spot, then," the man says. "Some entrance. You who we can thank for that big job the other day?" He eyes the scattered diamonds on the floor.

The Spot leans back in his chair and shrugs. "I might know a thing or two about a thing or two, especially if some of those things are diamonds, rubies, and emeralds," he says with a nasty laugh.

"Oh my," the waiter says, with an equally nasty inflection. "Then what say your first drink is on the house, Mr. Spot. And we hope it's with the understanding that we'll see you again."

The Spot has to hold in a shudder of excitement. He makes sure his voice is even when he says, "I'll have a macchiato. No sugar."

The man tips his head and walks off to put the order in. Around him, Spot can feel people staring, and he likes it. He hears whispers and conjectures about how he did it. He lets the words wash over him and can't help the grin painting itself on his face. No one here is going to judge him for his results; no one is going to mock him for getting things done. They didn't care about the *ethics*.

"Just wait," a sullen voice says from a table in the corner. "Just wait till the bug catches up to you. You ain't got a prayer against him." The Spot looks over to see a large white man leaning over a mug. He's got a nose like some-one took a bat to it, and small, angry eyes.

"Psh," the Spot says, bravado raising his voice. "I could take that guy. He's pathetic." The Faithless might be handling Spider-Man for now, but if the Spot can pull off the job he just pulled off . . . why couldn't he take Spider-Man, too?

"Yeah, right," the big man says. He stands. "Whatever you say, new guy."

"It's the *Spot*," Spot grits out in response.

"I'm just sayin', the bug'll take you down eventually." He shrugs, and then he limps to the door. The Spot is too angry to say anything. "See ya, Bobby," the anonymous jerk says to the bouncer, and heads out into the evening.

Oh, so I'm still "new guy" huh? Just wait. I'm going to take down the bug.

When Peter shows up at the *Bugle* after school, the energy is *intense*. People are running this way and that, and when he gets to his desk, he sees that Kayla is nowhere to be found. He takes his seat and turns to the long-term proj-ect Kayla started him on of organizing old print photos. There's a huge stack of folders to go through, so he picks one at random, opening it and starting to go through the pictures so he can organize them into piles. A few cubes over, he hears someone on the phone asking for a quote from someone. "Can you tell me when you realized the Enlow Diamonds were gone? Sir? Hello? Hello?" Then the sound of a phone crashing into its cradle. "Argh! Why won't anyone talk to me?!"

Peter winces. *Yikes, that did not sound good.* It's like that all over the floor. At one point, Peter gets up to use the restroom and swears that he can hear Jameson from two floors away screaming for *more information on his desk, right away.* He still hasn't been one-on-one with Jameson since his fake firing, and Peter is content to keep it that way. He ducks his head and goes back to the photographs.

About a half an hour later, there's a whirlwind of energy behind him, and Peter turns to find Kayla collapsing into her chair. She's fanning herself and sitting low in her seat, slouched in a way Peter's not sure he's ever seen her before.

"Uh, hi?" he says, unsure.

"Remind me that I asked for this promotion and that I knew what it was going to be like going in," she says by way of a greeting.

"Um, you asked for this promotion and you knew what it was going to be like going in?" Peter asks more than states. Kayla grins, but Peter can see she's tired behind it. "What's the deal around here? Everyone seems like they're bananas," he says, gesturing around. The person from earlier is back on the phone, and Peter thinks it sounds like he's on the verge of tears.

Kayla leans forward, and her eyes are wide with excitement. "There's a *new* super villain in New York."

Peter grimaces. "And that's . . . good, because?"

"News, Peter! It's hot, exciting news! And the first person who gets the story out gets to name him, gets to decide how the rest of the papers will probably cover it, will get the recognition, so when the inevitable well-researched long-form piece comes out, they'll be in serious running for the awards. Everything moves so fast now; you have to get *in the game*." By the end of her last sentence, Kayla's eyes are wide, and her fists are clenched under her chin, and she's not even looking *at* Peter anymore, but rather something off in the distance.

"Oh . . ." *Does this have anything to do with that jewel burglary I missed?* "So . . ." He stumbles, trying to figure out how to ask what he wants to ask. He finally settles on "What do we know?"

Kayla's gaze comes back to Peter. "Well, we're calling them Dots, or maybe Spots—Jonah was yelling, but also not articulating well, so I'm not sure what he and Robbie landed on—and they leave behind these black circles, but no one knows why. Somehow they were able to get in and out of a fully armored truck with the *entire* haul without anyone seeing them. I think the dots are like a calling card, and that they can probably go invisible."

Throughout Kayla's explanation, Peter's face has fallen further and further. A few short weeks ago, this person was just hitting random ATMs and Peter didn't catch them. And now they're cleaning out entire armored trucks? Peter knows things can only escalate from here.

"And then—" Kayla looks at Peter's face and cuts off abruptly. "Is everything okay?" she asks.

Peter rushes to school his features into something more neutral. "Yeah! Yeah, sorry. Just . . . these guys always lead to so much trouble in the city, you know? That guy in the rhino suit attacked my school once, and it was under construction for *months* . . . still is actually."

Kayla's face softens, and she leans forward in her chair. "You're right, Peter. Sorry about that. It's just—from a news perspective, this *is* exciting. And they haven't hurt anyone, so I hope they get caught before anything happens, of course."

"No, you're totally right!" Peter says, not wanting Kayla to feel bad just because *he* feels responsible.

"Kayla!" Jameson's voice is closer now, and Peter can't help but flinch. "Has that masked menace been anywhere around the new guy? Any word of it?!" he yells, storming onto the scene. Peter swings his chair around so fast he nearly falls out of it, so that his back is facing the direction Jameson is coming from.

Kayla takes a deep breath and turns to J. Jonah

Jameson, who is now leaning over the top of her cube wall.

"No, sir," she says.

"That's strange, isn't it? That's the story! 'Masked Menace Misses Mastermind Behind Jewel Heist.'"

Peter has to resist the urge to put his head down on his desk and groan. From behind him he hears Kayla say, "You got it, Jonah. I'll start writing it up right away."

"Good!" Jameson says, already hurrying back the way he came.

Peter lets out a relieved breath he didn't even realize he'd been holding. *Great, more wonderful publicity*, he thinks, frowning at the remaining folders on his desk.

Later, Spidey is on his way home from the *Bugle*, swinging through the streets of Queens. He's disconcerted by how much everyone else seems to realize he messed up by not being there for this one big heist. *MJ was right. There's something really off about whoever is running that account.* TheSpideyCode0285 never actually messaged him back after this morning, and it is making him nervous. There is no reason that he can think of for the radio silence *other* than that this person is mad about being questioned, or frustrated that Spidey has figured out TheSpideyCode0285 has their own agenda.

"MJ!" Spidey says, suddenly remembering he has somewhere to be. "The town hall!" He shoots a web diagonally at an upcoming corner and uses the angle to swing around and make a hard left. He completely forgot to text her when he was leaving, so preoccupied with Dots or Spots or whatever this new bad guy was called. *Now she's really going to feel like she can't talk to me about this stuff,* Spidey seethes. *I can't let her down!*

He pulls another diagonal web trick and takes the next left. As he turns the corner, his lenses go wide at what he's facing, but he's moving too fast to avoid it. There, hanging in the air in front of him, is a gigantic black hole, and Spidey flies right into it.

MJ looks down at her phone again, and there's still no message from Peter. She and Maia are seated in the second row of the town hall Councilman Grant has put on, hoping to get some face time with the man. She unlocks her phone and types out her third message to Peter in the last half hour.

> JUST CHECKIN IN, AGAIN, THE TOWN HALLS
> ABOUT TO START, WHERE R U?? IF UR
> NIGHT JOB GOT IN THE WAY JUST CALL ME
> AND LET ME KNOW AT LEAST.

She hits send and frowns down at her phone. She hopes nothing is wrong, but she also hopes Peter didn't just forget that he was supposed to meet her at the town hall.

"Excuse me, everyone!" a loud voice at the front of the room calls out. "If you would please silence your cell phones. We're about to get started." There are only eight other people in the space besides MJ and Maia. *A town hall for a local councilman on a random weeknight isn't exactly the hottest ticket in town*, MJ reasons, even though the sight of the empty room makes her a little sad. Next to her, Maia shifts in her seat, trying to get comfortable in the cheap plastic chairs.

"At least we'll *definitely* be able to ask a question," Maia says. "Wait," she adds, "should we use fake names? Since he's already called you at school?"

"Oh . . . that hadn't occurred to me, but . . . can we lie to a councilman?" MJ asks, and Maia laughs in response.

"I bet he lies *all* the time," she says. MJ gives her a wry smile. "Actually, I'll ask. He doesn't know who I am yet."

"Fair enough. And also, it's a simple question! Plenty of people might want to know how to start a community garden if they don't know who owns a particular lot and if that lot's been empty for *years*."

Before Maia can respond, a tall white man walks out into the front of the room. He's got mousy brown hair and a pair of gold-rimmed glasses. His tailored blue suit and red tie look expensive.

"Hello to my Queens community. I'm Councilman Grant, and thank you for coming this evening. All ten of you." There's a round of quiet, polite laughter. "So, should we get started?" he asks.

The councilman walks around the front of the room talking about developers and bringing money into Queens; he mentions a few names at the top. *He's pretty charismatic*, MJ thinks, frowning. *But there's something I don't like.* A finger taps her thigh, and she turns to look at her seatmate. Maia is frowning.

"Something sketchy about him," she whispers to MJ. MJ just nods in agreement.

Then the councilman says, "And I'll be working closely with a brand-new organization—KRT Technologies—to get a lot of this done."

Both MJ and Maia sit up straight and lean forward. *That's the company that holds that lot!*

Unfortunately, Grant doesn't go any further in depth on that particular corporation during his speech, despite MJ and Maia waiting for him to. He spends another ten minutes on dog parks and some local business ordinances before he finally opens the floor for questions. Maia raises her hand immediately.

The councilman's pale blue eyes dart to her, and he

points. Then MJ swears that he does a double take when he realizes she's sitting next to Maia.

"Actually, give me one moment, please," he says, stepping away from the front of the room and leaning down to speak into the ear of the person who had initially introduced him. Then the councilman never comes back. He jogs out of a door on the side, and the person he whispered to moves forward.

"I'm so sorry, everyone, Councilman Grant had an emergency and had to run out of here. We'll see you in a few weeks for his next appearance!"

"Are you freakin' *kidding* me?!" Maia erupts.

MJ leans against her chair and throws her head back in frustration, closing her eyes and letting out a deep sigh. "This *sucks*," she says. She pulls her phone out to see if Peter's called or texted, hoping that he'll have something good to say. Her eyes sting when she sees that there are no notifications, and she bites her cheek, furious that she's on the verge of crying. "Ugh," she says, closing her eyes and taking in a deep breath to stop the tears from actually falling. *Why am I even crying? This is so annoying! I'm just frustrated!*

"We'll get to the bottom of this," Maia says next to her. "I am not letting *that* guy win."

CHAPTER THIRTEEN

When Spider-Man comes to, the first thing he notices is the *smell*. It smells like . . . garbage. *Like parts of the city on a hot summer day, but worse somehow.* He's lying on something hard, and he hasn't opened his eyes yet. Trying not to gag, he takes a second to go through his body and make sure nothing is broken. He wiggles his toes and flexes his fingers. Everything seems to be in working order. Opening his eyes doesn't help much; it's all darkness around him. He finally presses against the ground and moves to stand up. He immediately lets out a pained groan and puts a hand against his head. He must have hit it pretty hard. He closes his eyes again and stands still for a moment, trying to will the pain to go down. Finally, he pulls his phone out and turns on the flashlight.

"I'm in the *sewers*?!" Spider-Man gags. Lifting his fingers to his face, he considers pulling the bottom of his mask up just in case but doesn't want to lose the one layer of protection he has against the disgusting scent around him. He makes a concerted effort to breathe through his mouth. "What the actual heck?" He moves his flashlight around to see if there's anything he can see that will clue him in to how he got here, but there's nothing. The last thing he remembers is . . . "THE BLACK HOLE! I went . . . I went *through* it." Spider-Man has been through a lot, but he has never been dropped into a *Looney Tunes*–style black splotch of paint in the middle of the sky. "But," he says, starting to pace, "how *did* I go through it? The spots on the ATM were, like, *painted* onto the machines. I touched them. There was nothing about those that seemed like something could go inside or go outside. I need to talk to—MJ!" He slams a palm against his forehead and immediately lets out yelp of pain. Gently, he runs his fingers along the top of his mask. He gets about two inches above his right eyebrow and winces—there's a raised knot there, and it's tender to the touch. *"Ouch,"* he says. *I must have fallen headfirst out of that hole.*

Spidey groans again and takes a deep breath in through his nose to settle the pain and then immediately gags for the second time.

"That's it. I have to get out of here before I throw up and die, or vice versa." He looks up and down the long corridor of the sewer. A short distance away, he can see the dim pinpricks of a streetlamp shining through the small holes of a manhole cover. A few minutes later, he's pushing hard against the heavy disk and climbing out from the dank darkness. When he makes it onto the street, he takes a second to gather his bearings.

"Spider-Man?" There's a young Asian woman standing on the corner pointing at him. "Hi, Spider-Man!" she says again, more enthusiastically.

He glances at the street sign above her. *"Canal Street?!"* he cries out. "I was in *Queens*, and now I'm all the way back in the city. Are you *kidding me?!*"

"Uh . . . Spider-Man, are you—" the woman says for a third time, like she's not sure if it's really him, or maybe some impostor.

He evens out his tone and waves. "Heh, sorry, hi, yeah, I'm Spider-Man," he says. "Good to see you, but now I have to go." And before she can say anything else, he shoots a web out to the top of a building and flies up to the roof. The second his boots hit the roof, he pulls his phone back out. It's after eleven, which means he's lost around four hours of time and that he— There's a little red circle with the number seven in it sitting on the corner of his messages app. Grimacing, he taps at the icon. Five of them are from MJ.

HEY, HAVEN'T HEARD FROM YOU, ARE YOU ON YOUR WAY? MAIA N I ARE HERE ALREADY. C U SOON!

HEY PETER, DID U LEAVE THE BUGLE ALREADY?

JUST CHECKIN IN, AGAIN, THE TOWN HALLS ABOUT TO START, WHERE R U?? IF UR NIGHT JOB GOT IN THE WAY JUST CALL ME AND LET ME KNOW AT LEAST.

WELL U MISSED IT BUT IT'S PROBABLY GOOD BC IT WAS HORRIBLE

OK PETER I'M STARTING TO GET RLY WORRIED, WHERE ARE U????

Spider-Man wastes no time and texts her back.

IM SO SORRY! GOT HELD UP BY NIGHT JOB AND AM HEADING HOME NOW, GONNA STOP TO CHANGE REAL QUICK (LONG STORY) BUT WILL SEE YOU RIGHT AFTER???

Three little dots pop up to indicate her typing, but when the message comes through, all she says is *k*.

That doesn't bode well. . . .

The Spot falls back onto his bed with a happy sigh. *I just owned the Spider-Man! By myself! I did that! Me! Now let's see what that guy at the CWNN has to say.* He puts his hands behind his head and crosses his feet at the ankles. There are a few takeout menus sitting on the ground near his bed, and he thinks about ordering a celebratory feast for a dinner. A loud buzzing from the living room interrupts his musings, and he pushes himself up off his bed to see what it is.

The stolen phone is vibrating loudly on the coffee table, moving a few inches to the right with every buzz. The Spot grabs it and slides to answer.

"This is not what we wanted. This is not." The voices are *loud* this time around, and the Spot frowns.

"It's what *I* wanted," he says, iron in his tone. "It had to happen."

"Why would you—" The voices stall and stutter for a moment. "Sabotage. Why would you sabotage?"

The black dots all over his body dance and move as Spot gets more and more frustrated. *Sabotage?*

"That wasn't *sabotage*. That was a lark. A prank. That was a *calling card*," he says, the devious tone of his voice juxtaposing with his mock innocence. "Look, I saw that red-suited jerk flying around the corner and thought, *Why not?*" He flings his free hand out in a wide arc. "The universe dropped him right into the palm of my hands and I *wasn't* supposed to go for it? Think of what'll happen to the guy who takes out *Spider-Man*. People would know his name *forever*."

The Spot's not even really thinking of the phone in his hand anymore. He's thinking of a future where it will be his name on everyone's lips. Where the big bosses come to him for help.

"It was not. It was not smart. Not smart. We have Spider. Spider being dealt with. Plan. Plan happening," they say, voices rising with every word, interrupting his reveries. There's a twinge of *something* against the Spot's arm. Like something is pushing at it, but it's so weak he can't be sure it's even really happening. He looks down at his arm and then at the phone.

"Is that . . . you?" he asks. "Are you trying to *do* something?"

"You must. Listen. You must *listen*!" come the voices, loud and angry.

"Give me one good reason why," the Spot says.

"We will *give* you everything. But you help us. First. You find home. Our home."

Peter crawls into his bedroom and nearly slips on the window ledge. He looks down to find that his boot still has some sort of slime on it from the sewer. He shivers in disgust and tries to wipe it off against the side of the house so he won't bring it inside. In doing so, his toe gets caught under one of the slats, and he pitches forward, his stomach landing heavily on the windowsill with his legs hanging outside and his head on the inside. "*Oof,*" he grunts out on impact.

He hears his aunt's voice call up from downstairs. "Peter? Is everything okay?"

Peter hurries to yank himself inside the room, close the window, and start ditching his suit. He pulls everything off and shoves the balled-up mess under his bed, then reaches for the dirty pajamas he'd left lying on the ground that morning. He's just pulling up his pants when there's a soft knock at his door.

"Peter?" Aunt May's voice comes through muffled.

He dives into the covers and settles before calling out, "Yeah?" in a low voice.

The knob twists, and Aunt May pokes her head in. "I thought I heard something falling up here," she says. Her glasses are perched on the end of her nose, and Peter realizes she must have been working downstairs.

"Oh, I knocked over a stack of books," he lies. "Sorry about that." *And for lying,* he thinks.

May's eyes go soft, and she smiles. "That's fine, Peter.

I just wanted to make sure everything was okay." Then her nose scrunches, and her eyes narrow. "What *is* that smell?" she asks, looking around his room.

Peter keeps his face smooth. "What smell?" he asks, hoping she can't tell that he knows exactly what she is smelling.

"I don't know. . . . It just smells *awful*. Did you leave food rotting in here or something?" she says, moving to take a step inside.

"No! No. Nope. I just— Oh, maybe it's left over from an experiment I was working on," he says, the words tumbling out of him in a rush. He swings his legs out from under his blankets. "Do you want me to check right now?"

May raises her hands and shakes her head. "Oh, no, you rest, Peter. I feel like you've been running yourself ragged since school started. Maybe schedule some time for a break soon?" Her tone says she's asking, but Peter's heard it before and knows she means that if he doesn't schedule some downtime, she'll do it for him.

"Yes, Aunt May," he says. "Though, you know it takes one to know one." A quizzical look settles onto her features in response. "Someone who works too hard," he says meaningfully.

"That's enough cheek out of you, Peter. Don't forget who the adult is here," she says, the faux irritation in her tone belied by the big smile she has on.

"Yes, Aunt May," he repeats, mirroring her smile with one of his own.

"Next weekend, we'll *both* take time off and we can spend a Saturday eating junk food and watching movies," she says, turning away to head back downstairs.

"That sounds awesome," Peter says, meaning it.

"All right, now go to bed! Good night."

"Night!"

Peter waits in his room for fifteen minutes before he rises to throw on a heavy sweater and a pair of thick socks. Then he slides his window open and crawls out of it, careful not to step against the smudge from earlier. He crawls to the edge of his roof and looks left and right to make sure the street is quiet before launching himself over to the Watsons'. He makes it to MJ's window and taps softly at the glass. She opens it without saying anything and is already seated on her bed by the time he makes it inside. She's got a thick, dark robe on belted around her middle. She looks very cozy, but it's at odds with the way she's holding herself. Her arms are crossed against her chest, and she's got her legs folded under her.

"Hey, MJ," he says sheepishly, rubbing the back of his head. "I—"

"Where *were* you?" she says, voice breaking. "I was

worried. You said you'd be there and you weren't, and there was no information and I didn't even know who to call. I was *worried*," she says again, and Peter's heart falls. He steps forward, and she holds up a hand. "No, wait, you have to tell me."

He nods once and moves back to take his seat on the beanbag. Then he opens his mouth and lets it all out. About Jameson and the *Bugle*, about missing a new super villain, and about the black hole in the middle of the street. When he's finished, MJ's face has gone white.

"Peter, I know I have to figure out how to be okay with all of"—she waves her hand around in a wide arc—"all of this. I know that. And I *definitely* think we need to figure out some kind of system to help you in case something happens. Like, what if you didn't wake up in that sewer?!"

"But I did!" Peter protests. "I woke up. And, MJ, I know this is scary, but . . ." He stops and considers how he wants to say what he needs to say. "I've been doing this for a while now, and sometimes things happen. I might get hurt. I know that." He shrugs. "I'm used to it. Honestly, my head barely even hurts anymore."

"But what if it's something . . . worse?" MJ asks, curling in on herself and with sudden clarity,

Peter realizes what she's asking. "Oh, oh, no, MJ." He stands, and she finally allows him to sit next to her and put his arm around her shoulders. "MJ, I . . . I *have* been doing this on my own for a little while, and it's definitely gotten dangerous. But I'm also pretty good at fighting," he jokes weakly.

In response, she shoves at his ribs lightly with her elbow. "It's not funny," she says, her head bowed. "We need a system. I can't be— We're sixteen. We need a *system*."

Peter squeezes her shoulder and nods. "Okay. Okay. We'll come up with something if something *horrible*—but unlikely!—happens. Remind me to tell you about the time I took down Electro and the worst thing that happened was I got a splinter."

MJ lets out a small laugh and then surreptitiously wipes her face. Peter makes a show of looking away. "We have to figure out who this Spidey Code guy is soon, Peter. I don't like how easily Dots or whatever has gotten bigger."

"I agree. It's at the top of my list. I don't like being played." His voice is low and angry for a moment before he shakes himself out of it. "*Anyway,*" he says finally. "Tell me about the town hall."

"That's the *other* thing!" She pushes him again in the same spot, just in the middle of his ribs. "I *know* your Spider-Manning—" Peter raises an eyebrow, his cheek indented like he's biting it to keep from laughing. She rolls her eyes. "Your *Spider-Manning* is important and that you do so much good for people in the city. But my stuff is important, too. And I don't like feeling like it isn't. I want to change the world, and help people . . . just in a different way."

Peter leans back on his hands. He thinks for a moment before turning to her to reply. "You're right. I should have remembered to text you before I left the *Bugle*, even if this other stuff *was* going on. I should have remembered where I was supposed to be—with you—way earlier, because what you're doing *is* important," he agrees. "I don't want you to think I don't know that. Though these were kind of extenuating circumstances. I don't think I could have seen that big black hole in the sky coming." He tries to make it sound like he's joking, but it falls flat.

MJ twists the edge of her robe belt in her hands, pulling it back and forth and wrapping it around her fingers. "You *should* have remembered to send me a message. And Spider-Man stuff is probably going to always get in the way." Peter opens his mouth to say something, but MJ keeps going. "This is something I have to figure out on my own, I guess, to not compare the things we do, or whatever."

Peter bobs his chin to indicate he hears her. "I don't— I mean—" he starts, unsure of what he can say. Then he shifts so he's sitting up straight again. "I can't just stop."

MJ gives him a long look before getting up to step away from him. Peter bites back a sound of frustration. "I'm not asking you to; no one's asking you to stop. But I don't think you've had to really think about . . . consequences."

"You don't think I think about the *consequences*?" he asks, unable to keep the incredulity out of his voice. "All I do is think about the consequences! What if someone gets hurt? What if—"

Peter's phone vibrates in his pocket, interrupting him. He frowns; he can only think of two people who would be messaging him so late at night, and one of them is right next to him. The other one still owes him a response.

"Do you think that's . . . ?" MJ asks, assuming the same as Peter. But her voice is tight, and Peter isn't sure what he can do.

"I don't know," he says, pulling the phone out to see. When he reads the notification, he's surprised. "Oh,"

"Well?" MJ asks. "Was it them? The Spidey Code?"

Still looking at the screen, Peter shakes his head once before shifting his gaze back to MJ. "No, it's that reporter, Swapna Subhaiya. She's back in town and wants to meet me."

CHAPTER FOURTEEN

The next night, Spidey swings back to that same apartment building in midtown. He crawls to the correct window this time and settles back, leaning against the flat concrete. He glances at his phone and sees that he's a few minutes early. Swapna had asked him to come by at 7:15, and he told her to meet him at the same window Kabir had opened a few days earlier.

He looks down at the sidewalk below for a little while, watching the dots of people going about their business. He can't help but think about his fight with MJ the night before. It hadn't really resolved so much as it had just ended, and he's still unsettled. *I don't want her to think I don't support her. And I definitely don't want her to be worried about me. But . . . what am I supposed to do?* Before he can continue that line of thought, the window next to him slides open and a dark-haired head pops out.

"Spider-Man! Hi!"

Where Kabir Subhaiya was a little awkward and reserved, Swapna Subhaiya is all vibrance and excitement. Her hair is deep, dark black and cut into a short bob, and her lips are painted a bright red. She's already changed out of her work clothes—*unless she goes to work in a Nirvana T-shirt and sweatpants,* Spidey thinks. *What do I know?*

"Hi," he says. "Thanks for getting in touch with me."

Swapna grins. "I have to ask, do you have all your conversations like this?" She gestures to herself inside and Spidey stuck on the side of the building.

He takes a second to think about it. "It happens more than I'd expect, actually," he settles on answering.

She laughs in response and then launches into another spiel. "How could I not get in touch with you? Have you *ever* talked to a reporter? I mean, I know I'm not technically the person who covers your . . . uh, beat, but . . ." She trails off. "He might complain about you, but even Jonah wouldn't turn his nose up at an exclusive with *the* Spider-Man," she says, her teeth showing in a bright, wide smile.

Spidey is thrown and tries to find his footing. "Oh, uh, no. No, that's not why—no, thank you," he finally says. "I don't want any kind of interview. I was actually wondering if I could get your help with a . . . a case I'm working on."

Swapna's dark-lined eyes go wide, making them seem even larger than they already do. She leans forward, resting her elbows on the windowsill. "Oh, I hadn't thought— Of *course* you'd work cases. You're not just *stumbling* on all these crimes." Spidey makes a mental note to not reveal how many times he does actually just "stumble on" people doing bad things. "I'm happy to help if I can. For a favor." Spider-Man isn't sure he likes the sound of that. "How'd you find *me*, anyway?" Swapna adds before Spidey can say anything.

He's ready for this question. He and MJ had discussed possible explanations before he'd left the night before. "Oh, a friend of a friend of a friend works in the media," he says, hoping the vagueness will be enough to put her off from investigating further.

She gives him a long, considering look. Spidey waits to see if she'll call him out. "Okay," she says, apparently deciding it's not worth continuing that line of questioning. "Tell me about what's going on. What can I do for you?"

Spidey's lenses narrow. "What did you mean by 'favor'?" he asks, instead of answering her.

Swapna grins, only he can see something sharp in it this time. "Look, I can't just let this opportunity go. You haven't talked to *any*one in the press, ever. I'm not saying I want to know your secret identity, but maybe if I come through for you on this question you have . . . you could do me a solid. That's the offer, Spidey. Take it or leave it."

Spider-Man looks at her, thinking it through. He isn't sure what his options are, and as long she's not trying to figure out who he is exactly . . . maybe he can go for it. "Okay," he agrees. Then he pulls his phone out and opens up his Twitter account and tells her about the anonymous user sending him tips. But he doesn't give her specifics about the tips outside of the handle.

When he's finished talking, she taps a finger against her chin and looks off in the distance, thinking. "So," she says once she's processed what he's told her, "my first question is, is that your personal phone? Like, that's the phone you use even when you're not, you know"—she gestures at Spider-Man—"dressed up like that?"

Spidey shrugs, wary of where she's going with this. "Yeah, I guess?" he says.

Swapna takes a deep breath. "Some free advice, kid? That's got to change. You can't use your *personal* phone! Do you know how easy it would be to figure out who you are? You have got to get a prepaid phone, one that you can set up by just putting a few dollars on it and not needing any sort of identifying information to kick off service."

Spidey slaps a palm against his forehead. *I cannot believe I didn't think of that six months ago, especially after that conversation with MJ about the Spidey Code user!* "You are the most right person I've ever met," he says, holding in a groan. *Because* that *would be unprofessional.* Under his mask, he rolls his eyes. "That'll be the first thing I do after this. Could you—"

Swapna gives him that same sharp grin. "I told you, I'm not interested in leaking your identity or anything—I think we get more good stories with you than without you . . . and I have a vested interest in my newspaper continuing to sell copies. But, uh, maybe reset your personal phone to factory settings and then never use your prepaid to sign onto your Wi-Fi at home. In fact, to be safe, don't tweet anywhere near where you live, ever."

"The internet is scary."

She shakes her head, laughing. "It's not. You just have to be careful. Now"—she turns away for a moment, and when she pokes her head back out, she's holding a pen and notepad in her hand—"the handle is TheSpideyCode0285?" she asks. Spider-Man nods. "Okay, cool. I'll look it up and then tell you what I can find. And tonight, I'll send you a list of apps to download that will allow for secure messaging and my contact info for those apps."

"You're a lifesaver, Mrs. Subhaiya," he says, and then quickly says, "Swapna, I mean. Swapna." *Grown-ups use first names!* She doesn't comment on it, but Spidey can see that she's looking at him strangely now, like she's trying to figure something out.

"Oh, one more thing. Is there any way you could figure out who owns a URL for me?"

"Is this part of the same case?" she asks.

"No, this is for . . . a different case." *Which isn't entirely untrue,* Spidey reasons, *it's just not* my *case.* He taps a finger against the wall behind him, trying to settle his nerves.

"Two questions . . . two favors," she says, and Spider-Man frowns under his mask, wondering if he's out of his depth.

"Okay. It's for a company called KRT Technologies."

Swapna scratches her pen across her pad, making note of the company name. "K . . . R . . . T . . . Tech," she says quietly to herself as she writes. "Why does that sound so familiar . . . ?"

Spidey shrugs again. "I've never heard of them, and there's no contact info or employees listed on the site. It's confusing."

Swapna is nodding at her pad, likely thinking through her next moves. "Okay, give me a few days with this. I'll be in touch, Spider-Man! Get that burner!"

The first thing Peter does after his meeting with Swapna Subhaiya is drop into an alley and change into street gear. Then he finds the closest electronics shop, which is just a few short blocks away, and starts walking over. When he makes it, he sees a sign for JT's Electronics over a small space tucked in between a hair salon and a pizzeria on 39th Street. The bright fluorescent lights of the shop bleed out onto the sidewalk through grimy windows. Peter pushes on the door, and a bell jingles to announce him.

"Hello!" sounds a lightly accented voice from the back of the shop. A small, dark-skinned man with a white kufi covering half his forehead and a bushy gray beard turns the corner. "Hello," he says again when he spies Peter. "How can I help you?"

Peter glances around. The shop has a plethora of electronics—radios and tablets, cameras, the works.

"I'm looking for a cell phone?" he asks. "But one that doesn't need, like, an account or something. Like, I can just put some money on it and use the minutes." *Yeah, that doesn't sound weird or shady, Parker.*

But the man isn't looking at him strangely, he's just nodding and looking at his merchandise. "Hm, yes, okay. I think I have just the thing for you," he says, turning around and reaching high up to a shelf of plastic-wrapped boxes. "This one is very nice and is just one hundred and twenty-nine dollars."

Peter balks. The man frowns and nods. "I see we're in the market for something else." He kneels down and grabs a different plastic-wrapped box from a low shelf. "This one is forty dollars."

Peter lets out a stream of air and takes the box from

the man. "Does it . . . ? Can I download apps onto it?" he asks, looking at the box in his hands. It's not a brand he's ever heard of before, but it looks like a regular smartphone.

The man nods. "Yes, but the life of the machine won't be very long."

Peter pulls out his wallet and looks at it. He tries to put away a few dollars from his *Bugle* paycheck for emergencies, and some for dates with MJ—the rest he passes along to Aunt May, much to her chagrin. In his wallet he has a twenty, a ten, and two ones that he had been saving to buy MJ a Valentine's Day gift. . . . *But this is more important; MJ would agree.*

"I have thirty-two bucks," he says. The man steps back and considers him. He comes to some kind of decision because he steps away from Peter and moves behind the counter. "You seem like a nice kid," he says once he's situated. "Thirty-two bucks it is."

Peter grins and moves up to stand before him across the glass. He can see some scarves and what looks like a rolled-up prayer mat stored in the clean space behind the counter.

"Thank you so much!" Peter says, dropping the money on the counter and immediately unwrapping the box.

"Please don't. My wife would say I just can't say no to a sad boy."

"I'm not sad!" Peter can't help but bite out, mildly affronted.

The man gives him a patient smile. "Scared, then. No, wait. What is the word, not scared. Anxious. You are anxious."

"Okay," Peter agrees. "I can't deny that. But either way, I appreciate it, sir. Really. This is a huge help."

Ten minutes later, Peter's at a Starbucks down the street, with his new phone plugged in and turned on. He's logged into the free Wi-Fi at the coffee shop and nursing a tall black coffee. He's unearthed an old gift card he won in some kind of school event the year before that had exactly $2.67 left on it. A tall black coffee was $2.52. *Maybe that ol' Parker luck is a thing of the past*, he thinks, grinning and waiting for the phone to download Twitter. He's turned his own phone off. Logging into his account, he quickly brings up the messages and is gratified to see that there's a new one from the Spidey Code, sent twenty minutes earlier. They're finally replying to his question from the day before.

Apologies for the delay, but I wanted to look into this further. I'm troubled by the mistake because this program should be stronger than that. It shouldn't be failing. I don't understand how it failed us here.

TheSpideyCode0285

Peter's eyebrows shoot up. This is more emotional than the person has been before. They're usually very business-like and almost terse in their messages.

> Okay. I just don't want to worry about this again. Is there anything I can do to help?

The response comes back immediately.

> No! No! I will handle this. I will fix this. Don't worry, Spider-Man. I'll make this better and then no one else will get hurt or taken advantage of.

TheSpideyCode0285

"And what did they say after?" MJ asks Peter. They're sitting next to each other at the table in her kitchen after school, ostensibly to work on their project, but really, Peter is telling her about his evening with the *Bugle* tech reporter and what the Spidey Code user had told him. They seem to have reached an unspoken agreement to not talk about their fight, and MJ isn't sure how she feels about that. Things were somewhat awkward when he'd gotten there a few hours earlier, but once he'd started telling her about his evening, they'd slipped right back into easy conversation.

"That they were going to fix it and that no one would ever get hurt again," Peter says, and he sounds uncomfortable. "I don't know, MJ. I feel like maybe this is someone who got hurt because you-know-who wasn't around. . . . Which seems to be a running theme in my life, lately." He groans and runs a hand through his hair.

MJ smiles a half smile and reaches up to grab his wrist, stilling his movement. "Peter," she says, "you can't be everywhere all the time unless you had, like, a million clones or something. Don't take *everything* on your shoulders."

In response, Peter just sighs and lifts the corner of his lip in an attempt at a grin. "I'll work on that," he says, and settles his hand back down in his lap.

"You do that," she says. "I mean it."

"Yes, ma'am." This time, his smile is genuine, and MJ feels a warmth in her chest.

"Okay, let's get into our OSMAKER stuff," she says. "Maia's going to kill us if we don't map out our pieces of the app today."

Peter's face twists up, and he lets out a sound that tells MJ he'd definitely rather be doing something else. MJ's about to make a joke when she hears the front door open.

"I'm home!" her mom calls.

"We're in here!" MJ calls back, and a few seconds later, her mom walks into the room holding a stack of envelopes and flipping through them one by one.

"Hi, Mrs. Watson," Peter says, and MJ's mom looks up, surprised.

"Oh, hello, Peter. I didn't realize you were here," she says pointedly at MJ.

"I did say 'we,'" MJ mutters, but then apologizes. "Sorry, Mom. I thought I told you Peter was coming over today to work on our project."

Mrs. Watson tucks a strand of bright red hair behind her ear and shakes her head. "You might've. My head is all over the place." Then she turns to Peter. "You're always welcome here, of course. So don't feel like you're not!"

"He doesn't," MJ says at the same time Peter says. "I don't!"

MJ's mom lets out a loud laugh in response. She steps to the counter to drop envelopes down as she goes through them.

"Anything good?" MJ asks from her seat.

"Just bills and junk," her mom replies, and then stops. "And, huh, something from a law firm?" MJ hears the sound of the envelope tearing and then a sharp intake of breath as her mom reads through the letter.

MJ turns fully to face her mom, then: "Is everything okay?"

"Mary Jane, is there something you want to tell me?" her mom asks in response.

MJ looks at Peter, and she's sure his expression is mirroring her own. His brows are drawn in confusion, and his lips are turned down into a frown. "I . . . don't think so?" she says after consideration.

"So you're not stalking this . . . Councilman Grant?" her mom says in a stern voice that MJ doesn't hear very often.

"What?!" MJ says, completely shocked. Peter drops his pen on the table. "I . . . No! I emailed his office twice because my boss told me I should, and then I went to the town hall, but I didn't even *talk* to him!" she blurts out.

Mrs. Watson gives her a measured stare and then looks back down at the sheet. "I think maybe . . . I think they're hoping we'll just be scared of this sheet of paper," she says quietly, like she's working it out as the words come out of her mouth.

Peter takes MJ's hand and squeezes it tightly. She looks over at him, and he has his eyebrows raised in askance. MJ squeezes back and shakes her head. *I'll handle this.*

"Mom, I didn't tell you, but they also got me in trouble at school."

Mrs. Watson slams the paper down on the counter, and it's her turn to ask MJ what she means. So MJ explains about being called to the principal and the empty lot she and Maia found.

"MJ, I know you won't want to do this, but would you mind pausing on this garden idea for a little while? Just so we can figure out what's safe and what's not safe."

MJ bristles. "That's not fair!" she says. "I didn't do anything wrong!" She feels those frustrated tears start to gather behind her eyes again, and she curls her hand in a fist. Next to her, Peter shifts like he's unsure if he should do something.

"I didn't say you did," her mom says, voice placating. "I'm just saying, let's think this through first."

MJ takes a deep breath, trying to calm herself down. "Okay, Mom," she says. Her mom isn't wrong, but she's not going to just give up on this project because someone is trying to scare her. She'll just have to be smarter than *Councilman Grant.*

CHAPTER FIFTEEN

Home!

   Pieces. It's in pieces. But it's so close. Close.

He will find it for us.

     We will rise.

Power will return.

   Power.

    Home.

So far down.

    Down below us.

The Spot rubs against his arms trying to create some friction, but it's a force of habit more than anything else. *The old me would be cold, though, standing on Brighton Beach in the middle of the night, talking to random aliens on a cell phone I stole from a child.*

He shakes his head to clear out the negative thoughts and stares at the black ocean in front of him.

"Okay, we're here," he says, holding the phone up to his mouth. "Now what?"

"Now . . . now we search," the voices say, and the Spot isn't sure, but he thinks they might sound stronger. The Faithless has sent him here, telling him there is some kind of powerful thing they need to find, and they need him to do it.

"So . . ." He looks out at the expanse of water. "I just . . . guess?" To the west, he can see the shadow of Coney Island's Luna Park in the distance.

"Coordinates. Try 40.56, -73.9," they say.

"I know I seem like an all-knowing super villain," the Spot says. "But let me just enter that into the maps app so I can figure out what direction I need to go. And tell me what I'm looking for."

"Home. We find home."

"Okay," the Spot says, irritation bleeding into his tone. "What does that *mean* for someone who has never seen your home?"

"You call. You call it meteor. Space. Rock."

"Is it . . . like . . . is there a color, or a texture?" the Spot bites out through gritted teeth. "You've got to give me something to go on here."

"Red. Red and solid. Rock. Smooth. Hollow in middle. Air pocket," they say.

The Spot lets out a deep sigh. "I guess that's something . . ."

He types the numbers into the search part and the map shifts and moves to a space a few miles offshore, and the Spot takes a step back. "*And*," he says, "I'm going to need some kind of scuba gear or something. I can't breathe underwater."

"*Hurry*" is all the voices say. "*Hurry.*"

The Spot opens a hole in the dark and pops in, jumping into an athletic shop somewhere in Miami. He hasn't been worried about the distance. The last few weeks have shown him how few limits there are on his powers. So he's not surprised when he lands right where he wants to. It's quiet in the store, but he can hear people yelling in the streets. He looks around, finding a tank of oxygen, a mask, and a pair of flippers in his size. Something near the cash register catches his eye, and the Spot grabs it—the powerful flashlight fits perfectly in his hand. He pulls the gear on, and holding the flippers in his other hand, pops back into the Spot world.

"All right, now I'm ready." He situates the oxygen tank and pulls the long tube and mouthpiece to his face, and steps into the flippers. He lets the phone go, leaving it in the Spot World before finding the hole he needs, the one that will take him to the coordinates he wants to get to. It's straight below him, so he takes a step and hops in and is immediately surrounded by the ocean.

The Spot glances to the left and right and doesn't see anything that could possibly be what The Faithless described to him. He's far enough down that it is pitch-black around him, and the Spot hopes that doesn't mean there are animals nearby that he can't see. He shivers in the cold water and flips on the flashlight. He squints in the darkness, the beam of light moving this way and that. There are tiny motes floating in the brilliance, but nothing that seems to match what The Faithless told him about. He pokes around for a few more minutes before swimming back and popping through his portal, ending up in Spot World.

"Home! HOME!" the voices on the phone say, not waiting for him to start speaking.

"Sorry, there was no smooth red form down there. We'll have to try again."

A scream so loud rends from the phone speakers that the Spot finds himself jumping into the hole leading to his apartment just to get away.

"You're sure this is okay?" Peter asks for the third time.

MJ lets out a frustrated whine and stops on the sidewalk suddenly, pulling him backward by their clasped hands. He stumbles lightly, but she can tell he's doing it to be funny, considering he has actual spider-agility. *I think.* MJ can tell they're both trying hard to ignore the thin sense of awkwardness that's still hovering around them after their unresolved fight and the scene with her mom. But all MJ wants to do today is hang out with her *boyfriend* on what is supposed to be a romantic date.

"Peter, for the *last time*, yes, I am fine with our Valentine's Day date being *simple* because, first of all, it's a fake holiday—"

"Hey!" Peter protests. "It's, like, the paragon of romance!"

MJ looks at him, incredulous. "It's a *fake holiday*," she says again. "And second, I understand why you had to buy that phone," she says meaningfully. "I'd rather you spend it on something that will help us fight the bad guys than, like, I don't know—chocolates? Cards?"

"I hope you know I'm more original than that," Peter says with a crooked grin.

Around them, there are couples holding hands and walking down the street, and groups of friends popping in and out of restaurants.

"I know, I know," MJ relents. "I just want to you know

that I am *fine* with us just being able to hang out with each other." Then she pauses. "Wait, Peter, did you want, like, a really romantic movie Valentine's Day date?" she asks.

Peter's cheeks go radioactive red, and he looks away. "No, no. Definitely not. Not me."

MJ takes the opportunity of his avoidant gaze to poke him in the stomach. "Peter Parker, if you wanted to do something like that, you just have to tell me. I don't *really* mind it," and it's MJ's turn to go bashful. "I just don't want you to feel bad."

"Well, I don't want *you* to feel bad."

"*Excuse me!*" A well-dressed white man with a bouquet of flowers breaks through between them, rushing to the subway stop on the corner. MJ can hear him mutter something about "tourists" and "sidewalk is for walking" as he brushes by.

"Not a tourist!" Peter yells at the man's retreating back.

"*Could've fooled me!*" the guy yells in response.

"Oh, New York transplants." MJ grins, retaking Peter's hand and pulling them along their path. They're in Williamsburg again that evening, Peter leading them toward a free hot-chocolate tasting happening in a newly opened bakery off the L train.

"I hope this place isn't expecting a purchase alongside that free hot chocolate," he says, but there's laughter in his tone and MJ knows he's not serious. "The website did not say anything about a purchase being required to attend. I read it three times to make sure."

"My favorite kind of event." She smiles, interlacing their fingers. They chat amicably for a few blocks and are about to cross the street to get to the baker when MJ feels Peter shift beside her. He pulls her quickly to the right so they're standing under an awning of a shop. He's grabbed something from a display and got it hidden behind his back. MJ gives him a quizzical look, but she's still smiling.

"Okay, not a ton of romance happening tonight—that's fine. But for you, my dear," Peter says, flourishing out a single wrapped rose from behind his jacket.

MJ's mouth drops open into a little O before settling back into a soft smile. "Where did this come from?" she says, reaching a hand out to take the rose from him. Something occurs to her just then, and she leans to her left to find a bucket on a stand behind him full of *Valentine's Day Roses, only one dollar!* A snort of laughter escapes her, and then MJ is doubled over, laughing into her fist and still gripping the stem tight. When she finally catches her breath, Peter's got that same crooked grin back on his face.

"So, romantic . . . but broke-Peter-Parker style." He laughs. "Here, I still have to pay for this," he says, taking the flower back from her. MJ starts to protest, but Peter just holds a hand up. "We can't just return it! It's got all *our*

gross boyfriend-girlfriend Valentine's Day germs on it."
He chuckles, and the sound is warm and soft in MJ's ears.

"Okay, okay," she says, light teasing in her tone. "After you, tiger."

He steps into the shop, and she's hot on his heels. But when they get inside, the easy atmosphere they'd been enjoying is nowhere to be found.

"I *said* I didn't need a bag! Can you not understand a simple statement?! God!" someone near the front of the store is yelling at a cashier. "And this is the *wrong change*! Is counting beyond you, too?!"

Peter slides a look to MJ, his face contorted into an expression that can only be described as *yikes*. MJ nods subtly in agreement. That's when she realizes the screaming voice is familiar.

"Peter"—she rests a hand on his arm—"is that . . . ?"

Next to her, Peter stiffens as if he's just had the same realization. "Dr. Shah?" he breathes out.

They creep forward a few steps, through the narrow aisles, and peek around a corner. Sure enough, standing with his back to them is the familiar form of their science teacher. He's got his hands on his hips, and he's angled forward, clearly trying to intimidate the young Indian woman standing behind the counter. Peter steps forward resolutely, and MJ moves with him.

"Hey, Dr. Shah!" he says brightly, and MJ is struck by Peter's ability to do what's right even when it's undoubtedly going to be very uncomfortable. In front of them, their teacher's shoulders tense, and he turns around slowly. There are deep bruises under his eyes, like he hasn't slept well in a long time, and his right hand is holding a black shopping bag and shaking.

"Peter, MJ," he says, and there's only cold recognition in his tone, nothing more. "Good to see you. If you'll excuse me." And without another word, he takes his groceries and exits the store.

That was weird. . . .

"What a jerk," the woman behind the counter mumbles before turning her charm back on for Peter and MJ. "Can I help you?" she asks, with a smile on her face again. Peter holds up the rose.

"Just this, thanks," he says, pulling a couple of quarters out of his pocket. The rose purchased, they exit the store and Peter presents it to MJ with a flourish, but there's an awkwardness to his movements now, like he's trying to force them to rewind to the mood a few minutes earlier. MJ takes the flower with a faint smile, and Peter cringes. "Too much?" he asks. "Yeah, too much. That was weird. Dr. Shah's being weird."

MJ agrees. "Yeah, he *really* is . . . but there's something . . . That aggression . . ." She trails off and Peter lifts his eyebrows expectantly.

"There's something what?" he asks her.

"I don't know yet," she says slowly, trying to work

something out in her head. Finally, she looks back down at the rose in her hand and up at Peter. "Let's not let this ruin our night, actually. We can figure it out later."

Peter beams and takes up her free hand. "You're right. There's two cups of free cocoa with our names on them."

Laughing, they walk off toward the bakery, leaving the strangeness of Dr. Shah behind them for now.

CHAPTER SIXTEEN

"Peter," Aunt May says, leaning against the back of the couch where Peter is currently sitting with his books spread out and his notebook open, writing furiously. It's a Sunday morning, and the house is quiet.

"Mm-hmm?" he asks.

"When are your friends getting here?"

Peter's head whips around and he stares at his aunt. There's something in her voice that's putting him on edge. He narrows his eyes. "Soon . . . Why?"

"Just excited to meet some of your crew!" she says, trying not to smile too widely.

Peter groans. "Aunt May, please do not call them 'my crew' when they get here. That is not what they are."

"Okay," she says, but in a way that tells Peter she's not making any promises. "Maybe I'll offer them up some wheat cakes."

Peter lets out a pained sound, and behind him, Aunt May lets out a hearty laugh. He turns around and wrests his arms over the back of the couch, dropping his chin in the dip between them, looking up at his aunt from under his eyebrows. "You know I love your wheat cakes, but I also know that it is *weird* that I love wheat cakes as a sixteen-year-old," he says.

"It is not *weird*," Aunt May says, sounding mildly offended. "My wheat cakes used to win awards, I'll have you know." She tucks a strand of gray hair behind her ear.

"Aunt May," Peter groans.

His aunt laughs again and places a hand on his head, rubbing his hair affectionately. "I promise not to offer your friends any of my weird wheat cakes. Only the most normal snacks for your crew," she ribs.

"Thank you," Peter says, grinning. "Please know your desperate nephew appreciates it greatly and promises to make *you* wheat cakes next weekend." May tries to hide a flinch, but Peter catches it. "What? My wheat cakes are pretty good," he says.

"They definitely are, dear. They're very good," Aunt May says placatingly.

Distrust etches across Peter's face. "I feel like you're just saying that to be nice."

The doorbell rings, interrupting any chance Peter has to find out if his aunt is playing him or not, and she just smiles her enigmatic smile and goes to open the door. Peter rolls his eyes, but it's good-natured and full of affection for his aunt. He hears her greeting MJ at the door.

"Mary Jane! It's so nice to see you," Aunt May says from the hall.

Peter jumps up and starts moving his mess into some sort of organized piles, hoping it doesn't look as chaotic as it feels. Then he flips around and stands as MJ enters the living room.

"Hey, Pete." She gives him a small wave.

"Hey, MJ," he says, unwilling to give his aunt any more teasing fodder.

"Oh," his aunt says. "I think I left the stove on. I'll be back in just a minute."

Peter takes her absence as a chance to vault over the couch and give MJ a hug and kiss in greeting.

"Okay!" Aunt May announces herself a moment before she steps back into the living room, and Peter realizes she went into the kitchen so he and MJ could have a minute alone. He blushes, but thinks, *I'm lucky to have a cool grown-up in my life.* "How are you, MJ?" she says once they've all settled onto the couch to wait for Randy and Maia to join them. "I have to say, I think you've had a very good effect on Peter—I think the number of calls I've gotten about my tardy nephew is down at least fifty percent," she jokes.

MJ laughs and agrees. "It took some doing, but I think we're *almost* at the point where we don't have to run for the bus every day."

"Almost," Peter echoes, content to see two of his favorite people in the world laughing together.

They spend another few minutes in happy conversation, when the doorbell rings again, announcing what is likely Maia or Randy. Peter stands up and says, "I'll get it." He walks to the door and opens it, surprised to find both Maia *and* Randy on the front stoop.

"Hey, man, let us in. It is *freezing*," Randy says, pushing Peter aside the second the door is open wide enough for him to make it through.

"We ran into each other on the bus," Maia says by way of explanation. "Sorry we're late, the subway was a killer this morning." She follows Randy into the hall and starts pulling off her layers to hang up on the hooks situated on the wall.

Peter closes the door and gestures to the living room. "S'fine. MJ's already here, the living room is that way."

"MJ's already here, huh?" Randy says, waggling his eyebrows under the thick red beanie still on his head.

"Yeah, nerd." Maia laughs. "She literally lives next door."

"Oh," Peter says, pointing at a closet off of the main door. "You can leave your boots in here."

Randy hastily doubles back and leans down to untie his boots with a sheepish grin. Peter waves him off, and the three of them walk into the living room to join MJ and Aunt May.

"Oh, hello." Peter's aunt rises to greet his friends, and there's a rowdiness that the Parker household hasn't seen in a long time in the air. He steps back to take it in and sits in the happiness for a second. Eventually, Aunt May says she'll leave them to their work and heads into the kitchen to rustle up some snacks for the kids.

"All right," Maia says, pulling out her own tablet, having forgone the one the school gave them since she already had one. "My cousin mocked up a sort of working version of our app, and I think we should go through it together." The four of them are seated on the floor around Peter's coffee table.

"Also, our list of names," Randy says, dropping his tablet onto the table with a loud *thunk*. He flinches at the sound, but then continues. "I have a few good ones, not gonna lie."

MJ nods, pulling out her binder and flipping it open to her own list.

"Where're your shiny new toys?" Randy asks.

Peter and MJ shrug. "Left it in my locker," Peter says, at the same time MJ says, "It's at home, I haven't set it up yet."

Randy looks between them while Maia taps on her screen. "Sure," he says. "Whatever you guys say. If you want to go analog, that's on you."

"I trust analog." Peter laughs, tapping his pencil against the blue-lined paper in his notebook.

"*Okay*," Maia says, getting everyone's attention. "Peter being a Luddite aside—"

"I do not know what that means, but I'm offended," Peter interjects, and MJ throws a paper ball at him.

"*ANYway*," Maia tries again, but she's laughing while she says it. "My cousin came up with a pretty cool design, but we need to write up a list of fake causes to give him so he can design what a real screen could look like without all this placeholder text." She holds up her tablet so they can see that one of the screens says ORGANIZATION DEDICATED TO BRINGING BACK THE CHICKEN SLIDERS TO MR. MANNY'S KITCHENS.

"That's a solid cause, though," Randy says. MJ throws a second paper ball Randy's way, and he flings his hands up in defense.

"I think one of our fake causes should be something about the tech industry," MJ says, and Peter thinks she's probably thinking about her own issues with KRT Technologies.

"That's a really good idea, MJ." Maia's fingers tap against her screen as she notes it down. "What else?" She looks at Peter and Randy.

"I think . . . something . . . with . . . plants?" Peter's voice goes high at the end of his sentence, and it ends as a question.

"The environment's a great idea," MJ says, gesturing to Maia to write it down.

They spend a few minutes coming up with a variety of fake causes to list in the Potential Projects to Join section of the app. Then Maia goes to the big cause section they've created, using the Go! Go! Gardens! group as their pretend page.

"Maia, that looks *awesome*," Peter says. "Like, it looks like an actual application people could use."

"I know, right?!"

The hours pass by pretty quickly. Aunt May pops in once to drop a tray of cookies and a bowl of chips on the corner table for them, but other than that they get through their work without interruption.

Finally, MJ closes her binder with a loud *smack* and grins. "I feel really good about this."

Maia nods enthusiastically. "Seriously, I think this is gonna blow everyone away." She glances down at the time on her screen and shoots up. "Oh crap, Randy, we're gonna miss the bus if we don't leave in the next ten minutes." There's a flurry of activity, and she and Randy rush to put their things in their bags.

"Oh," Randy says suddenly as he starts to move toward the entryway. "MJ, I totally forgot to tell you. I'm sorry I haven't had a chance to ask my dad about that URL yet—I already told Maia on the bus, but he's been *super* busy with this new super villain, Dots, or whatever."

Peter's ears perk up, and he watches MJ tell Randy that it's not a big deal.

"What's going on with the Dot person, anyway? Does your dad know?" Peter asks once she's finished talking.

"You'd know better than me, man. With your gig at the *Bugle*? My dad doesn't tell me anything. All I know is that Dots can get in and out places without a single trace. And all the authorities are super confused by it. Well, not without a *trace*," he amends. "There are those weird black dots left behind at every crime scene. But what kind of calling card is a plain black circle in a bunch of different, random sizes?" he asks.

From the front hall, Maia calls out, "Randy! We gotta go." She pops her head back in, and she's already got her winter coat and boots on. "I'll see you both later," she says to Peter and MJ. "And I'll email everyone the updated file so we can all look at it before we have to show it to Dr. Shah this week."

"Sounds good!" MJ says, waving. Randy rushes to join Maia.

"Good-bye!" Aunt May's appeared in the hallway.

"Thank you for having us!" Maia says. "And sorry we have to leave so fast."

"Gotta catch a bus!" Peter can hear Randy yell just before the front door slams shut.

Aunt May comes back to join MJ and Peter in the living room. "I'm digging your new crew, Peter," Aunt May says with a bright grin cutting across her face.

Peter has to laugh.

"I'm honestly impressed you waited so long to say something," he says.

"Sorry, we're your crew?" MJ asks, her tone full of suspicious disbelief.

"Jokes!" Peter says. "Aunt May's working on her new act as a comedian."

His aunt raises her hands in a conciliatory gesture. "I haven't even made it to the stage, and I'm already bombing," she says. "Okay, I'm going to finish up some work for the shelter. Is there anything you two need, or will you be okay in here?"

"We'll be fine. Thanks, Aunt May," Peter says, and MJ agrees.

When the two of them are alone, sitting on the couch, the silence feels heavier than it usually does between them. They've been carefully avoiding talking about their fight, and Peter wants to put it to rest. He's about to bring it up when MJ starts talking about Dots. "So that's not good, right? Did you ever hear anything else from the Spidey Code?"

Peter recalibrates his thoughts, thinking about the case. "Nope. That reporter—Swapna—said she'd need a few days to track them down, but I really hoped she would have gotten in touch with me by now." True to his word, he isn't checking the burner phone unless he's far out of the vicinity of his own home, so he hasn't had a chance to look today yet. "But something's really bugging me about this new villain."

"Yeah?" MJ says. "Because something's really bugging me about Dr. Shah, but I cannot put my finger on it."

Peter turns to her and grips her hands. "Exactly! Like, it's on the edge of my brain—"

"But it can't get to my mouth," she finishes. "Okay, what is it about this Dots?"

"Well, I'm thinking he's got to be using interdimensional travel somehow—which I *really* wish I was experiencing under cooler circumstances—because I don't know how else I could fly into a black hole in Queens and end up in a sewer under Chinatown."

"Though you were unconscious," MJ points out while twisting her hair into a high bun and poking a pencil through it to keep it stable.

"True," Peter says. "Someone could have carried me

there . . . though I don't know why they'd leave me my mask, if that was the case. I do remember flying *into* the portal. It's the last thing I remember, but I know I went inside of it. Dots uses *something* to create these portals. Because I know that much. It was definitely a portal."

"But what could they even use to make something like that?"

Peter shakes his head, frustrated by the lack of answers. "That's what we've gotta figure out, MJ."

"Everything. Everything is fine. Working."

"Everything is working as it should. As it should be."

"Do not. Do not worry, friend. This is . . . This is good."

"We are here. We are here to help."

The Spot startles awake in his bed—he was dreaming of *the beach.* He groans, taking his hands and rubbing them against his face. "I've got to take a break from that beach. Being in that water is giving me weird dreams," he says out loud. They'd been back at Brighton Beach every night for the last week and a half and had almost nothing to show for it. The Faithless are getting more and more frustrated, but the Spot is just tired. He pushes himself up off the bed and takes a second to appreciate the room around him. It's completely full of all the wonderful things he's stolen over the past week: examples of his prowess. There's a painting he liked the look of from the Met; some jewelry from Tiffany's; he'd even taken one of the mannequins from the Armani store in SoHo.

He flips open his actual phone to look and see if there's a report about him yet. He pulls up the *Daily Bugle* and there, on the front page! He skims the piece, getting angrier and angrier as he goes on.

"They keep calling me *Dots*, like I'm some kind of children's cartoon character?! Oh, no. Oh, absolutely not. I did not go through decades of schooling and then experiment my way into become a powerful super villain to not get to choose my own moniker. I *knew* I needed to go bigger," he seethes, now pacing back and forth, avoiding his new treasures. "I'm going to go bigger," he decides. He steps into the living room and stares at the other phone, the stolen one, that's charging on the arm of his couch. Considering it, he tilts his chin up and his head to the side. "What to do about you, though? I can't mess up any big paydays, so I can't risk you finding out. But . . ." He thinks of the *Bugle* article *again*. "I'm also not going to be disrespected by the likes of a New York City trash mag."

He walks over to the stolen phone and picks it up, holding it by the corner.

"If I look at the evidence, everything points to you all living in this piece of electronics."

He opens a hole in the air in front of him and tosses the phone in and then pulls the hole back onto his body.

"There. Now you're stuck there unless *I* get you out, *and* I think it should contain you nicely while I go make my *big* break."

CHAPTER SEVENTEEN

Spider-Man hops off the edge of one of the higher sky-scrapers in Midtown and dives down before shooting a web to swing forward. He's found that the more velocity he can get falling, the farther he'll swing on a single shot of web and the less time he'll have to spend making his web fluid. He flies forward and lets go of the web behind him, careening forward into a flip before landing on the side of a building. His legs are braced against the red brick, and he's got one hand perched on the wall, holding him steady. The other digs into his suit to grab the phone that's just started vibrating against his hip.

It's his new side-hustle phone, and there's an alert that Swapna has finally reached out! The message is short, just apologizing for taking so long and asking him if he can come by. Spidey takes a quick scan to find the closest street sign.

> **I'LL BE THERE IN TEN MIN** ✌️

He's early. It takes him eight and a half minutes to make it the two avenues and five city street blocks to her apartment, but this time he taps on the glass immediately. Spidey's surprised when Kabir pops his head through and says something, holding a hand over his mouth. It looks like he's chewing. He takes a second and swallows, and then says "Hello, Spider-Man" again, followed by "Apologies, you caught me right as I took an embarrassingly big bite of a burrito, and Swapna's just on a quick call."

"Hi, Mr.—Kabir," Spidey says. "Thanks for letting me know. I'll just hang out and wait for her here, if that's okay?"

"What? You don't have to do that. Oh, why don't you come in?"

"That'd be awesome, thank you. Nothing like New York in February to help you remember how much you love our horrible radiators."

Kabir laughs while stepping back from the windowsill,

and Spider-Man crawls in after the way is clear. Once he lands on the hardwood floor, he shakes his hands out, trying to return some feeling to his fingers. It looks like the window he was knocking on leads to their living room. There's a small teal love seat with a large circular ottoman serving as a coffee table. On it are two cardboard containers with half-eaten burritos in them, and two glass Mexican Coke bottles. Like in many a New York City apartment, the kitchen is easily visible, separated from the living room by a high counter and the couch Kabir is heading back toward.

"Sorry to . . . disturb you during dinner," Spider-Man says, hanging back awkwardly as Kabir sits down.

Kabir waves him off. "It's really no worry at all. You can take a seat there." He points behind Spider-Man, and Spidey turns to see a bright green statement chair behind him. He drops into it. "So," Kabir says, picking up his burrito, "how's Spider-Manning going these days?" Then he laughs. "Sorry, I just don't really know what to say when there's a super hero sitting in my living room. Would you like . . . something to eat or drink, I guess, water or coffee? I think there's still some in the French press. Or do you want to leave your mask on?"

Spidey lets out a short laugh. "Coffee would be amazing," he says. "But I can get it if you're eating! I mean—"

Kabir stands and says, "Nonsense." He moves into

the kitchen and pours some dark liquid into a large mug before placing it in the microwave. While they wait for the coffee to reheat, he turns back and leans forward onto the counter looking in Spidey's direction. "So, how *is* Spider-Manning?" he repeats.

Something tells Spidey Kabir really means what he says, and he appreciates that kind of sincerity in a person. So he answers just as honestly. "It's okay. In the middle of kind of a doozy of a case—"

"With that dotty-dots man?" Kabir asks.

"Person," Spidey corrects. "We don't know who they are yet, so they could be *anyone*. But yeah, that's part of it, for sure. I really appreciate your wife helping me out with some of this stuff."

Behind Kabir, the microwave beeps, and he grabs the mug, bringing it over to Spidey before taking his place on the couch again. Spidey pulls up the bottom of his mask and lets it rest over his nose. He takes a deep sip of the coffee, feeling the warmth flow into his chest and belly and letting out an appreciative sigh.

He opens his mouth to speak when Swapna comes through an open door near the kitchen, padding barefoot into the room.

"Oh," Spidey says. "Should I take my boots off?" *Please say no, please say no, please say no, my feet are not fit for other humans to see them.*

Swapna shakes her head as she joins her husband. "Hey, and no, that's okay. Those look"—she takes in Peter's suit—"complicated."

"It looks worse than it is." Spidey laughs.

"Okay." She puts her hands on her knees. "Thanks for meeting me on such short notice, but I didn't want to type what I had to say into a digital message—even one that's supposedly secure."

"I did get that new phone," Spidey tells her, pulling it out and holding it up for her to see.

She gives him an encouraging smile. "That's great! But even this . . ." She hesitates. "Actually, maybe we should go into the office."

Something in Spidey's stomach drops. *This sounds serious.* Swapna makes to get up, but Kabir puts a hand out to stop her and starts gathering up his food and drink.

"No, no, I'll go finish eating in the bedroom. Wanted to watch the rest of that *Top Chef* episode, anyway," he says, kissing her on the crown of her head as he rises. "Nice to see you again, Spider-Man. You're welcome anytime." Then he looks incredulous, like he can't believe the sentence just came out of his mouth before quickly schooling his features back into something kind.

"Thanks for the coffee," Spidey says, ignoring the look, and Kabir gives him a nod before heading off to the bedroom.

Swapna waits for the sound of the door shutting before

she starts speaking again. "So, I'm still working on the Twitter handle—I'm waiting to hear back from some of my contacts. It's kind of a . . . dicey thing," she says shiftily. Then she laughs and adds, "Whatever favor I call in is going to be a big one. I have half a mind to really ask for an exclusive interview with you for the *Bugle*." Spider-Man isn't sure what to make of that. "Now, the URL, that was another puzzle." She falls back into the couch and the loose, dark bun she has on top of her head bounces in reaction. Swapna presses her hands together and starts tapping the points of her index fingers against one another. She twists her mouth, like she's considering how to move forward and finding it distasteful. Spidey's hackles raise. *This is gonna be bad*, he thinks. "So, that KRT Technologies company . . . is owned by an FLT Tech, which is owned by a BYS Tech, and *that's* owned by an SYQ Tech. There are, like, seventeen shell companies, just stacked on top of each other."

"But what's at the top?" Spider-Man asks, his leg bouncing allegro in anticipation.

Swapna takes a deep, tired breath. "Oscorp."

Swapna can't offer much more beyond the fact that Oscorp is somehow involved. Spidey comes clean about *why* he is looking into KRT Technologies.

"What does Oscorp care about some random empty lot in Queens?" Swapna asks, mostly to herself. "This might be a bigger story than you think, Spider-Man. I'm going to keep digging into this."

"But you won't tip off—"

Swapna cuts him off. "I am a professional, Spider-Man. I'm not going to give away where I got any of my intel."

Spidey nods. They chat for a few more minutes, but neither one of them can come up with any solid reasoning as to why Oscorp might want something like that lot. As he's leaving, she pats his shoulder. "I'll hopefully have something to give you soon on that Twitter handle. Just need my friends in high places to come through. Once they do, I'll figure out a way for you to make good on the favors you'll owe me."

"Favors?" Spidey asks, grimacing and a little unsure of what he's gotten himself into.

Swapna just grins. "Don't worry about it. I should have news for you soon."

Spidey thanks her before crawling out of the window to make his way back home. *I gotta talk to MJ.* Before launching off the side of the building, he pulls out the phone, puts in his headphones, and dials MJ. Once it starts ringing, he presses his soles against the wall and pushes forward, flying high into the air and then arcing downward before shooting a web out to catch a ledge.

"Hello?" MJ's voice comes through clear into his ear.

"Hey, MJ!" he yells over the sound of rushing wind.

"Peter?" Even with the headphones in, MJ's voice is difficult to hear. He *thwips* out a web and swings to a stop on an empty rooftop. The shooter on his right wrist sputters a little, and he makes a mental note to refill his canisters of web-fluid when he gets home. MJ's voice cuts in again. "What's up?" she asks. She sounds like she's in the middle of something.

"Are you— Can you talk right now?" Spidey asks.

On the other end of the phone, MJ lets out a frustrated noise. "Yeah, I wouldn't have answered if I couldn't."

Spidey tries not to groan. It's been like this for a while now, and he misses how easy their conversations were. He breaks down what Swapna told him. He can hear her sharp intake of breath when he says who owns the lot. "What would Oscorp want with a lot?" Again, it sounds like she's asking herself more than anything else, but Spidey answers anyway.

"We couldn't come up with anything, but I was going to head to yours so we could talk it out in person. Swapna seemed really spooked at the idea of dealing with any of this over phones. Even ones that are difficult to trace. It's actually why I called instead of texting."

"That makes sense. I think Oscorp actually owns the internet we all use in most of New York," MJ says. "It might not be safe. Look, I'll dig into things here. Thanks for getting the info, though!"

"I'll come over when I get home so we can work on it together," Spidey says.

"Only if you can—otherwise I can totally handle it," MJ replies.

"It's not a problem, MJ." Spidey hopes she believes him. "I'll see you soon," he adds and hangs up the phone. Spidey drops back onto the street, swinging toward home. Then he turns a corner at 68th Street and runs directly into a brick wall. Spidey flies backward and lands on his back in the middle of an alley. "What the . . . ?" A groan of pain escapes his lips, and he gingerly touches his forehead. His mask is torn, and when his fingers come back into sight, there are traces of blood on his gloves.

He pushes up into sitting position and stares at the wall directly in front of him, and then looks back at the opening to the alley behind him.

"Where the heck am I?!"

MJ's sitting in her bedroom when she hangs up with Peter. She throws herself back onto the bed and stares up at her ceiling and considers the news he's just dropped on her.

Oscorp . . . the company that is sponsoring our competition . . . which has its hands in everything . . . wants a tiny lot in Forest Hills, Queens, for . . . reasons?

MJ picks her head up once and slams it back down

against her pillow like it will unlock something in her brain that will tell her the answer. She lies there a few more minutes before she finally lets out a loud and frustrated whine.

"Come *on*—think!" she says to herself before rolling over onto her stomach and pulling out her phone to text Maia. She knows she can figure this out if she just works through the problem.

> HEY, U THERE?

> YEP WHAT UP

> VIDEO?

> GIMME 2 MIN BESTIE

A few minutes later, MJ's phone vibrates and announces that Maia is video-chatting her. She slides it open immediately and starts speaking without letting Maia get a word in greeting out. "Hey, so, a friend of Peter's at the *Bugle* found out who owns the URL . . . and it's Oscorp."

"What?!" Maia's eyes go wide, and her mouth opens in shock. "One, why would they hide that? Like . . ."

"And hide it *well*," MJ cuts in. "Apparently there's a *ton* of shell corporations or something."

"And I'm assuming they have to know about this

Councilman Grant, who is being so completely extra." Maia bites at her lip and goes quiet. "Oscorp's probably the one telling the councilman to do this. Who else would be?"

"I just don't like how deep this is going," MJ says. "Or that apparently someone at that company is fine with terrorizing high school students." She flips her bangs out of her eyes, and a look of disgust flits onto her features. "Should we . . . ? I don't know. It makes me feel really weird about being in the OSMAKER thing."

"I hear you," Maia says carefully. "But I don't know what our options are, really? Not to mention, we don't really have any proof. . . . And I think OSMAKER is really coming from Norman Osborn. That guy's always talking about investing in the young builders and inventors and scientists, et cetera."

"Ugh, you're right," MJ says, banging a fist against her mattress. "I just don't like how . . ." She trails off, like she isn't sure how to finish her sentence.

"Powerless we feel?" Maia offers.

MJ sighs. "That's it. What are we supposed to do against a corporation like Oscorp?"

Spider-Man is still sitting on the ground, completely thrown by his circumstance. He's not sure where he is, and his skull is throbbing like he ran face-first into an incredibly hard surface. *Which I did, somehow.* He finally pushes up off the ground with his hands and tries to stand, but is immediately rewarded with a spinning head. Stumbling a few feet to the right, he braces himself against the side of the alley. All of a sudden, his spider-sense goes haywire, and Spidey wastes no time in shooting a web at a fire escape two floors up and yanking himself toward it. He lands in a crouch, head still swimming. He surveys the concrete below him.

There's a figure standing just a few feet away from where he'd been moments earlier, and Spidey's lenses narrow as he frowns under his mask. The guy is wearing a *really* weird suit, all white and covered in black dots—*dots!* he thinks.

"Hey!" he yells down. "Are you Dots?!"

The person in the weird suit throws up his hands and lets out a guttural scream in response. Then he takes a deep breath and squares his shoulders. He looks up at Spidey and points at his own chest. In a loud, surprisingly deep voice he crows, "I am the Spot!"

Spidey stares at him for a second and then lets out one loud guffaw.

The Spot seems to grow angrier. "Are you *laughing* at me?!" he cries. "You can't *laugh* at me. I've been taking stuff from under *your* nose for weeks."

Spidey's still laughing, but at that he quiets down.

He's not wrong. Spidey jumps and flips forward so he can land back on the street and get a closer look at what he's up against. He lifts two hands in apology the second he lands. "Sorry, sorry, I didn't mean to be rude. That's just what the newspapers are calling you. Maybe you should try leaving a note next time?" he asks, the faux innocence layered heavily on his words.

The Spot scoffs in response. "They told me you liked to try and be funny. That you'd try to distract me with jokes."

All of a sudden, Spidey sees something move across the Spot's chest. Focusing below the man's strange mask, he comes to a sudden realization: *That's not a suit he's wearing.* Spider-Man is horrified to see the spots on the man's body are shifting around, moving in a sluggish way. It's almost enough to make Spidey nauseous.

"Are those . . . spots *living* on you?" he asks.

"This is what I *am*, Spider-Man. What I made myself! I'm the Spot!" The Spot throws his arms wide and laughs, and then, without warning, he launches forward. Spidey's spider-sense goes wild again, and he flips out of the way, only to find the Spot's already thrown a hole up, so Spidey flies into the hole and back into the alley, running directly into the Spot's fist.

chest, only for it to fall uselessly into one of the black dots littering the Spot's body. Under his mask, Spidey frowns.

"The things *on* you are portals, too?!" The Spot seems to realize he's made a mistake, and he takes a step back. "Oh, no, no, no, it's time to *connect the dots, Dot,*" Spidey singsongs, launching himself forward. "We're just getting acquainted! You can't leave now!"

The Spot turns around, and his shoulders are heaving. Spider-Man can't discern actual features on his face, but if he had to guess, he'd say the Spot is furious. "My name," the Spot says, "is *the Spot.*"

Spider-Man falls through the floor and realizes the Spot has snuck a hole directly below him. He falls out of the sky back into the alley with a painful *thud. I need to end this*, he thinks, somewhat dazed from the fall. His head and his cheek are still tender to the touch, and he thinks his knee might have just been cut open from his rough landing.

Spidey gets to his feet, willing his legs not to shake. *I can't give him the time to get me with another one of those things.* Directly in front of him, the Spot is flinging out another dot his way, but Spidey's too close. He throws a first forward as hard as he can—only it goes *through* the spot, and before he can stop, the last thing Spidey sees is his own fist coming toward him.

The Spot stares down at the spider-jerk lying passed out on the ground before him. Leaning forward imperceptibly, he reaches out his good hand. *Maybe I can get a glimpse at what's under that mask*, he thinks. But as his fingers stretch forward, the Spider spasms like he's on the cusp of coming to. Panicking, the Spot drops into one of his black holes, portaling away from the alley before his adversary wakes up.

He goes directly to his apartment, and suddenly he realizes he was able to bypass the Spot World entirely. *That's new. . . .* He wonders if it was the fact that he just wanted to be somewhere safe. "That's good, though," he says to himself, still cradling his injured hand against his chest. Dipping his other hand into a spot on his side, he pulls the stolen cell phone out of Spot World and drops it onto the table, then falls onto his couch. The phone rings immediately. The Spot lets a long rush of air out through his mouth and leans forward to answer. "Hello," he says, his tone flat.

"You—you lost. Lost against the Spider-Man."

"Tell me something I don't know," the Spot says, leaning back against the couch. He tentatively stretches his hurt hand out in front of him, flexing his fingers. *At least this isn't broken.*

"Lost. You lost," the voices say again, loudly.

"I know!" the Spot yells out. "I was *there*! I know!"

"Need us. Need help," they say.

The Spot nods at the empty air. "You're right," he says. "I shouldn't have tried this on my own. That was hubris. This kid has taken down some top-tier villains, and every time it was because they went at him *alone*." He's speaking more to himself than The Faithless now but nodding at every one of his own words. "New plan," he says finally toward the cell phone on his table. "I'll still help you find your home, but you help me take down the Spider-Man."

"That. That is acceptable. Acceptable."

This time when Spidey comes to, he's completely alone. Panicked, his hands fly to his face, and he heaves a huge sigh of relief when he finds his mask still down and covering his identity. Then, groaning, he slowly sits up. The blood on his forehead has dried by now, but he looks down at his knee and twists his face unpleasantly. Under a tear in his suit, there's a long gash across the kneecap and the blood has soaked into the edges. *That's going to suck to clean* and *repair*, he thinks. His head is pounding something awful, and briefly he feels a pang of remorse for anyone he's ever punched. *That hurt.* The phone sitting snug at his hip vibrates, and in his ear his headphone beeps; he flinches at the sound of it but taps the side of his head to answer.

"Hello?" His voice is little more than a croak, and he clears his throat to try again. "Hello?" He's pleased that at least this time he sounds more normal.

"Peter?!" MJ sounds panicked, and he realizes she must have expected him back ages ago.

"Hey! Hey," he says quieter. "I'm so sorry. I got— Well, I got waylaid by the Spot. But I'm okay!" he gets out in a rush. There's a pause on the other end of the phone as MJ processes what she's heard.

"O . . . kay . . ." she says slowly. "Who's the Spot? Wait, is that who Dots is? Wait, *did you see Dots in real life?!*"

Spidey stands and winces as he puts weight on his knee. He looks down at his web shooter and sees that the right one has enough for maybe a two-block swing, and the left one another six. He lets out an annoyed whistle through his teeth.

"I did, and he *is the worst,*" he says, limping his way out of the alley to figure out where he is. *Please still be in New York, please still be in New York, please still be in New York,* he thinks. "Oh, thank goodness," he says as he steps onto the sidewalk. He's on Christopher Street.

"What? What happened?" MJ says.

"I'm in New York," Spidey says joyfully.

"Is there a reason you wouldn't be in New York?" MJ questions, confusion apparent.

"I'm heading your way, but I have to take the subway.

I'll see you in"—Spidey looks up at the late night sky and lets out a tiny moan—"an hour and some change."

When Peter crawls through her window, MJ already has her first-aid kit ready for him. She takes in the look of him: his mask is torn at the forehead, and there's a deep purple bruise surrounding a cut that's already scabbing over. His suit is torn at the knee, but that abrasion looks just the tiniest bit fresher. *He has a healing factor*, she reminds herself. *He's going to be fine.*

"I think I like it better when you come by in your pajamas for secret hot chocolate and binge watching," she jokes, trying to bring a sense of normalcy back to the room.

Peter smiles at her weakly, pulling off his mask with a slight cringe. She squeezes his shoulder and then passes him the first-aid kit before settling onto her bed.

"We're gonna need to come up with that plan for what happens if I can't find you sooner rather than later, my non-eight-legged boyfriend," she says. Peter nods but doesn't answer as he cleans his knee with antiseptic. "Peter, I'm serious."

"I hear you," he says. "We will."

"Peter." MJ can't help it, and she knows she sounds irritated and that it probably seems like she's nagging him.

But she's tired of feeling helpless whenever he disappears. It isn't *fair*.

"MJ, can we table it for now? I just knocked *myself* out."

That snaps MJ out of her irritation. "What?! What happened?"

"Oh man . . ." Peter starts, but pauses to let out a light hiss as he passes the alcohol wipe over the cut on his forehead. "So, Dots is actually the Spot and is *very* mad that people don't know that. And so he ambushed me like it was *my* fault or something. I'm also really tired of all these implications that super villains and crooks are bad-mouthing me and gossiping all over the city like they don't have anything better to do." He tells her how the rest of the fight went in another rush of words before leaning back into what she's begun to think of as his beanbag. "And now here I am, after a very long subway ride because the R, apparently, isn't running into Queens right now."

MJ shoots him a sympathetic look. "I'm sorry you had such a terrible night," she says. "And I'm sorry that guy was such a complete jerk. But so . . . he's covered in actual, like, black-hole portals?"

"I think so?" Peter says. "I don't know what else they could be. When I was flying through one, I *thought* I caught a glimpse of . . . I don't even know, some other world? Something that was covered in black dots like the Spot, but I was moving too fast to really see it."

"I feel like there are all these pieces of things happening

right now, and my gut is telling me there's a connection, but I can't figure out what it is." MJ worries at her lip. "Is it a coincidence that this Spot stuff is happening, Oscorp is buying random lots in Queens and having me hassled by a local government official?" she asks.

Peter doesn't have an answer to that, so he just shrugs. "Honestly, I have no idea. They could be disparate occurrences. I don't know how the Spot and Oscorp could possibly be connected, but I also have no idea what Oscorp gets out of any of your stuff. The Spot at least . . . I think he just wants people to know who he is. He was *so* mad when I called him Dots." Peter lets out a laugh and immediately blanches and clutches his middle. "Oh, okay, note to self, ribs are also bruised."

He's going to be fine, MJ thinks again. *I'm not going to play the nervous, worried girlfriend. I can help.*

"Okay," she says, businesslike. "I'm going to figure out what Oscorp wants. Maia and I talked earlier, and we both feel weird about the OSMAKER event—"

"Oh man, yeah," Peter says, sitting up straight and cringing again.

"But there's not much we can do there," she continues, giving him a look that says *please let me finish talking*. Sheepishly he leans back into his seat, waving a hand in apology. "I bet there's a system that the OSMAKER event uses that I might be able to use to hack into Oscorp. I've been watching a *lot* of how-to videos on YouTube. And I'll think about the Spot. There has to be *something* that will stop him. . . ."

"MJ, you don't have to . . . you know, do all of this," Peter says, gesturing in a wide, all-encompassing arc.

"I want to," MJ says, with a little bite to her tone. "Or are you the only one who's allowed—"

"No, no, that's not . . ." Peter cuts her off. "I'm sorry. I just—I don't want to hijack your life."

MJ's face twists, and she turns away from him. "You're not, Peter. I've got this."

And even though Peter must notice how her voice shakes at the end, he has the grace not to say anything.

CHAPTER NINETEEN

Peter walks home from the bus stop but stalls outside his house. His shoulders are tense, and he's pretty sure he's started grinding his teeth while he sleeps. There's been no sighting of the Spot for days, and it's making him nervous. MJ's had no luck on the Oscorp front, and it seems like all their leads are dead. She's brought up trying to create a Spidey-system a few more times, but Peter isn't sure what that could even look like. It edges too close to people finding out who he is for his comfort. Plus, TheSpideyCode0285 account has been dead silent, except for pointing him toward one single kid lost in the Central Park Zoo, and then going back to complete silence. He stands on the sidewalk and looks up at the sky accusingly. "If there is anyone in charge of life, the universe, and everything, if you're listening, please stop making *my* life so hard."

Then he pulls his backpack higher up on his shoulder and trudges up the stairs to the front door. His phone goes off just as he sticks the key in the lock, and Peter realizes with a start that it's his *other* phone, the one he usually keeps off. Leaving the key in place, he pulls the phone out and glances at it. As he reads the notification, his entire face lights up. It's a message from Swapna saying she'd cracked the Spidey Code, finally. Peter never makes it inside.

Spidey's back in the accent chair in Swapna's living room. She hands him a cup of coffee and sits down on her couch.

"Thanks," Spidey says. "So, what'd you find?"

She doesn't look nearly as tense as she did the other day. In fact, when he showed up at the window, she laughed and said she could have told him everything over the phone. He was thankful for the mask to hide his red cheeks as he climbed into the apartment.

"I can't believe it took me so long to find this, but it turns out the account probably belongs to some high school teacher out in Brooklyn—or he lives in Brooklyn. He teaches at a school in the city."

Spidey's ears perk up. "Oh?" he asks, trying to be cool.

"Yeah, someone named Samir Shah? The same computer that logs into the Spidey Code account logs into his personal account. So it's likely there's a connection there."

It takes everything Spidey has not to drop his coffee-filled mug on the floor. *Dr. Shah?!* There's a slight accent in the way Swapna says Dr. Shah's whole name, with the stress on the first syllable instead of the last. "He used to be a professor over at ESU but lost his family to an Electro event—"

"I know," Spidey says without thinking. Swapna's eyes narrow, and Spider-Man doesn't like the analytical way she's looking at him.

"You . . . know him?" she asks. "A random high school teacher in the city?"

"I mean"—Spidey flounders for a moment—"I've heard of him. I worked that Sandman case last year? The one that ended at the Museum of Science? Dr. Shah used to be on the ESU team that was doing that big research project out there." *Nice save*, Spidey congratulates himself. "But I don't, you know, *know him* know him," he says, rambling just the slightest bit.

Swapna gives him a long look but finally nods, seemingly believing him.

"Can I ask you a favor?" Spidey asks before he amends, "Well, *another* favor?"

Swapna nods, shifting so her feet are folded under her. "Honestly, after the contacts I pulled to get this information, you're racking up quite the tab."

Under his mask, Spidey grimaces. But there's nothing to be done for it, and he has to ask. "Can you—" Spider-Man considers how to say what he wants to say before just blurting out "Can you keep this between us for now? Just don't . . . go after this guy? I want to talk to him."

Swapna frowns. "I don't think there's anything solid to pursue right now, but I can't make any promises if something big comes out of it. Like . . . you're not my beat. My beat is technology, so that would be the angle." Spider-Man moves as if to interrupt, but Swapna plows on. "I don't see this becoming a story, so there's no reason for me to bring it up or talk about it now. That said, if I need to, I will."

Spider-Man gives her a short nod. "I can respect that . . . and I'll do my best to make sure it *doesn't* become a story. Or at least . . . any kind of, like, technological one?"

"You do what you gotta do," Swapna says, rising. "Now, as much as I enjoy our chats—and I do, really, not being sarcastic, Kabir tells me people can't tell sometimes—he's on his way over with his mom and she will not be interested in meeting you, I am sorry to say."

"Oh man, does she hate me?" Spidey asks, groaning. "I'm a good guy!"

Swapna starts laughing and shakes her head. "No, no, she just doesn't know who you are, and she does not care for strangers."

"I hate to say it, but that is a *relief*," he says, rising. "Thanks again for your help, seriously. And I understand the whole reporter thing. I appreciate it even if you do find something you might need to write about."

"I can at least promise to wait two days before I start thinking about why a high school teacher in Brooklyn would be doing this kind of thing," she says, walking him to the window. "And I think I'm starting to have an idea of how you can help me out. . . ." Spidey isn't sure he likes the intense look she's giving him. "I'll be in touch."

"Ah, okay," Spidey says awkwardly before climbing out the window.

Swapna just laughs.

Now I have to go find Dr. Shah . . . and get to the bottom of this.

MJ texts Spidey the address she'd found for Dr. Shah. They know he probably lives somewhere in or near Williamsburg, and so he's not surprised when he swings to a stop and lands on top of a parapet in Bushwick,

Brooklyn. There's a church in the near distance, and a school behind him. He surveys the ground below, which is busy with kids leaving after-school programs and adults getting home from work. *I should wait until it's a little less crowded* . . . he thinks, and then hops off the parapet and onto the roof. *Should've brought my backpack—at least I could have worked on my essay for English.* . . .

It's another hour and a half before he feels comfortable dropping down onto the street. Next to the door, there's a list of names and a row of buzzers. Spider-Man puts a gloved finger against the list and starts running down them, reading through until he finds *Shah, S. 614.* Taking a step back, he looks up at the building to count the windows and is distressed to realize there's no way he can tell which of the four windows above him would be 614. So he presses the button next to the name and is surprised when there's a loud buzz and the distinct click of a lock freeing. He pulls the door open before it can lock again and steps inside the building. It looks newer on the inside than it did on the outside, like the interior was gutted and reconstructed for entirely new apartments but the developer didn't want to spring for a fancy new facade. Spidey scrunches his nose in distaste; there's no personality to the gray-and-white decor around him. He doesn't see an elevator, so he jogs lightly to the narrow staircase a few feet ahead and starts the climb up. From a few floors above him comes the sound of a door opening, and heavy footsteps start down the stairs. Spidey makes it to the fourth floor before he runs into the very person he was looking for heading down.

"You!" Dr. Shah says, eyes wide with shock as he falls backward against the banister with a hand against his heart.

"Hey, Doc," Spider-Man says genially. "What's up?"

Dr. Shah spins around, but Spider-Man still catches the fury painted across his features. "You can't be here," he spits out with his back to Spider-Man. It sounds like the words are being pulled from his lips with a vise, like he hates having to say them at all. Spider-Man doesn't listen and instead trails Dr. Shah up the stairs to his sixth-floor apartment. His teacher gets to the door and walks inside. With a deep sigh, he leaves the door open behind him, and Spidey takes that as an invite, stepping over a welcome mat that says NO NAZAR HERE. Dr. Shah has kicked his flip-flops off and left them near the door. *Maybe I should come up with an easy boot removal . . .* Spidey thinks, laughing awkwardly to himself. This is an uncomfortable situation for anyone to be in, and he's not sure how to handle it. That same feeling of being untethered washes over him.

Dr. Shah's voice breaks over him from somewhere deeper within the apartment. "I don't suppose you saw the delivery guy outside when you rang the buzzer? I hope *someone* enjoys my sushi."

Spidey steps further inside the neat apartment and

hears the last part muttered under Dr. Shah's breath. It's punctuated by a tired sigh. They're standing in his living room, and there's a small kitchen off to the right side.

Dr. Shah rubs a hand against his forehead in what Spidey can read as irritation. "What are you *doing* here?" he asks. "I didn't want you to know who I am."

"Yeah, about that. I don't make it a habit to deal with strangers for too long," Spider-Man says nonchalantly. "They tend to get cocky. Or shady. Or both. And it never ends well for me."

"You shouldn't have come," Dr. Shah mutters. His eyes are dark with anger, and his hands are fisted at his sides. He takes a step forward and lifts his arms like he's going to shove Spidey out the door and into the hallway, but then seems to think better of it. "Just get out," he finally says, his voice wavering.

"I told you I have—" Spidey starts.

But before he can finish, he's cut off by Dr. Shah screaming loudly, *"I SAID GET OUT!!!"*

And it's like a dam has unleashed as Dr. Shah starts to stalk toward him. "You broke my *trust* by coming here, Spider-Man. I tried to help you, and look what good it did for us! Nothing!" There's spittle on his lips under his mustache, and his skin is waxy. The bruising under his eyes has gone deep purple, like he hasn't slept in weeks.

"I can't leave, Dr. Shah. There's something wrong with your code—it has me missing huge crimes in favor of little, distracting ones. I've heard of you. I know you're not a bad guy, so . . . what's going on?" Spider-Man doesn't move from his spot between Dr. Shah and the door, waiting for the man to make a choice.

Dr. Shah stares at him, his entire body tense and breathing heavily. Spidey can see his fist twitching at his side, like he's aching to hit something. It's a few stressful minutes with the two of them standing still in Dr. Shah's living room . . . until, finally, *something* inside of him seems to crack and he deflates. It's almost like Spidey can see the fight go out of his teacher.

Dr. Shah steps backward, away from Spider-Man and moves around the couch to fall into it. He sits heavily and leans his elbows on his knees, dropping his face into his hands. He mumbles something to the floor. Spidey hesitates. There are a million different ways to react, but he's not sure what the right one is. *When in doubt, ask a question*, he thinks.

"What did you say?"

Dr. Shah lifts his head and turns back to look at Spider-Man. "I said, I don't know what is wrong with the code. I never should have—it's not even really mine. It just seemed like a way that I could help. How could I say no?" Suddenly, he stands again and speeds to another room before returning a few seconds later with a laptop and a cell phone. He drops them both onto the table in front of the couch with a loud *thud*, and Spidey flinches. "I've been looking and looking for days. Why didn't it tell me about those missing jewels? It should have told me about those jewels!" His movements are frenetic, and his voice is getting louder again. The scene is unnerving Spidey, who isn't used to seeing his usually even-headed teacher so . . . out of it. "How could it have been so *wrong*?!" Dr. Shah says.

And before Spidey can say anything, Dr. Shah grips his ears and he *screams*. The sound is sharp and loud, and then cuts off abruptly. Spidey shudders, like something is crawling up his spine. *What do I do . . . ?* He looks on helplessly as Dr. Shah's knees come up and he curls into himself, rocking back and forth on the couch. Spidey steps forward to get closer and maybe put a comforting hand on his teacher's shoulder. And then he hears Dr. Shah mumbling, so he ducks his head closer to parse the words.

"I'm sorry, I'm sorry, I thought I was doing the right thing. Please don't hurt me. I'm so sorry. I'm sorry. I just wanted to help. I thought this could help."

Spider-Man's spider-sense buzzes lightly at the base of his skull, and he flings his head backward just as Dr. Shah throws a punch.

"*Whoa!* Let's talk this out with*out* punching the Spider-Man, who might accidentally break your hand if you try too hard to hit me. I do not want that on my conscience."

"Oh," Dr. Shah says, and stares at him, openmouthed

for a second. Then he stands and spits out, "You want something on your *conscience*, Spider-Man? How about my *family*? Where were you—"

Spider-Man's heart drops into his stomach. He *knew* this about Dr. Shah. He remembers reading the newspaper article like it was yesterday. Dr. Shah losing his wife and daughter to one of Electro's disasters. Spider-Man itches to say something. *I'm sorry*, he thinks, *I know what this is like. I know how much it hurts.* But he doesn't get a chance to say anything because Dr. Shah lunges forward fist-first!

CHAPTER TWENTY

Spider-Man ducks and grabs his teacher around the middle. He makes an effort not to squeeze too hard, but he wrestles Dr. Shah back onto the couch and grips his hands at the wrists, holding them down.

"Dr. Shah! What are you doing!" he yells. "This isn't like you! Why are you *fighting* me?! I'm the good guy!" Beneath him, Dr. Shah struggles and his eyes are wild. There's something familiar about the way he's acting, it's reminding Spidey of someone . . . if he can just put his fingers on it. MJ's words from Valentine's Day pop back into Spidey's head. *She mentioned his aggression, and when*

was the last time I saw someone lose it with anger this intensely?
"Sandman!" he says out loud.

Dr. Shah stops struggling, his eyes focus, and he looks at Spider-Man, completely confused, like he has no idea how he's gotten there.

"I . . . Spider-Man, I'm so sorry. I don't know . . . I don't know why I'm so angry these days. I . . . This is not like me. You have to believe me. I am not a violent man," he says, his voice breaking.

Spider-Man lets go of Dr. Shah's wrists, and then Spidey falls back onto his haunches, resting his forearms on his crouched knees. "I do, and I have a very important question for you, Dr. Shah. Have you been to the New York Hall of Science in the last six months?"

Dr. Shah sits up, rubbing his wrists, and gives Spider-Man another strange look. "Yes. How did you know that? *Why* do you know that?"

"Did you connect to the Wi-Fi there?!"

"What?"

"It's important—did you?! And was it with this phone?" Spider-Man pinches the corner of the phone from the table with this thumb and pointer, and dangles it in front of Dr. Shah.

"I— Yes, yes, I did. It was after that big fight you had there a few months ago. Some colleagues asked me to help them work through some of the issues that . . . resulted."

Without hesitating, Spider-Man takes the phone into Dr. Shah's kitchen and opens the fridge. He's going to do exactly what Mary Jane did all those months ago. He finds a jar of pickles—*vinegar!*—and drops the phone into it, screwing the lid on tight. He starts going through the drawers haphazardly before finally finding a heavy roll of foil that he can use the wrap the jar up tightly.

From behind him, Dr. Shah is yelling and asking what he's doing, but Spidey stays focused. *I have to get this thing out of the apartment.*

"I'll be right back," he says to Dr. Shah, and then hops onto the counter and, holding the jar, slips out of the kitchen window and onto the wall. He's back in twenty minutes after a quick jaunt to the Gowanus Canal. *If this gross canal can handle a shark, it can handle a jar of pickles with an alien anger virus thing inside of it. I hope. Not like there's Wi-Fi signals inside of the canal, anyway.*

When he crawls back into Dr. Shah's window, the man is sitting at the kitchen table. He's got his head in his hands again, and his shoulders are tight up around his ears.

"Dr. Shah?" Spider-Man asks, hopping off the counter and onto the black and white tiles below. Dr. Shah startles, and his head whips up to look at Spider-Man. "Sorry! I didn't mean to scare you. . . . I thought you heard me come in."

"No, no it's okay. . . . I was lost in—my head's just not where it should be these days." Then Spidey sees

Dr. Shah get a familiar shrewd look on his face. It's not one Spidey's seen in months, and he's heartened by the unexpected expression. "But I think you might be able to tell me more about that, unless you stole my phone for no reason?" he asks.

There you are, Dr. Shah, Spidey thinks, grinning under his mask. He moves to join his teacher at the table and takes the seat across from him. The table is empty save for salt and pepper shakers in the shape of two planets, and a napkin holder that has the numeric value of pi in iron looping around the base.

"I've got a story for you, Dr. Shah. . . ."

HE BROKE US.
 HE TOOK OUR MAN. HE TOOK HIM FROM US.
WE WILL BREAK THE SPIDER-MAN.
  REVENGE.
    REVENGE.
      REVENGE.
ENACT THE FINAL
 SPIDEY CODE
  DESTRUCTION
WE WILL SEE IT THROUGH.

It's late by the time Spidey has finished talking, and Dr. Shah is rubbing at his face. He still looks tired, but the wildness is gone from behind his eyes.

"So . . . it was inside the phone? Or probably part of the phone . . ." Dr. Shah says to himself. "It must not be strong enough, and so it needs some kind of tether to keep it grounded here. But . . . it must have been what sent me the algorithm? Why would it want to help stop crimes?"

"That's what I want to know," Spider-Man says, interrupting Dr. Shah's musings.

"I can't believe I spent the last several months being manipulated by a radio wave. For months, I thought I was finally fighting back and doing something good. It was always too good to be true. I should have seen that."

"You were fighting back!" Spidey interjects. "You *were*," he says again, putting meaning behind his words. "Even if their goal was to distract me, you still helped me help people, Dr. Shah."

"Please, call me Samir." Spidey's lenses go wide and he has to bite back the urge to say "No thanks." "Thank you for saying that, Spider-Man. I hope I helped. I . . . I don't want other people to go through what I did." His eyes go distant. "Nina—my wife—and I, we'd taken our daughter, Kiran, to the merry-go-round in Central Park one afternoon. This was seventeen months and four days ago." Spidey blanches—that was not too long before he'd started his side gig as the Spider. But it was still *before*.

"That villain, Electro, he came in out of nowhere, on the run from some bank job or something, I don't even know. But he just started going haywire—literally. And then before I could do anything, before I could get us away, they were both gone." Dr. Shah clears his throat, and his eyes look wet.

Spider-Man's heart breaks. "I'm sorry," he says. "I wish—"

"I do, too," Dr. Shah says. "I'm always wishing. I used the Spidey Code because I wished I could help you make sure no one else ever has to go through what I went through. I never should have trusted it. But when you put away Max Dillon, I was thrilled—not to see him go, but to know that he couldn't accidentally break an entire family apart again." Spider-Man isn't sure what to say. "I just hate that this thing I thought was good, was just a tool in another way to make your job harder. I hate that they were able to use me like this!"

"How did you get the algorithm, anyway?" Spider-Man asks.

"First they texted me asking if I was interested in helping you out. Then they sent me the code. I just had to run it."

Spider-Man taps his fingers against the table, and his eyes dart around, running through what he knows about the case. "This thing obviously wants to keep me away from something. Everything about the jobs you sent me screams distraction in retrospect. . . . But I don't know what it is."

"You don't think it's this Dots that the papers are talking about? That's who committed the jewel theft, no?"

Spidey nods thoughtfully but then disagrees. "I would have said so, but he just ambushed me completely out in the open a few days ago. Like he wanted to be noticed. He wants to make a name for himself, not fly under the radar. If it's about him, he doesn't know it. I don't think it's him, though. It makes no sense for him to come after me directly if they want to keep me off his tail."

Dr. Shah frowns, but he takes in what Spidey has said and seems to agree. "Okay . . ." he says. "I'm going to make this right. Let me look into this and figure out what I can. Why do they need you distracted? What is it they don't want you to think about, or to find? What is their goal?"

Spidey pushes against the table and lets out a whistle. "Those are definitely the right questions, Doc," he says. "And I really hope you can find some answers."

CHAPTER TWENTY-ONE

MJ's phone is vibrating on the floor next to her bed. She blearily opens an eye and rolls over to grasp at the thing. Her hand palms the floor a few times before she finally locates it, wincing at the bright glow of the screen in her dark room.

Why is Maia calling me at five in the morning?!

She lifts the phone up and slides to answer it, putting it next to her ear. "Hello?" she croaks out, her voice rough with sleep.

"Uh, so, sorry—I just realized how early it is. I was up to go for a run—"

"Who *are* you?" MJ groans into the phone, and buries her face back into her pillow.

Maia laughs on the other end, but there's an apology in it. "Anyway, I was up, and I checked my email and . . . somehow our request for that garden lot was approved?"

MJ shoots up into sitting position, wide awake now. *"What?!"* she asks. "I didn't even . . . Did you submit an application?"

"No! I wanted to see if you did? But how could we? Neither one of us wants to admit we know Oscorp owns that thing."

MJ twists her free hand into her blanket, her stomach roiling with anxiety. *I don't like this.*

"This feels super shady, doesn't it?"

"It does. I definitely did not submit anything to that site—especially after my mom got that letter scaring us off. I didn't want to do anything . . . you know, official. I was just digging into it on the side," she says softly, remembering how early it is.

Maia is quiet on the other end of the line.

"I . . . don't know," MJ says. "I guess we should . . . use the garden?"

"Should we?" Maia asks, and MJ can't tell *what* she's thinking.

"Let's talk about it at school today?" MJ finally says.

"Yeah, okay, yeah. Sorry for calling so early. I guess

this isn't exactly an emergency, but . . . it really freaked me out."

"No, it's totally okay! It's weird! And scary!" MJ says, validating her friend. "I just don't think there's anything we can do right this minute. But I'm glad you told me."

"Okay, go back to bed, MJ. I'll see you in a few hours," Maia says, and hangs up the phone.

MJ stares at the quiet machine in her hand and taps the screen to light it up. Opening the messages app, she starts to send a quick message to Peter. But her fingers hover over the screen, hesitating.

He's definitely asleep. Why would he be awake? You know what time he got in last night! Peter had come over the night before to tell her all about his conversation with Dr. Shah. MJ was still reeling. She *knew* the way their teacher had been acting was familiar, because she'd been through it!

Maybe I should . . . say something to Dr. Shah tomorrow? Or today, rather.

She feels an affinity with her teacher now. They both got affected by this thing that took advantage of their feelings, and of their circumstances. She knows that she can't actually say anything about what she knows. *But . . . maybe I could just be extra good and he'd feel okay. Wait . . . Peter talked to Dr. Shah last night, and now this morning Maia gets an email saying we got a vacant lot we never actually applied to?* She didn't like to assume coincidences, not since she found out who Peter actually was. But she can't connect the pieces between the two things—the aliens and the phones, and Oscorp and the vacant lot.

MJ sighs and pulls the blanket off of her. *May as well get ready for the day. . . . Maybe school will bring some answers.*

> **I GUESS I SHOULDN'T BE SURPRISED THAT DR. SHAH WAS ABSENT TODAY BUT . . .**

Spidey looks down at his phone. He's balancing on the edge of a fire-escape grate on the Upper East Side and reading a text from MJ about Dr. Shah. His teacher's absence made sense—*if I'd been in close contact with an alien rage monster for the last few months, I'd probably need to recuperate, too!* He toes the black metal beneath his feet, careful not to hit any of the lights strung up, or the huge dead potted plants crowding the area. They're all more husks than living things, but he still avoids breaking them.

His other phone buzzes, and Spider-Man can't help but rolls his eyes in response. *I hate this whole two-phones thing.* When he grabs the burner, balancing it on top of his personal phone, he sees that, coincidentally, it's a message from his teacher.

SM - CALL ASAP

That can't be good.

He dials the number, and before the first ring can finish, Dr. Shah's voice comes through in a rush of high energy.

"I was culling the code to kill the algorithm completely, and buried deep in the ones and zeroes was some kind of command that had run on its own. It listed out one last potential violent crime you may want to check out. I've gone through the rest of it five times, and there's nothing else like it."

"That definitely sounds like a trap," Spider-Man says, his voice flat and matter of fact.

There's a hum of agreement on the other end of the line, and the sound of something shifting, like Dr. Shah is nodding his head. "I thought the same . . . but do you think we can risk it being a trap?" He sounds uncomfortable asking the question at all. "The program may have distracted you, but it was never wrong about crimes."

"Do you think that means there something bigger going on somewhere else? Because that would suck really, really bad," Spider-Man says plainly.

"Let me keep an eye on it. I can probably tap into police scanners on my end. Or . . . at least keep an eye on local internet chatter."

Spider-Man takes a moment to appreciate how cool his teacher actually is. Still, there's something in his gut giving him pause.

"I don't know . . ." he says. "But text me where I need to be and when anyway."

"Okay . . . I'm following a lead on my end to see if we can figure out where this all originated, but I'll drop the information to you right now." There's a short pause, and then his voice comes through again, loud and clear. "Good luck, Spider-Man," Dr. Shah says, and disconnects.

Spidey rubs a hand against the back of his head and starts pacing along the thin edge of the wrought-iron fire escape. The text from Dr. Shah comes through:

9PM. CHELSEA PIERS. SNIPER.

Spidey's stomach drops. A *sniper*. He walks back and forth five times before finally someone cries out from inside the apartment to his right.

"You're makin' me dizzy, Spider-Man! Get off my balcony!"

"Balcony?" Spider-Man yells out as he presses the side of his ear to start a call "More like balco-fire-hazard!" He flies forward and *thwips* out a web. The phone in his ear rings once, then twice, then several more times before it finally goes to voice mail.

Hi! This is MJ's phone! I'm not here, but Mr. Voice Mail is, so leave a message and I'll call you back. Or just text me. Actually, I will definitely text you back. Who leaves voice mails?!

"Hey, MJ," Spidey yells against the rush of wind, "call—I mean, text me when you're around. There might be some stuff going down, uh, with the night job." With one fist gripped around his web, he uses his free hand to tap the side of his mask ending the call. *So much for that plan . . .*

At 8:50 p.m., Spider-Man is sitting on top of a building on the corner of 11th Avenue and West 20th Street, just across from the entrance to Chelsea Piers. The entertainment space looks fairly normal—there are families heading to golf or ice-skate, groups of friends making their way to pick up food before joining whatever activity they were there to do. There's nothing out of the ordinary that Spidey can see, nothing that gives him a clue as to what might be coming. Dr. Shah didn't have any further information for him, just the time and place and that it was a sniper. That probably means rooftops. Or it could mean someone hiding behind something. In the distance, he can see the lights of boats on the Hudson and hopes that the crime isn't going to happen on a *boat. How would I even swing over there?*

He leans his elbows on the parapet and groans. MJ

still hasn't called him back, but he's not worried. She has her own stuff going on. *That might be connected to* my *stuff.* They'd gone over it together during the day at school—this alien reappearing, the Spot, Oscorp, and the mysterious approval of an application that was never sent. He couldn't make heads or tails of it, but MJ was sure they had to be related. She just couldn't figure out how.

"What if this is all a lie," he says to himself, "and I'm sitting here like a chump while that Spot dude robs, I don't know, the New York Stock Exchange for hot tips or something?" He throws his head back and lets out a shout. "Argh!"

Distantly, he hears someone yell, "Shut up! I'm trying to watch a movie!"

"Sorry to disturb!" he calls back. "My bad!"

There's a flash of something across the street, and someone screams. Spidey's head snaps back toward Chelsea Piers—did he miss it? Did something already happen? He braces himself against the building about to swing forward, eyes searching for the disturbance. There are so many people! Then he finally sees it and sags in relief—just a family with two kids who are fighting over a sparkler and their mother is yelling at them.

Spidey lets out a breath. He crawls over the side of the roof and leans against the building, his feet and back braced against the bricks. He glances at his phone again; it's 8:54. There's only six more minutes until something might happen that Spidey needs to stop. There's the loud sound of a window snapping open a few feet away, and Spidey tenses. But it's just someone leaning out to throw their keys down to a friend waiting on the sidewalk. *I need to keep it together*, Spider-Man thinks. He can't keep jumping at every little thing. He needs to stay calm and be ready. If there is a sniper on a busy evening at Chelsea Piers, it would be the stuff of nightmares. Spider-Man finds himself hoping that it really is just a trap for him.

There's movement on the roof across the way—for a split second, Spider-Man sees something tiny and reflective from a spot just over where the golf course is. *Is that the freakin' sniper?!* Spidey vaults over the edge of the roof and swings over 11th Avenue and flying up to land on top of one of the many food trucks that litter the entrance to the piers.

"¡Mami! ¡ES SPIDER-MAN!" a young girl cries out in Spanish from beneath him, but Spidey doesn't have the time to stop and say hi. He jumps onto the side of the building and starts crawling up as fast as he can before he pushes himself into a run, his legs bounding large leaps until he makes it to the top. The roof of Chelsea Piers looks orange and dull in the low light of the city at night. It's not quiet—there are loud *thwack*s of golf balls being hit into an artificial green and children screaming on an ice rink below his feet.

He stops and twists his head around, looking for *any*

sign of someone being there, but there's nothing. His spider-sense is silent. Something scurries behind him, and Spidey flips around, arms up, knees bent, ready to spring. It's just a rat.

The ledge where he thought he saw something is several feet to his right, and he jogs over to check the scene out from this side. On the ground, there's a black hoodie and a tripod. *What the . . . ?*

"*Hey!*" a loud yell comes from behind him. "*Spider-Man?!* You can't be here!"

Spider-Man jumps up and does a backward flip over whoever's yelling at him and lands before shooting two quick webs out at the form in front of him and pulling him backward.

"AHHH!" the man screams, and then falls backward with a sickening-sounding *crunch*, followed by a *thud*. From the ground, there's a loud groan of pain. "Oh man, my head. My head's bleeding. And I think my shoulder's hurt. Why did you do this?" the man lying on the ground says, and Spidey can hear the thick threat of tears in his voice. He takes a step backward.

"Aren't you . . . ? Didn't you have a gun?" he asks, and hates that he sounds hopeful.

"A gun?!"

Spidey steps forward to get a better look at the man, and he sees that it's just some young East Asian guy. Under his T-shirt, his right shoulder looks swollen, and blood is pooling on the ground from a cut on the right side of his forehead. Spidey flinches. *This is wrong.*

"I'm so sorry!" he says. "I thought . . ." He looks back at the tripod and realizes that blending into the hoodie on the ground, partially obscured by the thick fabric, is a camera case. "I . . ." He gestures unhelpfully.

"Hey!" another voice shouts out before Spider-Man can continue. "What did you do!" A tall brown-skinned man rushes forward. He's got on a security-guard jacket and a baseball cap, and he's waving Spider-Man off. "Did you attack this guy, Spider-Man?! I knew the *Bugle* was right about you!"

Spider-Man sends a harried look between the newcomer and the man he'd hurt lying on the ground. He thinks the man's shoulder might be broken. "I'm—I . . ." he tries again, but can't get the words out.

The security guard pulls out a taser, and Spider-Man launches himself off the roof.

"Buddy," he hears the man on the ground say to the guard as Spidey's swinging away. "Can you please call an ambulance immediately?"

Spidey lands heavily on a roof nearby, close enough that he can still see what happens, even if he can't hear it. He watches as the ambulance shows up and paramedics take care of the man he's hurt. He watches as the security guard tells the EMTs what happened. He watches as people take pictures and crowd around the stretcher as the paramedics push it to the waiting ambulance. Spidey knows he hasn't heard the last of this.

The Spider is forsaken.
          He will not see us.
                    He won't find us.
Too broken.

CHAPTER TWENTY-TWO

"Peter!" Randy's voice cuts into Peter's thoughts, and his head drops off his hand in surprise, nearly slamming against the desk.

"Wha-what?!" he asks, heart hammering and eyes wide.

Randy and Maia are looking at him strangely, while MJ has something that reads as pity in her gaze. He looks away.

"I said," Randy finally answers, "do you have the calendar that Dr. Shah passed out at the beginning of the year? We think we wrote notes on one of ours, but it's not mine, MJ's, or Maia's, so . . ."

"Oh, right. Right. Yeah. Let me look," Peter says, leaning over and rummaging through his backpack. He's glad for the distraction. He didn't sleep a wink last night, the guilt and anxiety keeping his eyes open far past what was a reasonable hour to fall asleep. *I can't believe how bad I messed up*, he thinks for the millionth time. He had known it was a trap and he'd still fallen right into it, and he'd hurt someone in the process. Dr. Shah had apologized profusely when he heard. Peter risks a glance up at his teacher from under his bangs, and it looks like the sleep gods haven't been kind to Dr. Shah, either. His lids are drooping, and he leans far back in his chair with his arms crossed over his chest.

Finally, Peter locates what he's looking for. He pulls out the crumpled-up sheet of paper and spreads it across his desk, trying to un-crease it with his hands.

"Sorry," he says. "But here's mine. . . ."

Randy takes it from him and reads over it. "Nah . . . it's not here, either. I *know* we wrote it down somewhere," he says, but Peter's already tuning out again.

That poor guy. I hurt him so badly. How could I have just . . . gone in like that, without even considering the information was flawed? I thought it would be a trap for me, where I'd get hurt . . . not where I would hurt someone else.

A video of the security guard telling his story has gone viral, and it's been rough. He's telling everyone he saw Spider-Man attack an unarmed man, unprovoked. And he isn't wrong. *I don't even know what to do. . . . Do I turn myself in?* His stomach twists itself into knots at the thought. He doesn't have any friends over there, and it would probably be a death wish to do it.

"Excuse me? Dr. Shah?"

Peter's vision focuses to find that MJ has her hand raised and his trying to get their teacher's attention.

"Dr. Shah?" she says again.

With a start, Dr. Shah leans forward, and he looks at MJ like he didn't even realize he was at school. Like he's surprised to be in a classroom at all. "Um, yes, yes, Ms. Watson?" he says, and he sounds as tired as Peter feels.

"Can Peter and I go to the media center to look something up?" Peter's head twists back to look at her, but she's got her eyes on Dr. Shah.

"Sure, yes, let me write you a pass." He scribbles his signature on some blank passes, not bothering to fill out the rest of the sheet, and reaches out to hand two of them to MJ. Peter slowly unfolds from his chair and shoves his hands in his pockets. He's not sure what to make of this sudden trip. Behind him, he can hear Maia and Randy whispering, but he's too tired and distracted to focus on what they're saying. He follows MJ out of the classroom. The second they're in the hallway, without a word, she pulls one of his hands out of his pockets and holds on to it.

"It's not completely your fault," MJ says finally after another few minutes of silence.

Unbidden, the words "Sure, whatever you say" come out of his mouth. "It's not my fault that I shot my webs at a civilian and then yanked so hard he fell over and broke his shoulder."

MJ squeezes his hand hard and looks at him sharply. "I said it's not *completely* your fault, which is true. Some of it is." She shrugs. "And that sucks, because I know you would never intend to hurt someone."

"I wouldn't!" he says, completely earnest.

"I know, Peter. And I bet, if that guy wasn't so ticked off, he would probably know, too."

"I just wish I knew *why* they did that to me. Like, what was the point other than to make me feel like crap and hurt some poor guy?" He stops walking and pulls away from her hand before leaning heavily against the wall, head bowed. There's a finger at his chin a second later, and MJ is pulling it up and looking deep into his eyes.

"Peter, we'll figure this out. I promise." And she gives him a soft kiss before pulling back. "Actually, I think I have an idea. You should go see the guy. Talk to him. Explain it."

"I don't know, MJ. He . . . Why would he want to see me? The guy who hurt him." Peter's looking back down at the floor again and doesn't see MJ's face fall. "Besides, wouldn't it be illegal? Sneaking into someone's hospital room?"

"Then what's the plan? Just ignore it and hope it goes away?" she asks.

"No! I just . . ." Peter stalls. "I don't know. I just don't know."

MJ's words run over and over in Peter's head while he's at the *Bugle* that afternoon after school. *Should* he just go see the guy? Peter is sitting at his regular desk, listing out photo file names in an Excel grid along with their corresponding date and filing cabinet number. It's mindless work, and he's thankful for it. Behind him, there are several loud chimes in a row.

"Oof, people need to *relax*," Kayla says, sliding in her seat. Peter is about to ask her what she means when someone beats him to it.

"About what?" Ned Leeds's tall form leans over the wall of Kayla's cube.

"Hey, Ned," she says, and then: "The Spider-Man thing." Peter turns his seat fully around and finds that Kayla's gesturing at her computer screen. "The *Bugle* social is blowing up since we posted that video that Betty got. I can't believe she was there last night, by the way. Did I notice a familiar black watch in one of the frames?" Kayla asks coyly, and Peter has a moment to see Ned pull one of his arms off the top of the cube, but not before catching a slash of black at Ned's wrist. When Ned answers Kayla, his cheeks are tinted just the slightest bit red.

"I don't know what you're talking about," he says primly. "But what do you mean people need to relax? The guy messed up pretty bad."

"Something about this whole thing is rubbing me the wrong way . . ." Kayla says.

"Is it that Jameson might be right and we shouldn't actually support random masked vigilantes?" Ned jokes lightly, and Peter grimaces. "Okay, I can *hear* your eyes rolling, Kayla."

"This whole thing doesn't seem fishy to you?" she says, ignoring the comment. "There's something bigger going on here, I swear. This is not like Spider-Man."

His expression grateful, Peter makes to turn back to his desk. "That seems like a stretch, but whatever you say."

"That's right—whatever she says!" Jameson flies into the room in a whirlwind of spiked hair, too much coffee, and furious verbiage. "You'd know that if you were half the reporter she is, Leeds!"

Peter's looking at Jameson with the same slack-jawed expression Ned has on his face. Even Kayla looks shocked at Jameson's statement.

"Close your mouths! You look ridiculous!" Jameson says.

"Sir," Kayla starts. "Did you just . . . ? Was that a compliment?"

"It was an *insult* for Ned, and fine," Jameson mumbles, "a happenstance of a compliment for you. Because you're right. I hate that web-head with all my heart, but there's something weird going on here."

"Then why did we report that 'Spider-Man Succumbs to Shattering Civilian's Shoulder'?" Kayla asks, clearly confused.

"Because we report the facts, Kayla! And that—was—a—fact. But another fact," he adds, and Peter is surprised to hear a tenor of actual *thoughtfulness* in Jameson's words. "This is off-brand for that spider-freak. He's selfish and annoying, but he hasn't *hurt* civilians. Plenty of property destruction that he should pay for, and plenty of times teaming up with people who do hurt civilians, but Spider-Man himself? He's never done it. I don't know if he's escalating, or if he got set up. But there's something weird going on with that guy. Mark my words. You should follow your gut, Kayla," he says as he turns to leave.

"Wait, Jonah. . . . Did you need something?" Kayla calls after him.

"I need Leeds! Ned! Follow me!"

Ned's mouth is still hanging open, but he closes it with a loud snap and takes off in Jameson's wake.

Kayla looks back at Peter and laughs. "Nothing like working at the *Bugle*, right, kid?"

Peter nods but doesn't reply. *I can't believe J. Jonah Jameson doesn't just assume I'm a jerk like the rest of this city.* He'd seen no less than four different headlines about his fight throughout the day, and he was getting tagged in

multiple posts about how Spider-Man wasn't worth following, or that Spider-Man went after the little guy. *It sucks*,
he thinks, *and it's freakin' demoralizing!* He turns away
from Kayla and tries to put his head down, going through
his task again.

"Hey, Pete," Kayla asks, "is everything okay? You
seem a little down."

He swivels his chair back to face her again and gives
her a shaky smile. "No, yeah, I guess—people just turned
on Spidey so fast. I feel like he made a mistake—"

"But that mistake means that someone got hurt pretty
bad," Kayla interjects.

"I thought you were on his side!" Peter says.

"I am! But at the same time, I get why people are mad.
He's going to have to earn their trust back." She shrugs.
"Mine, too. I don't like what happened to that man. And
even if there is something weird going on, we know he
hurt that guy."

"What do you think he needs to do?" he asks her.

"What do *you* think he needs to do?" Kayla asks back
to him, and Peter sighs.

The Spot is back at Brighton Beach, and The Faithless
are in his ear, reverberating in his head. *"Find our home!!!*

We must. We must access our home. Weak. We are growing ever weaker."

"Look, you took Spidey's reputation down and set it on fire. As far as I'm concerned, we are in this together, friends." The Spot looks out over the water in the darkness and frowns. "But . . . I don't know how efficient this is. Just doing all this guesswork, picking up random coordinates. How many times have I been in that water? Too many," he answers his own question. Then he starts tapping a toe against the sand. "You know what, though . . . I used to, at one point, be a scientist." He steps backward and turns his back on the ocean. "If I could take this phone, where you— Do you live on it? How does this work?"

"In. We are in waves. The waves you use. The wireless waves. Host. The card in phone is the host."

The Spot stops short in sudden epiphany.

"I can feed you through a particle electrometer. If I can figure out what your chemical makeup is—you're connected to whatever this thing is in the sea, right? I think I'd be able to track it. I can figure out a way to track it. I was a *very* good scientist," he says, rubbing his fingers against his chest in pride.

"YES," the chorus thunders in his ears, and the Spot nearly buckles at the force of it.

When his head clears, he straightens and grins. "All right, you did me my solid. You broke Spidey's relationship to this city. He's gonna be so busy dealing with that garbage, he'll never see me coming. So now I'll scratch your back—well, metaphorically speaking, of course. This is what partners do, isn't it?"

We will be home today.
    Home.
        And stronger than ever. It will feed us.
    We hunger.

CHAPTER TWENTY-THREE

The Spot steps out of the hole and into the lab he used to frequent at ESU. The room is empty, and the darkness is interrupted by shafts of moonlight cutting through the large windows running along the wall. The last time he was here was when he became the Spot. He grins. He won't think about getting kicked out of the space for claims of bad science, or how his colleagues turned on him. He just focuses on the memory of success. It was a moment of triumph.

"Feels good to be back in a laboratory."

He surveys the room: There are some machines in the back corner, and a slew of desks with various detritus covering them—notebooks, machines in myriad states of repair, laptops, and tablets. There's a mostly empty one near the front, and he drops the cell phone onto it before rummaging in various drawers to find the tools he'll need. Situating himself on the stool behind the desk, he picks the phone up and takes a tiny Phillips screwdriver to it. Once the tiny screws drop off from the bottom, he takes a flathead to the seam between the screen and the metal running around it, prying the two apart gently, his hands moving into the rhythms of his old life quite easily.

The faceplate comes free, and inside, he finds all the workings of a modern-day cell phone. At the end of the desk sits a large microscope. He slides over and pushes the cell phone underneath, holding the phone steady with one hand and using a pair of thin tweezers in the other. The light from the microscope shines bright enough that the Spot can easily locate the tiny white card in the motherboard. He leans away from the scope for a second and carefully takes out a thin stream of cotton to wrap around the edge of the tweezers, which he dips in alcohol so he can get rid of the glue keeping the card steady inside the phone. Then it's just a matter of carefully lifting the card out of the phone and placing it gently onto the counter. Then he uses a sharp tool to scrape the *tiniest* amount off the Wi-Fi card and lets the fine powder rest on a thin glass slide.

When the Spot pulls back after the removal, he lets out a low whistle.

"I'm getting shaky in my retirement," he jokes. Then he leans in to put the Wi-Fi chip in the phone again and rebuild it. Crossing his fingers, he powers the phone on and waits with bated breath. It rings, and the voices of The Faithless creep into the quiet of the lab.

"We. We are. Here. We are here." But the sound is weaker than the Spot has ever heard, and he rushes to start the next step.

"Now let's fire up that particle electrometer." He feeds part of the sample into a medium-sized machine in the back of the lab and listens as it whirs to life. The motor inside hums, and a bright light shines out from the cracks between the metal. A blue light colors the Spot's white skin in its image as the screen next to the machine turns out, and a series of numbers rolls across it, followed by a visualization of what's happening inside of the particle electrometer.

"Work? Did it work?" the voices say from the speaker-phone.

The Spot steps back and folds his arms across his chest, looking over the output with an analytical gaze. "So this"—he looks at one piece of the detected chemical compound—"the mass charge of this piece right here indicates that twenty-two percent of the sample I took is oxygen and this"—he sees the line of the other piece— "this is . . . you. It's a chemical makeup I've never seen before, I think no one has ever seen before in their lives. And this part"—he looks at the piece of the compound that is still while the rest of it vibrates—"that's what I'm betting is the thing we're looking for." He taps his fingers against the keyboard. "Now to isolate that piece of it and . . ." There's a slew of furious typing. "Voilà. I am *still* a genius," he says, taking note of the series of numbers on the screen and writing it down on a piece of paper. "And now we just . . ."

He breaks open the particle electrometer and pulls out a few coils and a small motherboard. He moves back to the desk he'd first been at and opens his own cell phone and sets about soldering the motherboard and coils inside of it. The back won't fit on it anymore, so he takes a thick piece of plastic and tapes it around the edge. Switching it on, he brings up a map application and enters the numbers into the search function.

And then he waits.

The Faithless's chorus whines from the speakerphone. "Did it. Work? Did it work?"

In the bright light of his cell phone screen, the Spot's face morphs into a giant smile, and he breathes out a small "Woo." The map on his screen is solid red in color, and the Spot slowly moves until it turns to a slow green blink. "Did it work? Of course it worked. I built it," he says.

"This thing is going to lead us right to whatever it is you're looking for. I just input the signature that the particle electrometer gave me, reconfigured the GPS a little bit with some help from the ol' PE, and here we are. A map that tells us where to go."

Spider-Man crawls down the side of Mount Sinai Hospital. He's swung onto the roof and is now making his way toward the window he needs on the fourth floor. Working at a newspaper has its positives, and Peter is thankful, if feeling a little guilty, for taking advantage of it to find out where the man he hurt is staying. His name is Winston Lee, and he's a full-time photographer for several magazines in the city. *In another world, I might ask him to mentor me.* He sighs internally. *But nooo, I had to get bitten by a radioactive spider and now I crawl up buildings and no one pays me to do it. What am I even talking about?* Peter shakes his head. *I am losing it.*

He inches forward and finally sees the window he's looking for. It's cracked open just the tiniest bit, like someone out there is still in his corner. Crawling past it and underneath, he situates himself below it. His fingers dip into the space between the metal edge of the window and the sill, and he pushes upward slowly, willing it not to make any sounds. Once the gap is wide enough, he slips inside and stands on the cold linoleum floor in a darkened hospital room. There's a lump on the bed in front of him, shifting back and forth, and Spidey can see a faint glow on the side of it.

"No!" the lump cries out, and Spidey jumps into action.

"Oh my god, are you okay? Do you need me to call the nurse?"

"AH!!!" the lump yells, flipping around so Spidey can see that it is in fact Winston Lee sitting on the bed. He's up and holding his phone in the hand not trapped by the harness strapped to his shoulder. On the phone screen, Spidey can see the words *Game Over*.

"*Ooooh*," he says, thankful—not for the first time—that the mask can hide how red his face is. "AH, uh, sorry."

"Spider-Man?!" Winston asks, sounding incredulous. He turns on the lamp near his bed, and Spider-Man can see the tiny dots all over his hospital gown. "What the heck are you doing here?!" He narrows his eyes. "Are you . . . stalking me?"

"What? No! I came . . . I came to apologize," Spidey says. Winston glares at him.

"Save it." Winston rubs at his eyes. "I don't need your apology. I was just trying to get some cool shots of New York City lights, and I am pretty sure you broke my shoulder because you can't tell the difference between a thing that holds a camera and a thing that holds a *gun*."

Spidey flinches. He clearly isn't helping Winston by

being here. Maybe he's only trying to absolve himself. "You're right," Spider-Man says, and turns to leave. "I am sorry, though. Really." He lifts one foot and braces it against the window ledge, curling his fingers around the sides to pull himself out.

There's a loud sigh behind him, and then Winston says, "Wait. Hold on."

Spidey steps back down, turning to look toward Winston, who is sitting up in bed and staring at him.

"Tell me what happened."

"I'm sor—"

"And *don't* apologize again," Winston interrupts, his voice hard. Then he adds, "I don't know you, but everyone *knows* you—this isn't like you. Was I just in the wrong place, wrong time? Why would you attack *me*?"

There's an empty seat next to the bed, and Spider-Man moves to crouch in it. "Sort of," Spidey says. "Someone sent me a bad tip, and I should have spent more time working through it, but I was worried about people getting hurt. I . . ." He hesitates, and then adds, "I should have been better."

Winston looks away, but he doesn't seem quite as angry as before. "I don't like how my already weird situation is getting weirder," he says, but it's followed by a small, humorless laugh. "Look, I'm not, like, pressing charges or anything. No one even knows your name."

"I *really* didn't mean for any of this to happen," Spidey

says. "And if you really do want to . . . press charges"—
Spidey stumbles over the words—"we'll figure *something*
out. I can't tell people who I am. I don't want the people
I care about to be in trouble, but . . ."

Winston is already shaking his head. "I believe you.
That you didn't want this to happen, I mean," he says.
"Plus, one time, you stopped my friend Urika from falling off the George Washington Bridge last year, and that
definitely counts for something, all right? I guess we're
square. I don't know if I can forgive you quite yet, but I
get that you probably end up in tough situations all the
time. Can't always make the right call."

Spider-Man leans forward, surprised. "I remember that
bridge thing! I just like thwipped out a web and—"

"Sorry, you did what?" Winston interjects. "Did you
say 'thwipped'?"

Spidey's rubs the back of his head, self-conscious. "Oh,
yeah . . . that's the sound my web makes when I shoot it
and so now I . . ." He mimes pressing his web shooter.
"Thwip, thwip?" he says weakly.

Winston looks at him for a moment and then lets out
a huge laugh. It takes him a few seconds to calm down,
and when he finally does, he's wiping tears from his eyes.

"That's incredible," he says. "I gotta ask, though. . . .
Would you say, that when a problem comes along . . . you
must 'thwip' it?"

Spider-Man stares at him blankly. "I mean . . . sometimes, I guess?"

Winston returns the blank look. "No . . . I mean—do you not know the song—*how old are you?*"

"Well, I guess . . . we did it?" Maia steps into the empty lot and looks around before turning around to give MJ an awkward smile.

MJ follows in her footsteps and joins her. Behind her, there's a notice on the chain-link fence that designates the lot as a future community garden. Together, MJ and Maia take in the twenty-odd feet of space, with its hard-packed dirt and dead grass.

"Also, I think that weird teddy bear is staring at me with its one glass eye," Maia adds, gesturing to some suspicious-looking dirty stuffed animals at one end, surrounded by a lot of other trash.

From her bag, MJ pulls out a roll of industrial-sized trash bags and two pairs of gardening gloves.

"I can't believe we're doing this in *February*," Maia says, grumbling.

"This was *your* idea." MJ laughs. "I believe you said, 'It'll be good to get a head start because we'll be so busy with the app next month.'"

"Please don't use my own words against me. I am but a simple girl." Maia puts a hand against her chest and pretends to faint, catching herself just before she actually falls to the ground. Then she looks around, and there's a very real, slight shiver to her movements. "Let's, uh, stick together, yeah?" she says. MJ wholeheartedly agrees.

They move toward the far end of the lot. MJ hands Maia a pair of gloves and a bag, and they get to work picking up garbage.

"So," Maia says after a few minutes. "Do you think Oscorp just, like, gave up? Because everything about this is making me nervous. I feel like some guys are gonna find us and threaten us over this thing or something." She lets out a nervous giggle.

MJ stops what she's doing and looks around. *It is* really *quiet around here.* . . . She thinks of the letter her mom got, still sitting in her office. She hadn't brought it up again, and MJ hadn't, either.

"I know what you mean, but maybe they just felt like the whole thing was more trouble than it's worth? I mean, I have to guess Oscorp was the one who secretly donated all those tablets to the school, right? To what, bribe them into stopping us? And someone there definitely has Councilman Grant on the payroll. It feels wrong that they just . . . gave up, though."

"Mm-hmm," Maia says, ducking down to pull up a tangle of what looks like netting and several hair brushes.

She mimes gagging before shoving the mass into her bag. "Maybe next time we invite more people? Why does it feel like, for once, there's literally no one outside in Queens?"

It does feel a little eerie, MJ thinks. *Though it's also pretty cold outside. The gray day isn't helping anything.*

"Yeah, next time we'll ask, like, ten more people to join us." All of a sudden there's a tap on her shoulder, and MJ screeches out a loud, terrified sound.

"Sorry!" Peter's voice comes from behind her. "Sorry! I didn't mean to scare you!"

MJ flips around and shoves his shoulder. "PETER PARKER, YOU ANNOUNCE YOURSELF!"

He backs up a few steps with his hands raised in the universal gesture of *my bad*, and she can tell that he's trying to keep a straight face. His cheeks are bright red from the cold, and he's wearing the hat and scarf she got him for the holidays, though she notices they're a little worse for wear and remembers that he wears them while he's patrolling.

"Seriously, Peter, oh my god." Maia is clutching at her chest again, only this time it's in actual anxiety.

"Deal, sorry. I just came to see if you guys needed help. My hands are your hands." He wiggles his fingers at them, and they both end up laughing. MJ's heart is still pounding, though, so she takes a few calming breaths.

"So, Pete, you feeling better? Seemed like something

was up the other day," Maia says, considering the creepy pile of stuffed animals in the corner. MJ looks over at Peter, who seems chagrined. He had gone and talked to Winston, but not until after they'd disagreed over it.

"Oh? I think I just didn't sleep well the night before," he says, and waves his hand like it isn't a big deal. "I was just having an off morning. MJ talked me through it, though, because she's obviously amazing."

Peter throws an arm around her and gives her a big, show-off kiss on the cheek. MJ laughs awkwardly and pushes him away, wiping at the wetness he's left there. The actions were all right, but it still feels like there is something off between them.

"You're both gross," Maia says, and smiles. "Okay, I am gonna shove these weird stuffed moppets into the bag and then put it in the dumpster around the corner immediately because I feel like they're cursed." And she does exactly that, tying the bag closed the minute they're inside and then taking off to the dumpster. "BRB," she calls out behind her.

MJ takes the opportunity of them being alone to ask Peter how his meeting with Winston Lee had gone the night before. She'd fallen asleep before they had a chance to talk about it, and he hadn't wanted to hash it out over text messaging.

"It was okay. He didn't forgive me—but he says we're okay. And I believe him. Wish I could get the same from the city," Peter says, smiling and frowning in quick succession. "Did you see the *Globe* headline today?"

MJ's mouth twists up. She has. "'Spider-Man or Spider-Monster'? Yeah. They're just making stuff up now, straight up finding people who will lie about you. It sucks." She starts to pull off one of her gardening gloves intending to take his hand, but they're shoved into his pockets. MJ leaves her glove on.

"Nah, it's fine. I can still do good even *if* the city hates me. Just might not get free pizza from Sal's anymore."

"Sal wouldn't!" MJ says.

"He already did." Peter pouts. "I tried to grab some last night, and he shut the door in my face."

"We'll find a better pizza place," she says resolutely.

Peter surveys the lot around them. "How's this stuff going?" He gestures in a wide arc.

"I don't know. Maia and I are both pretty nervous about it . . . feels weird that this all just came together after everything was so fraught. I can't help but feel like the other shoe is going to drop. And soon."

"I know, but I also think you should take the win if you can. Let yourself enjoy the fact that the two of you did it—you're starting this thing! That's incredible."

"I don't know. . . . it still feels—"

"Dang right, it's incredible!" Maia's voice carries in before her as she returns, cutting MJ off, clearly thrilled to be free of the supposedly cursed stuffed animals.

Peter looks like he's about to say something else when he jumps slightly and then pulls his phone out of his pocket. He reads through the message, and his eyes grow big. "Ah, sorry, turns out I actually can't stay and help," he says, starting to back away before stopping to give MJ a quick hug.

She's thrown by his hasty exit but still manages to ask, "Everything okay?"

"Yeah, just a night-job thing," he says with a wink and a wave of the phone. "I'll see you both later!" And then he's off at a run, and MJ can see his elbows go up like he's started to unzip his coat.

"Man, he must really love working at the *Bugle*, huh?" Maia says beside her.

CHAPTER TWENTY-FOUR

Dr. Shah is waiting for him at his kitchen table when Spidey crawls into his apartment. The smell of various spices cuts through Spidey's mask, and he takes a deep, appreciative inhale. He carefully avoids the pots bubbling on the stove and hops down off the counter. There's an open laptop in front of Dr. Shah, and Spidey sees a new phone sitting next to it.

"Spider-Man! Hello!" he says, gesturing to the seat opposite him.

Spidey hops into it, sitting at a crouch with his elbows on his knees. "Hey, Dr. Sh—Samir," Spidey strangles out. "What's up? You said this was urgent?"

"I think I found out how to find who's responsible for all of this," Dr. Shah says, shoulders coming forward as he leans forward conspiratorially. "I figured out a way to hack the signal—"

"The signal?" Spider-Man asks.

"The Spidey Code—that last crime was fabricated by someone on an entirely different signal altogether.. A different wavelength."

"And . . . people can track that?"

"*I* can track that," Dr. Shah says proudly. "I was somewhat of a rising star when it comes to radio and electromagnetic wave research. So *I* was able to track it, and it pinged on a cell phone, a cell phone that was stolen several weeks ago. It used to be owned by someone named . . . Brad Evans?" The name doesn't mean anything to Spidey, but the words "stolen cell phone" do—he wonders if it's the elusive phone he and MJ haven't been able to find! "But I managed to figure out a way to track Brad's old phone, because it turns out whatever this thing is that lives in the waves of our Wi-Fi, has a truly unique makeup. A unique makeup that leaves a mark if you know to look for it."

Dr. Shah then launches into a lecture on the science behind his discovery, and while it does sound fascinating and definitely piques his interest, most of it goes over Spidey's head. *I wonder if I should tell him I've only ever taken two and a half years of high-school-level science*, he muses while Dr. Shah shifts into teacher mode. Finally, he slows to a stop. "This is . . . too in the weeds, isn't it?"

"It's a little out of my depth," Spider-Man says. "But I do appreciate the background! I'm not *not* a science guy, but I think I need a few doctorates under my belt before I can really internalize everything you're telling me. Can you give me the CliffsNotes version?"

"I *despise* CliffsNotes," Dr. Shah groans, pinching the bridge of his nose. "But I suppose it's the most expedient way to deal with this. Okay, the thing is, I matched up the pattern of the way this phone has been used over the last few weeks with another pattern, and I managed to clone the phone . . . and guess who's got it."

Spidey's stomach twists unpleasantly. "Who?" he says slowly.

"That man you told me about, with all of the black holes all over his skin!"

"The Spot?!" Spidey yelps. *"Ugh.* I still don't even know how to beat him. And now he's got this alien thing going for him, too?" Spidey remembers what it was like trying to fight Sandman with that thing on Flint's side. *It must be considerably weaker now, though. At least, I really hope it is.* "I can't *believe* I was wrong about him."

"The Spot keeps going back to a particular area of Brighton Beach, and then portaling into the water. I think he's looking for something that whoever sent me the Spidey Code wants."

Under his mask, Spidey's face pales. The last time this

thing had been looking for something, it almost turned the whole world into rage monsters.

"Tell me again about the fight with Sandman," Dr. Shah asks. "I think I may have an idea of what's going on."

Spidey goes into his fight with Sandman and everything he and MJ had figured out about the alien, making sure not to mention MJ's name. He tells Dr. Shah how the alien used anger and how they needed access to waves. Spidey even shares the story of the reclusive billionaire Addison Arledge and how an earlier Arledge generation found a meteor made of an element no one on earth had ever seen before—an element the alien seemed to need. An element that, when paired with electricity, caused a surge of anger in human beings. Spidey could still feel the strange non-weight of the element in his hands after Addison had handed it to him.

"So the lamp and everything with it was completely incinerated during that fight, yes?" Dr. Shah asks, and Spidey nods. He still remembers the terror of the old lighter not catching and how worried he was he wasn't going to get out of it. "But this thing, whatever it is, survived because there was so much signal around it. And now it's looking for a way to get stronger."

"It's the alien element. . . . There must be more of it here. It must have sensed it. That's what the Spot is looking for," Spider-Man says quietly, hit with sudden realization.

"I still can't believe it's actually *real*," Dr. Shah says.

Spidey tells Dr. Shah all about the research he'd done months earlier to figure out what was going on with Flint Marko.

"The tiny amount in the arc lamp had this thing turning Flint Marko's head round and round."

"The Sandman fight actually gave me the idea for how to destroy it," Dr. Shah says, pushing his chair away from the table. He starts pacing in the kitchen, slipping back into lecture mode. "If we were able to get the Spot's cell phone into some kind of vacuum, the thing living on it would have nowhere to go. We know—thanks to you— that the way it can travel is by inhabiting the Wi-Fi of specific devices. I think it must feel stronger if it's near the element, and maybe that means it will no longer need our radio waves to live. But if we can get it somewhere where there's no signal, no waves to speak of, it can't move."

"And where is that?" Spidey asks. "This all seems kind of impossible."

"If this was a decade ago, I would have said it was easy enough as going down into a subway tunnel, actually"—Dr. Shah starts nodding at whatever thought he's having—"*under* the river. In the tunnels under the river, it is a complete dead zone for signals. If you can get the alien into a tunnel underneath the river, you're good. I think you can end it by pulling the same trick you pulled with my old cell phone. Actually, give me a minute." Dr. Shah gets up and leaves the room before returning a few second later with a thin metal cup with a screw-top lid. He passes it to Spidey. "This should work better than foil. If you drop the phone in that, it'll weaken the signal considerably, though it won't completely kill it. It flattens into a disk, so you should be able to carry it in your suit. But you've got to get the phone, I think." Then Dr. Shah grimaces and adds, "The key is getting to it before it accesses whatever is left of their home world on Earth, though. *And there's the rub.*"

"There's a lot of ifs and hopes in this plan, Doc," Spidey says. "Is there anything solid I can go off of?"

Dr. Shah comes back over to the table and flips his computer around. On the screen, there's a map with a little red dot blinking and moving in bursts. "I'm tracking the phone. It keeps blipping in and out, and I assume that's when the Spot travels via the portals, but it's going to end up *somewhere.*"

Spider-Man is swinging in the direction of Brighton Beach. It's still pretty early in the evening, but that's where Dr. Shah said the cell has landed. He said he'd text any updates to Spidey as soon as they come in. Spidey's on the phone with MJ filling her in on what's happened. When he gets to the part about the stolen phone, she stops him.

"Brad Evans . . . I know that name . . ." MJ says.

"I didn't," Spidey replies, going over it in his head again.

"Wait!" Spidey can hear a loud noise over the phone, and then a lot of shuffling and banging. "Sorry," MJ says finally. "I ran downstairs to get on the computer. I *knew* I knew that name. That was one of the defunct accounts of the person who was at the Museum of the Moving Image the same day I was!"

"I thought so!" Spidey says. "I'm glad we finally know what happened there."

"So, then what?" she asks, and Spidey runs through everything Dr. Shah said to him. When he's finished talking, she's quiet for a beat on the other end before she says anything. When her voice does come through his headphone again, she sounds worried. "That's . . . an awful lot like a hope, a wish, and a prayer, Peter," MJ says.

"I know, but it'll be fine." He tries for nonchalance, but what comes out wavers too much to hit that level of confidence.

"We need a plan, Peter," she says, and it's almost too quiet for him to hear above the rush of air as he swings south through Brooklyn.

"I have a plan, MJ," he says, this time nearly sounding as confident as he wants to.

"You know what I mean. If you get hurt, what do I

do? Just sit here and wait and hope that you'll come out of it okay?" Spidey can hear how frustrated she is. "There has to be something I can *do*. I refuse to be that person, Peter."

Spidey doesn't know what to say. "MJ, I wish I knew what the system could be. I keep putting it off because I don't know what could work in a way that doesn't give everything away." There's quiet on the other end of the phone, and Spidey flips onto a tall light fixture. He crouches and waits a beat. "MJ, I—"

"Peter, if you get hurt, maybe that's the time *to* give everything away," she says in a rush, like she has to get it out before she can stop herself.

"MJ!" Spidey knows he sounds shocked, and he is. He's not sure MJ realizes what she's saying.

"I know, it's a big— It's a catastrophic kind of thing. But . . . if you're hurt . . ." She trails off. "I don't know what other options there are, and I'd rather you alive with the secret out than the alternative."

Spider-Man lets her words sink in. He processes them. And he realizes he doesn't have another idea.

"Okay . . . so you call someone."

"Good," she says. "So, if I don't hear from you by eleven p.m.—"

Spidey cuts her off. "Let's make it two a.m., just to be safe."

"Fine," she says tightly. "So if I don't hear from you until two in the morning, who do I call?"

Spider-Man thinks for a few minutes and swings down three more blocks, interspersing his webs with high jumps and ricochets off low buildings. Finally, he says, "Call Kayla Ramirez. Tell her everything about the plan, and ask her to call someone she trusts to help me. And I'll keep you updated as to where I am, I promise."

He can hear some typing come through over the phone and then a satisfied hum. "Okay. Was that so hard?" She laughs, but there's little joy in it. "Be careful," she says then, and it's serious and heavy.

Spidey takes a brief moment to flip onto top of a bodega. "I will, MJ. I promise."

The Spot is back on Brighton Beach. *Guess The Faithless was right about that much*, he thinks. It's early enough that there are still a few masochists standing on the freezing beach, taking evening walks in the icy wind. He's got a wide-brim hat on and a large coat. The hole at the center of his chest wavers as he tries to keep it together with his Ohn face. He's gotten used to being *just* the Spot lately, and he's loath to give up the power. He watches as a young couple, bundled up to the nines, walks arm in arm down the shore, and he sneers. *Why do The Faithless care so much about the beach being empty if they're just going to get stronger here. What does it matter?*

Then a loud, mocking voice cuts through the quiet of the beach. "Hey, Dots! Sorry, I mean *the Spot*!"

He looks up to find Spider-Man crouching on top of one of the streetlights, sitting smack between the two lights on the decorative filigree in between them. The Spot can hear the derisive laughter in Spidey's voice, and his head starts to vibrate with anger. He can feel the black dot breaking up and floating all over his body, morphing his skin to the white background with black polka dots.

"You! What are *you* doing here?!" the Spot cries, furious.

"I heard you're digging into something you shouldn't be digging into, so I thought I'd come see if you needed a partner," Spidey says, the lenses on his mask wide and unnerving. "Gotta say, Spot. You're trying to play with the big names, and I hate to tell you, buddy—you're not a big name. No one knows you. *I* asked around. *No one* knew who I was talking about." He crows, "You are a nonentity. Oh man, you're *Spotless*."

"That *does it*," the Spot says. He pulls a spot off his arm and throws it into the air, hopping into it, and in one more step, he's on the streetlamp, next to Spider-Man.

"Oh, Spotless Spotty," Spidey says, and the Spot can *hear* the smile. Spider-Man's voice is high and childlike, and the Spot hates him. The Spot yells something angry and inarticulate and throws a punch that Spidey dodges. So the Spot grabs him around the middle and yanks him back down to the beach. Spider-Man yells out loud and lands with an *oomph* in the hard sand. "Okay, I am *sorry* about that," Spidey says to him from the ground, like the Spot hasn't just pulled his butt down and thrown him onto the beach without so much as a "how do you do." "I was just trying to get your attention."

But the Spot doesn't want to hear it. "You think I'm not somebody. Just wait till you see what I'm about to do." From his pocket, he can feel the buzzing of The Faithless, but he ignores it. "Just wait—my friends are about to run everything, and you're gonna *wish* you gave me the respect I deserve. You think everybody hates you now, Spider-Man? Wait till my friends are done with this world. You're going down."

Spider-Man gets to his feet and has a hand up. One of his fingers presses against his head like his ear is bothering him. "Just hold on—wait. I just wanted to distract you so we could talk. Don't do this. This won't work out for any of us, standing here on *Brighton Beach*," he says, putting a strange inflection on the end of his sentence.

The Spot ignores it all. "You're just saying that because you know how powerful I'll be once they're better and on my side."

"They're probably lying to you—do you know what

they did to Sandman?" Spidey asks. The Spot hesitates, and Spidey seems to think that's his opportunity to talk. "They used Flint Marko up and then left him to be a giant mound of glass while *they* got away. They don't care about who they use to get what they want. And they'll use you, too, man."

The Spot frowns and actually takes a moment to consider Spidey's words. "Look," Spidey says, "give me the phone. I can handle this. I can—" The Spot's hackles rise, and Spidey redirects: "Or let's open one of those portals and take this chat underground, how about that? I know a great isolated spot in the tunnels under the city."

That's when the Spot realizes that with all of his action and Spidey showing up, waiting for the beach to empty is a moot point.

"Flint Marko wasn't smart," he says finally. "I'm *smart*. I know what I'm doing. So . . . *sorry*, my annoying arachnid. The game is already afoot, and we are a-footing the heck out of here!" Then the Spot flings an open hole into the air in front of him, and it cuts into the scenery, a deep black portal of opportunity. "Toodles!"

CHAPTER TWENTY-FIVE

"Don't!" Spidey yells at the Spot. *Oh, the super villain doesn't listen to reason, big surprise!* He presses two fingers against his palm, and a smooth line of web shoots out and sticks directly onto the Spot's back. Then Spidey gets dragged into the hole along with the Spot, but he doesn't land anywhere familiar. He doesn't land anywhere at all. He and the Spot are floating, still connected, deep in the ocean, and Spidey has to stop from panicking. He holds his breath. The Spot is swimming next to him and has a massive flashlight in his hand. He's shining it this way and that, and Spidey follows the beam with his eyes. Then he shakes his head—what is he doing? He can't stay here;

he'll run out of air. He's got to get to the surface! Spidey starts to kick in the direction he thinks is up, when the flashlight beam finally settles on something to his right.

Spidey stills his movements for a second and takes in the sight. The thing looks like a strange spherical red stone—smooth and about the size of the big Unisphere globe at the old World's Fair site in Flushing. He has the briefest moment to look at it before he's being pulled through another one of the Spot's portals thanks to the web between them.

And that's when it all goes upside down. Spider-Man lands heavily on the ground, wet and gulping in deep breaths of air. Then he looks around, and for a second, he's completely thrown. He's in a wide open white space, and there are thousands of black holes surrounding him. His web line is already taut and is leading him through another hole, where the Spot has clearly gone.

But Spider-Man doesn't have time to examine whatever this interim plane is, so he launches himself into the black hole, directly behind Spot. He lands hard onto smooth, deep red ground and finds the Spot already there, standing and speaking into a cell phone.

"Now what?" the Spot is saying. "We're here. Is it working? Are you stronger?"

"Question from the class," Spidey asks from behind him. The Spot twists around in shock. "Where exactly is *here?* Wait, are we *inside* that big red rock under the sea? How is there air down here?"

"You can't be *here!*" the Spot yells, and flings a spot in Spidey's direction, but he's already flipping up and over the Spot, landing on his shoulders.

"Ah-ah-ah, no sending Spider-Man to another dimension so you can kick off your evil plan," Spider-Man says, wagging a finger. Before he can say anything else, something pushes him off the Spot hard, and he slams into the red rock to his side. There's a loud *crack*, and Spidey isn't sure if the sound is coming from something in his body breaking or the walls around him. It feels like he's being smashed to death by an invisible anvil, and Spidey flails for a moment, pushing against the see-through assailant. It's as if every bone in his body is about to break, and his organs are screaming in protest. A strangled gasp escapes his lips. Spider-Man uses every bit of his strength to push as hard as he can, but the pressure still comes down on him. There's no give and he's panicking, but then he stills.

Maybe if I don't move, it won't know to push down. The thought is desperate, but it's all he's got.

Out of the corner of his eye, he can see the Spot taking a deep breath and starting to pull off his coat. Around them is just that same smooth red rock. And it's glowing. Spider-Man's never seen anything like it. But the low light lets him take the rest of the space in. There are no real edges, so it isn't quite a *room*. It's just a hollowed-out oval. The pressure on Spidey's sternum starts to lessen, and he waits one more beat before pushing himself away from the wall. The feel of the rock under his hands is nauseatingly familiar. Spidey's stomach drops. It's the same as the element from the arc lamp. This must be the meteor the aliens came from. The same kind of rock that Addison's ancestor found on that farm. He needs to end this before the alien is so strong he can't stop it. The Spot's back is to him now, and he's got the phone out again. It's yelling, "Leave us! Drop us! Home. We are home! We grow!"

I do not like the sound of that, Spidey thinks, and shoots a web out at the cell phone, pulling back at it hard so it smacks into his hands. The Spot and The Faithless scream in tandem, but Spider-Man is focusing. He yanks the cup disk out of his suit and expands it, dropping the phone into it and twisting on the lid. He shoves the whole cup awkwardly into his suit at his hip. *Not exactly aerodynamic*, he thinks, glancing at it.

"No!" the Spot yells. "You can't do this—you can't ruin this! I've earned this!" He reaches for one of the holes on his arm, but his movement is interrupted by the ground moving sluggishly and a loud crack. Spidey looks to the right, where he was slammed against the side of the space, and there's a large spout of water flowing into the room. *Well, I guess it wasn't my bones breaking, after all. . . .*

"Where *are* we?!" he asks, urgency threaded through his question.

"We're two hundred and fifty feet below sea level," the Spot spits out.

Spidey's lenses grow impossibly big, and he thinks of Dr. Shah's advice. "Well . . . I made it underwater, I guess."

"Let—them—*go!*" the Spot screams, and flings a hole at Spider-Man. He jumps to avoid it only to end up flying through a different one and directly into the stone behind the Spot. It's falling apart, though, and he manages to get through it without any pain whatsoever.

"So, this place, not exactly staying up to code, huh?" he jokes as he jumps to spring off and drops directly in front of him.

"They told me it would be safe here!" the Spot yells. "But you've ruined it!"

Spidey pulls his fist back to punch the polka-dotted villain, but, remembering his last experience, he hesitates. It gives the Spot the chance he needs to drop Spidey through a black hole and into that white space with all the portals.

Spidey twists around staring every which way. *I could pick any hole and get out of here. . . .* The Spot jumps into the space behind him and grins. "Welcome to my Spot World, Spidey. Think you can get away? Try it!" The Spot starts ticking options off his fingers, one at a time. "Let's see if you end up roadkill, or in the middle of the ocean *without* an air pocket, or maybe you'll fall into a volcano."

But Spidey isn't listening too hard. He's got a hand over his mouth and his lenses are half-moons. "Sorry, did you say *Spot World*?" And then he doubles over laughing, both arms around his middle. Something yanks him forward, within distance of the Spot's reach.

The Spot wastes no time in kicking Spider-Man hard in the stomach.

"Oof," Spidey says, falling backward, teetering on the edge of one of the black holes littering the space around him.

"No, I don't think so," the Spot says, grabbing the spider emblem at the center of Spidey's suit and pulling him back, both of them tumbling into the red rock again. There's a lot more water now, and the Spot is scrambling to get his hands on the cup at Spidey's waist.

Spidey hops up and sticks to the top of the cavern, crawling away as fast as he can. But he doesn't have far to go. The leak means that the air pocket they're in is small and getting smaller by the minute. *That water is going to be a problem*, Spidey thinks, eyeing the growing puddle behind them. He glances back at the Spot, and then he notices something strange. *Is it just me, or is he less dotty than he was five minutes ago?*

There's far more white than black showing on the

Spot's body now. *So, those things aren't infinite. If I can get a clear shot at the part of him that's white, I can end this.*

"Hey, Dotty, I'm comin' for ya!" Spider-Man flies forward, and as he hoped, the Spot flings out a dot for him to fly through, and another for him to come out of. Spidey has to be ready to swerve, experience telling him that there will be a hard wall on the other end of that dot. There's a loud splash as he lands, and the water doesn't even have time to settle before he's back in the air. He flips once to the front and then does a side barrel. The Spot watches him, his head jerking with every motion. Spidey does another flip forward, the Spot drops another dot directly in front of him, and Spidey flies through again.

"Stop, *moving*!" the Spot says as Spidey ends up right back inside the rock. "Give me that phone!" He flings spots out in quick succession and dips his hands in trying to grab at the cup at Spider-Man's waist, but Spidey is too fast for him. He jumps to the right, and to the left. Then he's up on the ceiling, scrambling forward before dropping down into another black spot and landing back in the room.

The Spot only has a few dots left, and Spidey thinks, *Now!* He flies forward with his right leg extended, waiting to make contact with the side of Spot's head, but then he sees a spot slide from the Spot's neck up and over his ear, and he knows he's messed up. Spider-Man's own foot comes out from a black spot to his side and kicks him squarely in the ribs. He falls with a sickening sound, and he can't help the whine of pain that pushes past his pursed lips. He's pretty sure at least one rib is broken, and it hurts when he breathes. *This is not a good sign*, he thinks before he pushes up from the ground to stand.

"That had to hurt, Spidey," the Spot says. "Face it, you can't hit me, you can't win." He shrugs. "So I'll just . . ." He takes a step forward, and Spidey jumps to the ceiling before coming down directly behind the Spot. He throws a fist at the Spot's side and a black spot slides to meet it, but then Spidey fakes him out. He pulls his right hand back and goes in with his left to the side of the Spot's head, and there's a loud *thud* before the Spot crashes to the ground.

"Sorry, you were saying something about 'can't hit'?" Spidey says to the Spot's unconscious form as he moves him into a sitting position against the wall so he won't drown. But his jibe is punctuated by a loud groan of pain. He tenderly touches the ribs on his right side and— *Oh no! Where is . . . ?*

The cup at his side is gone! Spidey thinks back. When did he last feel it on his person . . . ? *Before I . . . kicked myself in the ribs.* Desperately, he looks around the small cavern. *Okay, first, find the cup, then figure out how to stop this water from pouring in, and then figure out how to get . . . two hundred and fifty feet up without running out of air.* Spider-Man takes a second, puts both his hands against his face, and screams into his palms. Then he brings his hands back to his side and starts to take stock of his surroundings. The water's up to his knees now, and there's just a few feet above his head to spare. He walks over to the wall and pokes at it. The rock crumbles away at his touch. It's like he completely damaged the structural integrity when the alien slammed him into it earlier, and the meteor was starting to fall apart around him. *That's wei*— Before he can finish the thought, something pushes Spidey down into the water face-first!

Spider-Man struggles to breathe, his mask is trapping water in his mouth and nose, and he can't blow out fast enough to keep it from coming back in. There's something heavy on his back, holding him down. He's drowning! His legs are kicking out as hard as they can and he's scrambling to get a fingerhold on anything at all, but the rock around him is just disintegrating. Soon, he'll hit the ocean itself, and then it will all be over. *This can't be how it ends*, he thinks, *Aunt May and MJ need me, my friends need me, Dr. Shah needs me, New York needs me!* He knows he's got to stop moving, to stay still and reassess the situation, but it's almost like his limbs have a mind of their own. Still, the thing above him pushes, and pushes, and pushes. Spider-Man gags on a big gulp of water and tries to scream, but he can't.

This won't be how it ends!

He stops moving and presses both palms against the rock below him. With all his spider-strength, Spidey shoves against the floor, feeling the rock split below him, and he flies up into the air, coughing and sputtering. He can see the water nearly hitting the still-unconscious Spot's neck now, but . . . the Spot is blurry. Like there's something in front of him. The shape is hazy, and there's something unsettling about it. Spider-Man tilts his head, and realizes the thing is humanoid in shape. He can *just* sense two arms and two legs and something that might pass for a head. Above him, the red of the rock is actively bleeding into gray, and the thing in front of him starts to shimmer and stutter, the faint line around it beating in and out to a jagged rhythm.

"You see us," it says to Spider-Man, and its voice is a thousand voices all at once, deep and echoey.

"Unfortunately," Spider-Man croaks out, his throat raw and his tongue laden with salt.

"Even here, on the cusp of death, you joke. You are the worst of them, we think," the thing says.

"Who's *we*? What's your game?" Spider-Man says, trying to keep the thing talking. His eyes flit here and there, trying to piece together a plan—*any* plan. But there's nothing that he can find.

"We are The Faithless, and we will have this planet. It is ours now, little bug. We have taken what we need from this, the vestiges of our home." There's no red at all left in the rock around them, and Spider-Man realizes that The Faithless has been pulling strength from the meteor and now there's nothing more to pull. The shape pushes forward. "We don't need your puny little machines anym—" But then they stutter and the shape blinks out for a second, then two. Spider-Man holds his breath. *Is it over?* And then the shape is in front of him. "—ore," it's saying. And then it glitches again, disappearing and reappearing. *There's something wrong with it. . . .*

"You let me out of the water. Why?" Spider-Man challenges. "What's the point?"

"Because you are nothing, and we are everything. We are The Faithless. And everything will be ours." And then something puts a soft touch against Spidey's forehead and slams his head backward into the wall hard enough for another hole to gush water. Spidey's vision goes double, and The Faithless laugh before it cuts off abruptly as they stutter out of existence for a second. Then they're back, and there's something caressing Spidey's cheek.

"You were a decent adversary, Spider-Man. But this is our planet now. You will no longer be necessary." And then they're gone, and this time it's on their own terms.

CHAPTER TWENTY-SIX

Dizzy, and trying not to pass out, Spider-Man lunges through the water over to the Spot. The back of his head is stinging with salt water, and he knows The Faithless must have cut his head open with that last blow. The Spot is still out of it when Spidey reaches him, and Spidey pulls him up and starts shaking the older man.

This is our only chance to get out of here alive!

"DOTS! YOU JERK, WAKE UP. I AM NOT DYING IN A ROCK IN THE BOTTOM OF THE OCEAN WITH YOU OF ALL PEOPLE. WAKE UP." Spidey punctuates his words with tight slaps to the Spot's cheeks.

"Wake up!" he tries again, but the Spot's head just lolls from side to side. Tentatively, Spider-Man touches one of the holes on the Spot's face. His hand goes right through it, and Spidey squirms. "I do *not* like this . . . for whatever that's worth," he says to the Spot's unconscious body. Around them the water has gotten higher. There's only a few feet left of space and air. Soon Spidey's going to have to start treading to stay afloat. He tries not to think too hard about what comes after that. He tries to scratch at the black dot on the Spot's cheek, but it stays there, stubborn to the end.

"I can't believe I'm going to die in a rock with the most C-list super villain of all time," Spider-Man moans.

"A-list," comes a quiet, strangled voice next to him, and Spidey's lenses go wide. The Spot is blearily looking around. "Where're me? We? Who?"

"You're awake!" Spidey cries, and nearly throws his arms around the Spot. *Wait no, bad guy. Do not hug the bad guy.*

"Who're we, you. Who're you?" the Spot says. "My head hurts."

"Okay, I will explain everything when you take us to your weird Spot World, buddy."

The Spot looks down at where Spidey's holding him up in the water and then around them. "Did . . . ? How did—"

"Doesn't matter," Spider-Man says impatiently. His arm is starting to shake from the combination of his broken rib and the pain in his head. "Please do the weird creepy thing with the spots, and let's go."

Slowly, the Spot reaches up and grabs the spot off his face and puts it in the air right next to the two of them. Ever the hero, Spidey pushes the Spot through the darkness first and then follows suit, leaving the terror of drowning behind him.

He stumbles into the Spot World dimension, dripping wet, and finds the Spot sitting cross-legged, staring at all the dots around him.

"I really thought I could do this," the Spot says. "Like, I could be the worst thing the city has ever seen. I'm not even sure why I wanted it. Why did I care about any of this so much? The CWNN, the articles, none of it matters. I should have listened to the other scientists. I was so busy trying to be the best, at anything. At everything. I shouldn't have—" He's sounding a little more put together, but there's still something odd in his voice. "That thing just . . . left me there to die. I would have *died*. You beat me, Spider-Man. Fair and square."

"That was *not* fair. You had all the odds!" Spider-Man scoffs. "That was so unfair, I don't even know where to *start*. That was *horrible*. Horrible," he says for emphasis. The Spot stands up shakily, and he's favoring one leg. He puts two hands up in the universal gesture of surrender. "Oh my god," Spider-Man says. "I think you might actually be the worst." The Spot shrugs. "How do we get back to New York from here? Where are we, even?"

"It's my own portal dimension. I made it when I was a scientist."

"Man, you should have stayed a scientist. Figure out affordable mass teleportation so I can stop having to take the bus."

"That's what I was trying to do. I probably should have stayed a scientist," the Spot agrees, ignoring Spidey's grumbles and walking over to a black hole several feet away.

"You're making me feel bad for you," Spider-Man says flatly.

"I'm not trying to," the Spot replies. He waves at the hole next to him. "This one'll take us to the closest precinct," he says, pointing at it.

Spider-Man looks at it for a moment, thoughtful. Then he asks, "Is there one that'll get us to Forty-Seventh and Lex?"

"Maybe," the Spot replies, hesitant. "What's over there?"

"There's a rehab center for people like you," Spidey says. "I think you might need that more than a precinct."

It's *very* late when Peter sneaks back into his room; he's not even sure what time it is. His phone is shot, as salt water is not a great way to clean your machines out. It's possible MJ called Kayla and a reporter at the *Daily Bugle* officially knows that Spider-Man is Peter Parker. But Peter's so tired, and so full of pain, he can't quite bring himself to care.

There's an awful squishing sound when he steps into the room from the window ledge, and he wonders if he'll ever feel dry again. He takes off his mask and starts to pull at the bottom of his costume when he turns to his left and stops short. There's a dark form lying on his bed, and as he gets closer, he sees a hint of red.

"Mary Jane?!" he whispers as loud as he dares. The form twitches and then rolls over, and Mary Jane Watson is facing him, her eyes blinking open slowly.

"Mmm, Peter? What're you doin' in my room?"

"MJ," Peter says, somewhat hysterical, "you're in *my* room?"

MJ shoots up into sitting position, and Peter can see that she's wearing jeans and a sweatshirt under his covers.

"Omigod." She says it like it's one single word. "I—I got worried, and I didn't want to wait for you to come home and change and then come over. What happened? I had my alarm set for two a.m., and if you weren't here, I *was* going to call Kayla. What happened?" she asks again.

"How are you here?" Peter says instead of answering.

"Does Aunt May know? There's no way Aunt May knows," he adds. "Wait, actually, give me two minutes. I'm going to change and maybe do some light first aid. I will be right back. Don't move. I mean, move if you want, but . . ."

"Go," MJ says.

Peter grabs a pile of clothes without looking at them and hobbles to the bathroom as quiet as he can. Inside, he flips on the light and looks in the mirror. His face looks puffy and strange, and he's got bruising around his eyes and throat. He reaches up and touches the back of his head and immediately winces. There's definitely some kind of laceration there. Slowly, he changes into dry clothes, pausing to wind a long bandage around his middle a few times. When he pulls a shirt on, he realizes it's his old Weinkle's Daycare shirt, and he's struck with a strong sense of déjà vu of the last time he wore this shirt around MJ. *When I thought this was all over.* He lets out a deep sigh and leans over the sink, just breathing for a moment.

Then he washes his face and douses his hair with as much water as he can without turning on the shower. *I think I got most of the salt out, at least.* Bundling his suit up and sticking it under his armpit, he hobbles back to his room. MJ is still sitting where he left her, and she's fiddling with her phone. After shoving his suit into the closet, he turns a lamp on and sits sideways in his desk chair, facing her.

"Hey," he says.

"Do you want me to look at anything?" she asks, eyes knowing.

"If you wouldn't mind just glancing at the back of my head?" He's sheepish in his delivery, and she smiles softly.

"Yeah, I can do that, bug boy."

"Ugh, don't—that's what bad guys call me." He scrunches his nose in distaste.

MJ just laughs a small laugh and moves to stand behind him. Her fingers comb softly through his hair. "Oh, yeah, there's a small cut back here, but it doesn't look too bad. I think head wounds bleed a lot, but this one looks like it's already scabbing over." Her fingers still, and she pauses for a brief moment. "Do you wanna tell me what happened?"

So Peter does. He goes through the whole story, from the moment he got to Brighton Beach to confront the Spot to when he dropped the Spot off at a rehabilitation center. By the time he's finished, MJ's moved back to his bed and is staring at him with her mouth open.

"Peter, that's . . ."

"I know. The Faithless got away," he says, and he has a pang of horror when his voice breaks.

"What?" she says, confused by something he's said.

"They got away," he repeats. "I have no idea where they are, or what they're doing."

"Peter, I don't care—I mean, I *care*, obviously—but I am . . . you almost *died*, like, three times in that story. What the *heck*?!"

"Oh, right. I'm sorry?"

MJ falls back flat on his bed, and he hears her say, more to herself than him, "Guy almost dies, I tell him that's messed up, guy says he's sorry. Where is the self-help book for this specific problem?"

"Erm . . . MJ?" Peter asks, sitting up straighter to try and see her face in the low light of his desk lamp. She pushes herself back up and leans against the wall.

"The literal next thing we are doing is figuring out an *actual* plan so you don't *die*, Peter Parker, because if you *die*, I promise I will kill you. I can't— I would have called Kayla and told her your secret to save you, you know."

"Okay." Peter nods. "I'm okay with that."

"You are?" she asks.

"You're right. We can't do this without some kind of backup plan. That's . . . It's not fair to you. I'm sorry I didn't realize how much pressure it was putting on you. I didn't understand what you meant by consequences. Honestly, I'm all for the plan. I, too, would like to not die." He gets up to join her, taking a seat next to her on the bed. His legs hang off the side, next to hers, and she rests her head on his shoulder. Peter presses a kiss against her head.

"Thank you. I—I didn't know how to talk about it. Because you're the one who's *actually* in danger, it's hard to say anything when you're up against that."

"You can always talk to me, MJ. You said it weeks ago—it's not a competition. It's all important because we're important." He feels her nod against his shoulder. "So what are we going to do about this painfully powerful alien that is now completely mobile?" he asks.

"That is a good question. But you know what? We'll figure it out. I trust us."

Peter grins crookedly against her hair; he's remembering saying something similar to her just a few weeks earlier.

"So do I." Then he seems to realize something. "Wait, you didn't tell me how you got in here?!"

MJ looks at the window nonchalantly. "Oh," she says. "I climbed the tree and then hopped onto the roof, and then I climbed in your window."

EPILOGUE

Peter and MJ stroll into Dr. Shah's classroom. She's a few steps ahead of him and already has her backpack open to pull out a stack of packets.

"Hey!" She waves at Maia, who is sitting her seat.

Randy's in the back of the room, sharpening his pencil. "Hey, MJ. Pete," he greets, looking at them over his shoulder.

"'Sup, man?" Peter calls out, and lifts a hand in greeting to Maia before taking a seat at his desk.

MJ drops one packet on each desk before turning around to leave one on Dr. Shah's.

"He just stepped out to take a phone call, but said he'd be back in a few minutes," Maia says.

"Oh, we didn't see him outside. Weird," MJ mutters, but she's not really thinking about it. "Okay, this is every single page of our fully designed application, Alliance Activate." She grins. "Which I still *love*, Randy."

He's back at his desk now and is nodding his head. "Because it's a good name!"

Peter laughs, but there's the ever-present strain in it that's been there for the last few months, since his debacle with the Spot. The Faithless haven't shown their face anywhere, and his night job has almost been suspiciously quiet. Peter doesn't like it, but he doesn't know what to do about it . . . except keep searching. It's nearly summer break now, and Peter halfway hopes that whatever The Faithless are planning will happen before his junior year starts, but he's not holding his breath.

"Hello, Peter! MJ!" Dr. Shah steps into the room with a bright smile, and Peter is gratified that at least one thing has gotten better. After a few weeks clear of The Faithless's influence, Dr. Shah returned to his old self, which was a huge comfort to his OSMAKER team. He's been very involved since then, and has already given each of them an A for the semester. Peter has spent several evenings with his teacher as Spider-Man, going through where The Faithless might be, and how they could potentially find them. But so far, nothing has worked.